SERENE
VALLEY KILL

Derbyshire's DCI Forbes Thriller – Book 2

SYLVIA MARSDEN

In the Peak District of Derbyshire, in the heart
of England, a desire for love and a need for
revenge set 18yr old Simon on a dangerous
road. He knows who's trying to kill him, but
what he doesn't know is why. DCI Forbes and
his team don't believe Simon's claims – after
all – what could middle-aged women possibly
have to gain by murdering teenage boys?

***

This novel is dedicated to all those people who go the extra mile to help or to rescue animals in need.

***

Follow me on Facebook for updates on my novels.

***

From the first chapter **Serene Valley Kill** draws you in. The intrigue develops at speed. Yes you think you've worked it all out, but you never quite have! Absolutely brilliant with fantastic imagery. Whilst it was great to be reacquainted with characters featured in **Orphan Kill**, Serene Valley Kill can definitely be read as a standalone. Very highly recommended!

A Goodreads Reviewer

***

Sylvia Marsden was born in Mansfield, Nottinghamshire, and grew up in the heart of the Peak District of Derbyshire – an area she still thinks of as home.

She spends part of each summer in a campervan, touring the Peaks with her husband, her rescue greyhound, and of course, her laptop.

***

Her novels are also available as e-books on Amazon kindle and Amazon unlimited.

***

By the same author

ORPHAN KILL

***

MINE TO KILL

***

1

Far beyond the reach of her headlights, the December night sky met the rounded, dark outlines of the Peak District's rolling limestone hills. The winding road ahead looked almost too inviting, with its myriad of ice crystals sparkling against the black tarmac, tempting her on as if offering to lead her away from the nightmare she was living.

Tempting – but promising her nothing.

Arianne squeezed the steering wheel of the unfamiliar car until her fingers and shoulder muscles felt about to seize up. She slowed the vehicle to a crawl.

She had just one task to complete, and then she had to find her way back.

She had no choice.

With the heater set to maximum the air inside was heavy, each lungful feeling more unpleasant than the last, and each drawing the sickly-sweet taste of fresh blood and pine disinfectant into her throat.

She was unsure which of the buttons to press to allow in any of the ice-cold, night air.

Apart from the dead woman in the back, she was alone and lost, and following a single-tracked road further and further from civilisation.

The plastic sheet the women had wrapped the body in rustled and creaked at every bump and turn in the road. What if they'd torn it? How long would it take for blood to soak through threadbare carpet, and then through damaged plastic? She really didn't want to have to clean up any more of that poor woman's blood.

She looked into her rear view mirror and eyes she barely recognised stared back – her own, haunted, exhausted, fear-filled eyes.

"What if she isn't actually dead?" She broke the silence inside the car, but only with a hesitant whisper. "Then where should I take her... they never told me what to do if she woke?"

Rubbing the back of her neck with her left hand did nothing to ease the knot of tension. She'd had her orders, but it wasn't easy to find somewhere to dump a body – somewhere it wouldn't be found for a long time, if ever.

As she leaned forward in her seat another bead of sweat trickled down between her breasts, and after checking the rear view mirror again she squinted down through the semi-circular gap in the steering wheel. Almost ten miles on the clock, and yet the road ahead was still climbing.

Their instructions to her must have been wrong, either that or she'd taken a wrong turn somewhere. This road should have been taking her down towards the River Lathkill, where she'd been told to dump the body, long before now.

The further she drove the more sparkling clumps of grass she could see at the centre of the narrow ribbon of tarmac. It seemed very few people used this road; the last farmhouse with smoke eddying into the night air from its dark chimney pots was already a mile behind her. The next easily accessible roadside ditch would just have to do.

Then she had to find a place to turn the car – a farm gateway or a passing place. She couldn't risk adding to her nightmare by becoming stuck on a frozen grass verge.

Then it was simply a matter of finding her way back to complete the remainder of her day's more normal tasks.

2

Prunella Leath slammed both of her liver-spotted fists down onto the large wooden table in the centre of the vast, Victorian-styled kitchen. She took a deep breath and the two women stepped back. "For over twenty-three years, come rain or shine, fog or snow, hail or bloody sleet, I've come to Oakwell Grange every single, sodding day. And the first time I'm stuck at home, lying in my sick bed, for just two measly weeks, I have to come back to this. What the hell were you thinking?"

Neither of them answered.

She continued in a more hushed, syrupy tone. "I've been coming here since I was twenty-five and you two sisters were still in your teens; seventeen and nineteen years old." She flicked her gaze from one to the other. "Sheila and Hannah Hall, I've been wiping both of your noses since that very first day and still the pair of you can't make a sensible decision between you. So what if one of the women died, it isn't the first time it's happened, and it's not as though it's the middle of the summer and we're being plagued with bluebottles, is it? Why didn't you just put the corpse into one of the sheds and wait for me to recover? At the very least, you should have called me for instructions."

"We did phone you... several times..." Sheila Hall stammered under Prunella's unblinking stare, "but your husband always answered your mobile. He told us, in no uncertain terms, that you had the flu, you were extremely poorly, and that you weren't to be disturbed. And there was no point in either of us coming to see you up at the Keeper's Cottage... you know how your Brian feels about us... he would never have allowed either of us through the front door."

"That stupid girl hadn't listened to our instructions properly," Hannah Hall added in a vain attempt to shift the blame. "It's her fault the body's been found so quickly."

"And I suppose you're expecting me to feel grateful that you've decided to put me in the picture today – now that the council have found it?"

Hannah was still squirming. "How were we to know Arianne would fail to follow such a simple route? We thought the swollen river would take the body miles from here."

Words failed her. If she hadn't been struck down with that virus she'd have done the job herself, and made certain that the body wasn't ever found. "You two should never have sent that girl out there alone in the first place. She can barely drive. What were you thinking? Nothing I suppose, as usual. You should know by now to leave the thinking to me. If it hadn't been for my business brains, my original injection of cash, and my contacts, this wonderful property that you two own, together with the Oakwell Grange businesses, and the charity that you're both so bloody proud of, would all have folded years ago. And yet once again, here I am reminding you both of that fact."

"We appreciate everything you've done for us, and for the businesses, really we do," Sheila was always the first to grovel to her, "but when we couldn't contact you we did what we thought was best. No one will suspect the body came from here. We made sure it was well cleaned, and Arianne is far too fearful of the consequences for her family to ever say anything to anyone."

"Well let's just hope that you're right, shall we? And shouldn't you both be skivvying away in the school kitchens by now? You're late, and this place still needs your financial contributions. Get out of my sight, both of you. I need to think."

"Are you feeling well enough to come in for your lunchtime shift today?" Sheila was still trying to placate her. "I can cover for you, if you're not."

"Maybe tomorrow I'll feel well enough. My contacts will want to know why they are now a woman short, so thanks to you two I've got excuses to come up with, and grovelling to do."

"We'll see you later then," Sheila was following Hannah out of their kitchen as quickly as she could, but hesitated, turned, and then pointed to the small heap of envelopes on the kitchen worktop. "A letter came here yesterday, addressed to you. I put it on the top of the pile over there in the corner."

*

The main drawback to living out in the countryside and miles from anywhere, as far as Simon Carter was concerned, was that to establish any worthwhile level of independence, and therefore any kind of a life, a teenager had to have his own motorized transport. Against his parent's wishes, he'd used five hundred pounds of his savings to buy a Honda CBR1 125cc motorbike.

With Christmas a rapidly fading memory, he was again facing the wintery weather on his bike to attend the first aid, hygiene and safety course at the local college – a course which hadn't held his interest from its very beginning.

The first day back after the holidays was always the worst, but now it was over and he was heading home. He didn't mind the darkness too much; just as long as he could keep his overactive imagination under control. What was spoiling his journey tonight was the bitterly cold wind. That and the thought that he'd got to repeat the whole damn process over again the next day, and then the day after that.

The weather forecast for the remainder of the week was bleak, as his best friends John Lewis and Philip Booth had delighted in telling him. Maybe he ought to ask his mother to run him into college for the next few days. It might be worth the ear-bashing that he'd get from his father for enquiring.

He gently squeezed his leather-gloved hand on the front brake lever, but then quickly released it. That was another downside to living in such a remote spot. Between the moisture from the River Lathkill that his parents' property overlooked, and the fallen leaves from the hundreds of deciduous trees lining both the road and the hillside, the steep and narrow road was likely to be slippery more often than not.

Today was one of those seriously slippery days.

Snow had been flickering on and off for most of the afternoon, and the only thing preventing it from settling on the road now was the meagre shelter offered by the tangle of overhead branches. Unfortunately, the thin sheen of moisture which never seemed to disappear during the shorter winter days was already turning to black ice.

He had no choice other than to take this scenic route. It was the only tarmacked route to his parent's dream home;

their eight bedroomed, ex-farmhouse, bed-and-breakfast property.

Minutes earlier, he'd turned off the main A6 in Bakewell to drive along the road which eventually reached Monyash, but before that village, and deliberately ignoring the silhouette of the church and its adjacent graveyard at the top of the hill, he'd turned down the winding road which led to the valley floor, and his home.

It was a great place to live, really. Most of his friends envied him. He'd taught his school friends, John and Phillip, how to fish for trout while lazing on these river banks, and they'd all shared their first cigarettes and consumed their first serious quantities of illegally obtained alcohol at the side of the incredibly clear water. John's first proper girlfriend had even shared in some of their previously all-boy activities, but only until a colony of angry wood ants had persuaded the pair that courting in the great outdoors wasn't one of their better ideas.

The name, River Lathkill, he'd explained to them both one summer's evening when he'd been showing off, was supposed to have Scandinavian roots, and translated as 'narrow valley with a barn'. To Simon that seemed a fairly accurate description, though that wasn't what he usually called it. To him it was a little corner of heaven – his serene valley.

On nights such as these he regretted the times the three of them had tried so hard to frighten each other with tales of ghostly hitch-hikers, phantom vehicles, and unexplained sightings of strange, shadowy creatures darting back and forth across the road. The stories had been utter rubbish, of course, but still the old images lingered, playing tricks on his vision as he negotiated the mile-long stretch of road towards the valley floor. He blinked hard, determined to think of something else.

They'd moved here when he was twelve and he'd soon found casual holiday and weekend work helping neighbouring farmers with their harvests and their livestock. He'd learned how to fix fences and build dry stone walls, and been surprised at how much he'd enjoyed making and fixing simple objects. He'd loved the whole valley from the first day he'd seen it. Serene Valley, his mother had christened it on that very first day, and he'd borrowed that name for it from her, so that when he talked with his friends about their secret places, no one would know where they meant. But he could also see the merits of living in one of the smaller Peak District towns, at least until he was in his late twenties. He was saving for a deposit on a flat, hopefully not too far away, maybe somewhere in Buxton where there was at least a modicum of night life. Buxton wasn't exactly in the Peak District, but it was bordered by it on three sides, and it was close enough.

Anyway, there was no point in speculating. His first, unexpected taste of true love was a powerful reason for him to plan for the future, but his immediately task was to get home safely. Sleet had begun to fall. With his mind still drifting, and his cooling body on auto-pilot, he continued to squeeze and release the brake lever very gently as he descended into the valley. His headlights filtered through the skeletal trees closest to the road, and the few leaves which hadn't been bogged down in the undergrowth were being whipped up by the strengthening wind and were drifting across the road in front of him.

His journey was becoming more hazardous with each passing minute.

Looking through his visor was like trying to peer through a pane of frosted glass, and for some weird reason, the glass suddenly sparkled. He wanted to clear his visor but knew from experience that his wet glove would only create a smear. It must be the wet snow, he thought, but with every turn of his wheels, the tiny, fragmented specks of light became brighter. As he rounded the next bend, the specks exploded into dazzling lights. His brain froze. He blinked and instinctively squeezed on his brakes.

There wasn't room for a car and a motorbike to pass safely on this particular stretch of the road. He felt strangely disorientated. He felt sure the oncoming vehicle had just passed a purpose-built passing place. Why hadn't the driver pulled into it, or at least stopped, ready to back up? And why were his headlights still on main beam? Was the driver blind, crazy, or just plain reckless?

He released his brakes. He wasn't experienced enough to handle a full slide and something unfamiliar was happening beneath him. He flashed his headlight. Surely the driver had seen him. How could he not? But still the lights glared upwards, directly at him. Again he flashed his headlight and was forced to squeeze harder on the brakes. He felt both wheels of his motorbike beginning to slide.

"Shit... I'm losing it..." he swore into his helmet. "What the...?"

The idiot was still coming, and unless it was an illusion brought on by fear, was actually accelerating up the hill towards him.

Wet leaves slithered between rubber and tarmac.

His bike picked up speed.

It was an impossible choice to make, either solid tree trunks to his right or the swollen river to his left.

He felt his bike making the decision for him and leaned with it.

It was either that or risk going under the wheels of the idiot's vehicle.

He drew in one instinctively deep gulp of air before the ice-cold water rushed into his leathers. Before he could take in another, the strong winter current of the River Lathkill was pulling him downwards and sideways, ripping him from his bike and making him into the river's helpless passenger.

That one moment of calm was like nothing he'd ever experienced before. A shame about his bike, he thought quite calmly, it would be of no use to anyone any more, and his father definitely wouldn't be best pleased. Then he saw his mother's face looking down at him, with that disappointed expression that she reserved for the occasions when he'd gone too far with some inappropriate prank, or when he'd deliberately misbehaved.

Then air rushed into his lungs. He opened his eyes and realised his head was barely above water. He tore at the fastenings around his throat and then pulled his helmet clear only to feel it ripped from his grasp. His calmness turned to terror. It swept over him like an unstoppable tidal wave. The blackness around him looked dense and impenetrable, and the roar of the river was deafening. He felt as though he was on the end of a hundred ropes, being pulled along, forced to gulp in water along with precious air.

Desperately, he thrashed about. The water wasn't deep, he continually touched the river bed with his gloved hands, but everything was so slippery, and he was being pulled along at such a frightening speed. He had to get a grip on something solid.

He ought to at least try to swim, he thought, but in which direction? He couldn't see either of the river banks and there was a real risk of swimming into the centre. For most of its length the river wasn't all that wide, but the cold had already sapped so much of his strength that the wrong choice now could be his last.

The sudden impact into his side made him wretch. Then he gasped for breath. His body had folded around a hard, narrow object, and instinctively he reached out and clutched it to his chest. His legs wrapped around it as though it was a zip-wire suspended a hundred feet up in the air. A branch, a tree root, whatever it was didn't matter. Through his gloves it felt slippery, but against the force of the water it also felt wonderfully solid.

For several seconds he clung to it, too terrified to risk removing any of his limbs, and alternately taking in painful gulps of air and coughing up river water from the back of his throat. He prayed that his lifeline was a tree root, and not a broken branch which might splinter at any second with his added weight pushing it downstream.

There was no more time to think.

This could be his only chance to get out of the water alive.

He eased himself along, an inch at a time, then a little further and a little faster, all the time praying he was heading in the right direction. Some basic instinct told him he was, and that instinct was right. His left hand finally touched something much larger.

That same instinct screamed at him not to shout out for help. Someone had deliberately run him off the road. What if they were still around? He moved his left hand, trying to feel, trying to be sure it wasn't a false hope, and then he saw a few pale, shadowy strands of dead grass.

His arms had never felt so far beyond his control and his lungs burned. It was taking so much effort to maintain his grip on the slippery bank and the sparse vegetation, especially with his gloved hands, that he almost gave up hope of pulling himself free of the water. But slowly, and painfully, he managed to ease himself forwards.

With his chest on firm ground, he made one last effort to drive himself upwards. Jamming his feet against the tree root, or whatever it was that had saved him, he launched himself up and forwards like some grossly overgrown frog. It wasn't graceful, but it worked.

For a few moments at least, he wasn't fighting for his life.

The grass felt crisp and brittle against his face, and apart from that odd sensation, and the pain in his chest, his body felt alarmingly numb. He checked each of his limbs in turn. They were all still there – they hadn't been broken or twisted into grisly or obscene angles by the force of the water. They were just numb with cold.

His bike had gone, but he'd survived.

As quietly as he could, he coughed up what he hoped was the last of the water from his throat.

Then he lay still and listened. What kind of a bastard could have done this to him, and why, and could that person be lurking in the undergrowth somewhere, waiting to see whether he'd made it out of the water so that they could push him back in? He was probably too weak to offer much resistance, and definitely too weak to haul himself out for a second time.

He ought to be shivering, he thought, but he wasn't. His body must be going into shock. On the television they wrapped trauma victims in foil blankets, didn't they? Instead, he had water squelching around inside his leathers, which were designed not to allow moisture in and therefore making an excellent job of not allowing it out. There didn't seem any point in taking them off – he was quite literally soaked to the skin and the air temperature was well below freezing. He was alive, but at a considerable disadvantage.

"Get up, Simon... you have to move," he whispered through his teeth. His lips felt solid. The last thing he needed to do was to fall asleep. There was a distinct chance that he'd never wake up. "You've made it this far, so get up... now..."

He struggled to his feet but his legs crumpled after only one step and he found himself back on his hands and knees. "It can't be far to the road," he mumbled. "I'll just have to crawl."

If he wasn't so scared, if his chest wasn't so damn painful, or if either John or Philip could see him on all fours like this, he'd be laughing with embarrassment. Knowing them, they'd make sure his animal impressions were featuring on Facebook before either of them even considered going for help. But he'd forgive them anything if he could just see either of them walking out of the darkness and down that grassy slope towards him right now.

He could just about make out the line of trees along the side of the road. He was almost there. Then he could rest. He could get his breathing back under control, and maybe, just maybe, he'd be able to get to his feet and walk.

He was so damn cold. It was just a little further. He could almost smell the tarmac.

Somewhere close, too close, a car engine started up. Home was only about a quarter of a mile away but the sound wasn't coming from that direction. The tarmac had suddenly become a deadly place again.

Wracked with the pain of needing to cough but not daring to make a sound, he lowered himself until he was lying flat on the frozen grass and prayed that he was hidden from the road by the tree trunks and the undergrowth. He felt cold water seeping from his lower legs up towards his thighs. He closed his eyes and listened. The engine noise faded and the sound of the swollen river gradually replaced it.

He imagined walking home to a telling off from his father for losing something.

If only he could remember what it was that he'd lost?

*

"Deep breaths, Prunella," she whispered to herself as she stepped out of the Land Rover onto the darkest, quietest stretch of the road in the village of Ashtown. "Be calm. You are a chosen one, therefore you are powerful. You can easily deal with what needs to be done tonight."

Most Mondays were considered pool-nights by the regulars of the British Legion in Ashtown, and this Monday was no exception. Snow and rain had alternated throughout the day and she felt confident that no one would give her a second look in her grey, hooded duffle coat and her brown scarf, as she walked past the large bay-windows of the pool room. Very casually, she checked that all the usual local youths and their doe-eyed girlfriends were in there. There were curtains, of course, but she'd never seen them used, and as usual she had a clear view of the large room. And just as she'd hoped, the two youths whose hours were numbered, were leaning on the bar together and laughing at someone or something.

She'd noted their movements over many years, and now her surveillance was paying off, and was about to come to an end.

Let them laugh. This would be their last night out together.

The two youths normally left the Legion on foot, and their route home was one that she was familiar with, and one that she'd pictured over and over again in the hours since she'd read that letter. There was one perfect place for what she had in mind. It was a short stretch of road which was too narrow to allow for a pavement, and on which the council had painted a single white line to act as a narrow walkway. The eighteenth century, two-storey, limestone cottages which opened out directly onto each side of the road, created a perfect tunnel for what she had planned. There was no room for cars to park along there; providing her with the clear and uninterrupted thirty metre run that she was going to need.

And there was no one in the street to notice her.

She turned, pulled her scarf up over her mouth, and walked back to her vehicle. Before she could reach it she heard a car engine starting up, followed by a mind-numbing thump, thump, thump. Some of the youths were already leaving, but they were travelling in the opposite direction and weren't about to drive past her. The others wouldn't be too long now, and just as long as no one offered her targets a lift home, she could finish her night's work and be in bed with her mug of cocoa before one o'clock in the morning.

She climbed into the driving seat, pulled a blanket around her legs, and leaned back to wait.

*

Bill Harper, a pensioner for more years than he cared to admit, perched his stick-thin frame on his reserved wooden bar stool at the public bar of the Legion each and every night. A widower for twenty years, his pension was strictly allocated down to his last few coppers, which on pension days he ritually placed into one or other of the charity boxes on the bar. He allowed himself four pints of discounted beer each night. No one in the village could ever recall seeing Bill Harper drunk, and to his doctor's surprise, Bill's liver, along with his other major organs, had recently been given a clean bill of health. He was as much a part of the fixtures and fittings as the wooden bar stool itself. He'd waved off many of the previous landlords and landladies, and welcomed in their replacements with assurances of his *'special rates for such an old and valued customer as himself, and one who kept a watchful eye on the youngsters for them'*.

It was the first time that Bill had ever suffered the indignity of vomiting on the would-be pavement.

"It was the roar... the noise of the engine... that's what made me stop," Bill stammered to the group of uniformed and plain-clothed officers. "It wasn't right at that time of night... far too loud... it startled me... and it was all wrong because I couldn't see any headlights coming at me... just that noise. The bastard drove right past me... only missed me by a hair's breadth, it did. If I hadn't had my wits about me and stepped to the side, I'm telling you... I'd be as dead as them two poor young buggers over there."

DC Gary Rawlings looked at the man's misshapen and trembling hands. Unless they always shook like that, this old guy was going into shock. He didn't want to take any chances. His superior, DCI Michael Forbes, had made this witness his responsibility. "I'd feel much better if you'd let them take you to the hospital, just for tonight. I realise the vehicle missed you, but you've had a very nasty shock. Why not allow some nice young nurses to tuck you into bed, and then have a proper cooked breakfast brought to you in the morning. We'll need to interview you again tomorrow and take a proper statement, and I'd like to be sure that you're being well taken care of."

"I doubt I'll get much sleep wherever I am, young man. I just pressed myself up against that wall and watched. I've known both of those lads since they were nippers." A tear rolled down his lined cheek. "And there wasn't a damn thing I could do to help either of them. Straight into them it went, very nearly hitting that wall. The poor young buggers didn't stand a chance. Then the vehicle's reversing lights came on and that's when one of the lads screamed out. Terrible it was... terrible... I'll never forget it... he knew what was coming, you see... the poor lad knew."

"Just take it easy now, Mr Harper."

"But it accelerated back, right over them both. I heard the bump, bump of the tyres, and that's when the screaming stopped. Then the vehicle stopped and I really thought the driver was going to get out, to check their handy work, like. The driver's door opened a little way and I was so afraid... afraid that I might be next. I didn't dare to move. I'm far too old to run. I just froze. Then the door slammed shut, I heard that awful thud, thud as the car drove forwards over them again, and that was when the headlights came on and the vehicle roared away. I never saw any number plates, and I didn't get a proper look at the driver, but there was no mistaking the noise of those wheels going over those two poor young lads. I know I'll never forget that dreadful sound. How could anyone deliberately do that?"

"Come along now, Mr Harper; let's get you safely into the ambulance."

"But what about my cat... I've got a cat at home, waiting for me?"

"We'll make sure it's taken care of, don't you worry. In fact, I'll make sure of that myself."

3

DCI Michael Forbes was preparing for the Tuesday morning's briefing in the incident room of Leaburn police station, and like many of his officers, he'd only managed to grab a couple of hours of sleep since about six a.m. on Monday. "Settle down now, it's not been the best beginning to a new year that we've ever had. In fact, for our small, rural station it's an alarming record." He shuffled the papers on the desk in front of him. "Four days ago, the council's road department was called out to clear a gully on Hawthorn Lane. It's a little used road which most of us will never have driven along, and which leads up to only a handful of remote hill farms. However, the blockage was causing water to run onto the road on a particularly dangerous blind corner. Traffic lights had to put in place and debris was found to have backed up into an adjacent road drain, which meant that it was yesterday morning before the obstruction could be removed, and several more hours before anyone thought to take a closer look at the cause of the blockage."

"That in itself is something of a record for this council, in my experience," DC Harry Green added from the edge of the room in his strong Liverpool accent.

"Thank you Harry," Forbes wasn't about to allow his briefing to be turned into a political debate. "I'll listen to any sensible comments that you have, just as soon as I've finished speaking. The body of a female, fully clothed and wrapped in a carpet, and then secured in a length of black plastic sheeting, was the cause of the obstruction. As yet she remains unidentified. From the post-mortem late yesterday afternoon, we know she had been dead for at least two weeks, but the cold water and the plastic are making it impossible for Dr Alison Ransom to be any more accurate at this point in time. The victim appears to be of Middle Eastern origin. She'd had a small amount of dental work done, but not in this country, and not recently. She was in her late teens and had died as the result of a head trauma. But of equal concern, the victim had given birth possibly only hours before her death, and the baby had almost certainly been carried to full term."

"Oh, that's so sad. A mother who never got to care for her new-born baby," DC Emily Jackson came from a large family. She was the eldest of eight and had an understandably powerful mothering instinct.

"Quite..." Forbes had been looking at it from a different, equally distressing angle. When he was eighteen, his mother had died suddenly, leaving him and his father with a three-week old baby girl, his troubled sister, Louise. "Unfortunately, that turns it into a two-pronged investigation. We have an unidentified murder victim and a missing baby. There may be a healthy, new-born baby out there, one who someone has taken in and is hopefully caring for, or there may be a baby's body somewhere out there, waiting to be discovered. It could be in a plastic bag in a ditch, a dustbin, a skip, or on the council refuse tip.   We're going to need the public's help on this one and a press conference is due to begin in one hour."

He moved across to one of the three whiteboards in the room. "The second incident happened at around five p.m. yesterday. I've been told that eighteen-year-old Simon Carter is incredibly lucky to be alive.   According to one of the paramedics who attended the incident, Columbanus, the Patron Saint of motorcycle riders, must have been watching over Simon when an oncoming vehicle forced him off the road and into the swollen River Lathkill.   Simon was on his way home from college, on the route he takes every afternoon." Forbes had been given news of the Simon Carter incident only minutes before he'd begun the briefing.

"Couldn't that have been an accident, sir?" DC Robert Bell asked. "Weather conditions were pretty dire at around that time."

"Apparently Simon was insisting last night that someone had tried to kill him.   DC Bell and DC Jackson, you two can go to Calow Hospital today to take a full statement from him. The doctors have said that he should be well enough to talk about the incident by the early afternoon."

"Right sir."

"Right sir."

"Simon's incident takes on a far more sinister mantle in the light of last night's hit-and-run in Ashtown, which I know many of you were called out to attend for fear of the incident being a terrorist-related attack.   The two youths who were killed have been identified as John Lewis and Philip Booth, also both eighteen. I don't believe in coincidences. I want to know just how well Simon Carter and the two dead youths knew each other, and I want to know just what upset someone enough to make them want to kill all three of them."

Someone had already begun loading one whiteboard with the previous night's photographs of John and Philip, and the narrow stretch of road which still remained closed. DS

Adam Ross was preparing to add Simon Carter's details to the adjacent board.

Forbes looked at the first board for a few seconds. As soon as the press conference was over he needed to be back at the mortuary again. As Senior Investigating Officer he attended post mortems whenever possible in case something important was uncovered. Fortunately, unlike buses, they rarely came along three at a time. His one consolation was that he'd get to spend time with Alison again, even though it was over a pair of corpses.

*

Simon's had slept, but he'd no idea for how long. His eyelids felt stiff. He was in a hospital bed, but other than that he was unsure of anything. When he'd tried to look, his eyeballs had given the impressions of being two lumps of sand.

He remembered the distant, but reassuring sound of his father's voice growing ever louder, drowning out the sound of the river and frantically calling his name.

He hadn't been dreaming. He remembered now. After he'd crawled from the river, his father had found him. He'd survived. And now there was a soft, feminine voice at his bedside, offering him a drink and encouraging him to sit up.

There had been nurses last night – loud sirens, and then softly-speaking nurses.

Every breath he took was painful and his hands shook. It was almost too much effort to lift the mug of warm tea to his dry lips. He didn't remember feeling quite as bad as this when they'd fussed around him and tucked him into his bed last night. Or had it been this morning? He remembered that before he'd fallen asleep he'd been so hot – so very, very hot. They must have given him something, and it must have been good stuff.

Eyes blissfully closed again, he relaxed back into his pillow and listened. He should have thought to ask the nurse what time it was. He could hear people moving about, cutlery and crockery were being shown no mercy, and music from the sixties or the seventies was emanating from somewhere not too far away. But no familiar voices floated through his haze. If he had slept for hours, then the nurses could have changed shifts, he reasoned.

The smell of food arriving on something with a squeaky wheel could indicate breakfast time. He'd never had to stay in a hospital before, but he'd heard how insanely early the breakfasts were served. His raised his eyelids very gingerly and peered around the room for a clock, but the lights were all too bright, making it impossible for him to focus on anything more than a few feet away. He could really use some more of whatever they'd given him last night.

He remembered his mother fussing around him. She'd been telling him that she'd brought in his spare mobile phone and charger, so that shouldn't be far away. Memories were returning in disjointed flashes: the feeling of his face against the grass, one cheek slightly warm where he'd been lying, but the rest of it so, so cold... his father shouting out that he could see Simon's bike in the water... his mother's screaming... loud noises and bright lights... sirens. And he'd been right about the foil blankets. He'd felt so helpless hearing both of his parents crying. He remembered how he'd wanted to tell them he was all right, but his lips had refused to work properly and a weird noise had come from somewhere. He'd wanted to throw off the foil blankets but hadn't been able to. And he couldn't remember why he'd felt so hot.

"Severe hypothermia," a man's voice had come from somewhere close to him.

"Is he breathing?" a woman had called from further away.

Yes, of course I'm breathing, he'd wanted to shout out, *and I can hear you all.* But then he'd recalled reading somewhere that hearing is the last of the senses to go when you die.

He remembered being lifted onto a stretcher, and how much his whole body had hurt when they'd moved him, and then more sirens.

Someone was disturbing his pillows.

"Good morning Simon," the nurse who'd forced him to drink the lukewarm tea was back. And she'd brought help with her this time. "Can you manage a light lunch if we get you into a sitting position?"

Every breath made him wince.

"Cracked ribs," a distant male voice had said, but he'd no idea when he'd heard it.

He eased his eyelids open again, looked at the two nurses, and then looked around the room and saw the origin of some of the noise. It was coming from his left, from a television fitted onto an extending arm which was in turn attached to the wall behind the next bed to his. The occupant of the bed didn't appear to be watching the screen.

The sounds would be something to channel his fractured thoughts on while he worked his way through what looked like pureed carrots and lumpy mashed potatoes.

The local news headlines were being announced.

Suddenly his pain didn't matter. He stared across at the face of the immaculately groomed woman on the screen. He needed to concentrate on her every word. Projected onto the wall behind her were the familiar faces of his two best friends, John Lewis and Philip Booth.

He pushed the tray away and grabbed at the drawer of his bedside cabinet. His fingers scrabbled around and finally folded around his phone. He fumbled with the buttons. John's number didn't ring, but went straight to the answering service. Next he jabbed at Philip's number, but with exactly the same result. His ribs burned and he gasped for breath as he phoned his home number. "Dad, what the hell's going on... have you seen the news?"

He hadn't imagined it after all. He'd been right. Someone really had deliberately forced him into the river. "They tried to kill me... just like I told you... and then they went after John and Philip... you have to believe me now." He needed to cough; his ribs were so painful he could hardly breathe. His phone clattered to the floor.

The man with the television looked across at him. "Are you all right, shall I get someone for you?"

"I'm all right... thanks," he tried to whisper.

"Only you don't look it, mate. I'd pick your phone up for you if I wasn't connected to this damn thing," he pointed to the tube coming from his forearm. "I can see the screen. It doesn't look to be damaged."

"The police..." he croaked, "they were here last night, weren't they?"

"Yes mate, but you were pretty much out of it. They said they'd be back today to speak to you, but they didn't say when."

"Thanks." Presumably he was safe while he was in a hospital ward, but why had the three of them been attacked so viciously? And would whoever had done this to him want to try again?

4

The nurses had insisted to Simon that he remain in a sitting position, propped up in his bed by a mountain of pillows. It would help to clear his lungs, they'd told him. And they'd assured him the police were coming back to interview him, so why were they taking so long?

He'd been watching the corridor for the last hour. He needed to talk. He had information for them which could be vital. And the longer he lay in his hospital bed thinking about it, the more convinced he was that he knew exactly who was responsible for the deaths of his two best friends.

He closed his eyes, they were beginning to hurt again, and he let his head sink back into the soft heap. He wanted to get the sequence of events that he was convinced had led to last night's carnage, clear in his own mind.

His thoughts drifted right back to the junior school days he'd spent with John and Philip – all boys, together forever, they'd believed back then.

Maybe the three of them shouldn't have played quite so many tricks on the dinner ladies at their school. For years they'd tormented the weird, and definitely not wonderful sisters from Oakwell Grange, and their female groupies. But to bored and immature boys, the coven, as everyone had called the group of women back then, had proved an irresistible target. The three of them hadn't been the only ones tormenting the women, but they'd been the most persistent, and definitely the most ruthless.

On four separate occasions, they'd been suspended from junior school together, and each time they'd dutifully apologised to the women and promised to behave better, but with their hands clasped behind their backs and their fingers tightly crossed. John Lewis's father had taken his belt to his wayward son on each occasion, but no amount of punishment had stopped their fun for long. If anything, it had made the three of them more determined to eventually come out on top, and as young boys they'd used a pen-knife and sworn a blood-oath to each other that one day they would have the last laugh at the crazy women from Oakwell Grange. They'd progressed from slipping frogs and toads into the school kitchens, to daring each other to enter, when no one was around, to switch on a gas or an electrical appliance. They may have gone a bit too far on the odd occasion, and considering their ages it was probably only good luck and not good judgement that none of them had injured themselves or anyone else in the school. But the risks involved had been a major part of the attraction when they'd been too immature to understand the possible consequences.

Loyalty to each other had been another one of their sworn pledges – another of their blood-oaths, and while some of the young girls had obviously been impressed by their bravado, the three of them been too young to see most females as anything other than a nuisance.

The one exception had been their freckle-faced classmate, Suzy Randall. She had held the whole of their year in raptures, usually in the corner of the school playground, not with her wit or her charm, and certainly not with her looks back then, but with her stories of how her grandmother had never missed a single séance session at the mysterious Oakwell Grange, and how at just before midnight, whenever there was a full moon, the Oakwell sisters led a procession of women out into the fields behind their property and on towards the two stone circles hidden in the woods on the hillside.

"They carry lanterns and candles," she'd told them, "and they all wear nothing but long black gowns so that when they extinguish the lights you can hardly see them. Then they contact the Devil himself," she'd whispered to her mesmerised audiences. "They throw off their robes and dance around naked, and they chant and sing, and then the Devil rises up through the ground to speak to them. It's true... I've heard gran trying to persuade mum to go, but she won't. None of you must ever tell anyone that I've told you, or the Devil will know and he'll come and get you in your sleep. You won't be able to stop him from taking you."

Why the Devil never came for Suzy Randall was a mystery that had never occurred to any of them at the time. In the school playground, she'd been believed by everyone who'd had the courage to listen to her, and the three boys' successful dares and conflicts with the women of Oakwell Grange had gained them invisible badges of honour from their classmates. "It was worth taking a thrashing for," John would proudly announce after showing off his bruises to anyone willing to give up a sweet or pay a penny to see them.

During their final year at junior school, they'd bravely sneaked out of their respective bedrooms on one of those moonlit nights. They'd dared each other and egged each other on, and then battled their fears to witness for themselves that it hadn't all been fantasy on the part of Suzy Randall. It had simply been an exaggeration. To their relief, the Devil hadn't actually risen up out of the ground to speak, and to their disappointment, the women hadn't disrobed and danced around naked. But they hadn't let their classmates know that.

By the time they'd started secondary school, they were considered by most people who knew them, to be tough, fearless, and more than a little bit crazy. They'd developed reputations as three boys not to be messed with. At the request of their parents, and the recommendation of the headmaster of their junior school, they'd been placed into separate classes. Far from being big fish in a small town pond, they'd become insignificant minnows in a large lake. For two years, they'd settled into their school work and behaved like reformed characters.

It was Phillip who had first rekindled their obsessions with Oakwell Grange and its odd occupants. "Those women are all still working at our old school. I've checked," he was smiling as he spoke, "and it's my guess that they think we've forgotten all about them."

"Those women don't think." John could always be relied on for something amusing to say, "Not one of them have the right tools for that job."

That summer they'd all turned fourteen, and all suffered from acne. Phillip had made plans to keep the three of them amused over the summer break, and for differing reasons, none of their lives had been quite the same ever since.

They'd begun with tins of cheap spray paint, spraying the walls around Oakwell Grange with symbols of witchcraft, and then entering the grounds and spraying the defenceless flowering plants and bushes. And when no one had challenged them they'd moved on to the house and sprayed a cross, or a crucifix as Phillip had preferred to call it, on the huge front door. Amazingly, they'd got away with that as well.

"We want to make them feel more persecuted. We're going to drive those bitches out of our area if we possibly can.

Are you with me?" Phillip was never going to be content with just inflicting graffiti on the property; Simon had soon realised that. "Let's torch one of their barns, the one nearest to the house where they store that vintage tractor that they're so proud of. That will hurt them the most."

The blaze had been awesome. It had even scorched the gable end of the large property. And that had been a part of Phillip's plan, he'd revealed to them later. As it turned out, that had been one step too far, and their families and the local police had all put two and two together.

After being hauled off to the juvenile courts they'd been bound over to keep the peace for two years. John had taken another beating from his father and all three of them had been grounded for months. To many of their school friends, they'd been awarded yet another invisible badge of honour.

They'd found it easy to behave as model citizens for those two years, mainly because during that time they'd cultivated two female friends who'd kept them updated with news from Oakwell Grange.

For three full years, they'd amused themselves by concocting devilishly evil plans that they all knew would never be carried out. And when they'd turned seventeen, they'd taken the unanimous decision to cancel all but one of their blood-oaths, and consign their obsessions with Oakwell Grange to the dustbin.

"Our oath of loyalty to each other is for life." John had stated. And they'd all agreed.

It wasn't until a year later when most of their classmates had mapped out their futures, that Philip had recognised a trend. "How many apprenticeships and college places have the three of us applied for?"

"Dunno..." John was already in a black mood. His father had put a damper on his plans for the weekend by insisting they clear out the back garden together. "Dad thinks I'm deliberately flunking my interviews, but I'm not."

Simon remembered staring hard at Philip. "I even got turned down for a temporary holiday job at the new supermarket, but they're still advertising and taking on people who can barely speak a word of English. Are you thinking our present difficulties have something to do with our pasts?"

Philip shrugged. "We're all going to have to settle for low-paid jobs, or the dullest of college courses no one else will want. And right now, if we stay around here, we're all looking at a pretty bleak future. I know what I'm starting to think. What about you two?"

John looked sceptical. "Do the courts have that power? We were juveniles and we've kept out of trouble since the night of the fire."

"I'm not thinking about official channels..." Philip hesitated, "I'm thinking about a small-minded, vindictive headmaster, and the group of evil bitches from Oakwell Grange. We know that some of the women who go to those meetings hold influential positions in the colleges, and several others are married to men who are in positions to be able to affect our futures."

"But even if you're right," John still didn't sound convinced, "what can we do about it, short of applying for positions miles from home?"

"I'm beginning to think that could be their intention. If you remember, some years ago we made the mistake of letting them know we were trying to drive them away from this area. What if they're now returning the favour?"

Different voices came from beside his hospital bed. Simon opened his eyes to see that the man who normally left his television on, whether he was watching it or not, was reaching to switch it off and cheerfully greeting two female visitors.

Simon picked up his phone, flicked the camera icon, and scrolled back through his gallery of photos. He flicked through a multitude of pictures of three friends laughing, and generally having fun together.

He recalled how John had sounded impressed with Philip's reasoning on that day, not so many months ago. "It would explain why we are the only three in our year who haven't yet got options for next year, depending on exam results. Dad says…"

"Oh sod your bloody dad," Philip had playfully grabbed John around the scruff of his neck, "you're seventeen, almost an adult, stand up to him, or better still do what your mother did and walk out on him"

"She left because of me — because of the trouble we caused with that fire. Dad says she was ashamed to have her only son in that much trouble…"

"Rubbish, she left because your dad was regularly beating her, and she should never have left you with him. It's time that you grew a pair, and I say it's time for the three of us to let Oakwell Grange's crazy occupants know that we aren't going to accept their interference in our lives, and we aren't going to go away quietly."

Simon put his phone down on the bedside table, closed his eyes again, and allowed himself to relive the night that, until yesterday, had been the most momentous of his teenage years.

There was no easy route into the back gardens of Oakwell Grange, not without being seen. He'd clambered over two crumbling stone walls, ripping the skin off his shins when he'd stumbled into a dense patch of brambles, but he'd made it. And he'd been just in time to see the women leaving, as they still did on the night of a full moon. He'd entered the grounds with the scythe from Philip's father's garden shed, with the intention of causing as much damage to as much of the vegetable garden as he possibly could.

But that night, once the procession was out of sight, and as he'd crept between the wooden sheds, he'd twisted his ankle by almost falling sideways over a rotting, overgrown, wooden pallet. An extremely thin, frightened-looking girl had stumbled from her hiding place, and with one quiet sob she'd backed a few steps away from him and then stood perfectly still. She'd stared at him as though he was the worst thing she'd ever seen. He couldn't remember ever seeing anyone looking quite so scared.

Perhaps she'd thought he was the grim reaper, he'd thought afterwards.

After putting the scythe on the ground, and shifting his weight onto his uninjured foot, he'd tried to reassure her. "Don't scream... please don't scream... I'm not going to touch you. Who are you? What are you doing here? I expected this place to be empty."

Arianne had replied in her odd, foreign accent, although her English was good. "I saw you in the moonlight. I saw you climbing the wall over there. I thought you had come to rob the house. I am alone, and so I came out here to hide."

"What... do you actually live here; what's your name?"

"My name is Olesia Broozki, but everyone calls me Arianne. Please don't hurt me."

That was the precise moment that he'd fallen in love. "I would never hurt you. But you don't look as though you belong here."

"I was brought here from Afghanistan almost two years ago, and now I live and I work here. I cook and clean, and I help in the gardens. I know I am a servant, but I don't complain. I am well fed and safe. For some of my friends, life is very, very much worse. I work for my keep and to pay for my journey to your beautiful country. One day I will leave this house, but I cannot leave until all my debts are paid. If I go before, then my family back home will be hurt, and maybe even killed. Please... you must never let anyone know that I have spoken to you. I am not allowed."

"You mean you're a prisoner here? That isn't right. That's modern-day slavery. There are laws in this country to stop that, and there are people who know how to help you. There's a Human Trafficking Centre; I know because I read about it somewhere very recently. If you like, I'll find their number for you. I'm Simon Carter, by the way, and I live quite near here. Have you got a mobile phone so that I can contact you?"

"No, you can't... we can't... please... you don't understand," she'd looked as though she was about to cry. "My family will be in danger if I don't do exactly what these women tell me to do. The people who brought me here need their money, and I believe them when they say they will hurt my family. I have young brothers and sisters. Please... you cannot help me... I have to do this. I know there are many, much worse ways of paying them back. I am lucky really. I work for these women, but I am treated well. Please promise me you won't inform the authorities in this country."

"Are you allowed to contact your family?"

"I have one call each month to my parents, but the sisters who own this place, Sheila and Hannah; they stand by my side to check I do not say anything they do not like. And most times I can't get through to my parents anyway. Things are difficult where I come from."

"Can we meet sometime? I'd really like to be your friend. Is that possible?"

"Maybe... I'm not sure... I don't have a friend. I'm not allowed. It would have to be a secret."

"If I get you a cheap mobile phone and show you how to contact me, do you think you'd be able to keep it hidden from them?" That was the moment he'd seen the first hint of a smile from her frightened, but stunningly beautiful face, and he'd treasured that memory.

"Yes, I think so, if it's very small. But it will be dangerous for you too if they find out. You must be careful."

"Don't worry about me. When can you get out?"

"The sisters go out to work most mornings about half past nine, and the other lady who comes here every day, Prunella, she goes out about one hour later. I can't go far. I always have many tasks to complete before they all return."

"I can come here, just tell me where and when."

"At eleven o'clock everyone from here is always out. I could climb over the wall behind the orchard. It's out of sight of the road and I can be there tomorrow, or the next day. Would you really buy a phone just for me?"

His hospital bed rocked and he felt a body beside him.

"Oh, I'm so terribly, terribly sorry," one of the neighbouring patient's female visitors was struggling to regain her balance. "I haven't hurt you, have I? Are you all right? I feel so clumsy in these heels. I should never have worn them today. I had one hell of a job getting up the hospital staircase. Please tell me you're all right."

"I'm fine, don't worry, no harm done." He turned his back on the three of them and closed his eyes again. He didn't wish to get drawn into their mundane chattering. He wanted to cast his mind back to the events leading up to his friend's deaths.

Arianne had returned to the house and the sharp scythe had done a sterling job. Oakwell Grange's early summer crops had been almost completely wiped out, and although all three of them had been questioned by the police, there was no proof that any of them were responsible for the damage. If Philip's father had noticed that one of his tools had been missing for twenty-four hours, he hadn't said anything. It was John who had been the most nervous, and who had wanted them to wait a few months before targeting the women again with anything other than minor pranks.

Their next close encounter with the females had happened unexpectedly, just one week before Christmas, and less than three weeks before John and Phillip had been murdered.

The three of them had been enjoying some mid-winter sunshine, cycling along the narrow country lanes and occasionally stopping to eat chocolate and crisps and discuss their next potential move against Oakwell Grange. Simon had been ahead by about fifty metres when he'd heard the roar of a car's engine. He'd turned in time to see John and Philip careering onto the muddy grass verge and he'd just managed to steer his own bike onto the grass and out of the path of the speeding car before it had roared past him. He'd collided with a newly repaired stretch of dry stone walling and his left knee still bore the scars. He'd had barely enough time to reach for a loose coping stone from the top of the wall and launch the lump of limestone towards the rear of the car.

"Simon, are you hurt?" John had reached him first. "Did you see who was driving?"

"I'm all right. It was a woman, I think. She was wearing a headscarf. I didn't get a good look at her face, but I got a half-decent shot at her car. She should have a damn great dent in the back of it." He'd pointed to the coping stone resting on the opposite side of the road. "I was aiming at her rear window but I wasn't quick enough, and the stone was too bloody heavy."

"She could have killed us," John was checking over his own bike. "We ought to phone the police."

"We all know where that damn bitch came from," Philip had limped up behind them. "She was from Oakwell Grange. That was a deliberate act, and besides, who else would have tried such a crazy stunt on this narrow back-road? The problem is that it will be her word against ours, and who's going to believe us after some of the stunts we've pulled over the years. Let's not go to the police. Let's accept this incident as what it is; a declaration of war. What do you say?"

"Hello Simon, I'm Detective Constable Robert Bell and this is Detective Constable Emily Jackson."

Simon opened his eyes and grimaced as the stabbing pain returned to his forehead.

5

Jane Goodwin still had mornings when she woke from such a muddled dream that she would lie still for a few moments and listen for the familiar sounds of her mother pottering about downstairs in the kitchen. This was one of those mornings. But as the dream faded, and as she realised it was Adam downstairs preparing to go in to work early, tears sprung into her eyes. Her mother had always been an early riser, especially during the summer months. If the sun was shining, then she'd be outside, working away in her garden. And on cold winter mornings such as these, she would be baking, or sewing, or doing something else equally productive.

She missed her mother so much.

She threw the warm bedcovers from her legs and reached with her feet for her slippers. Her mother would never have approved of her stopping in bed with sad thoughts rattling around in her head. It still felt too soon to think about her mother and smile, even at the happy memories, though she really hoped that day wouldn't be too far away.

DS Adam Ross, and his four year old son, Ryan, had spent more nights with Jane and her daughter, Lucy, than at his own house since her mother's sudden death a few months earlier. They'd met at Leaburn police station where Jane was a special constable, and when she'd been in the middle of a very messy, very public divorce. At that time, almost four years ago, Adam had been struggling to come to terms with the death of his wife, and the practicalities of raising a baby. Jane's daughter was two years older than Ryan, and far from being jealous, as Jane had feared, Lucy had taken to mothering the infant boy almost from their very first meeting. Together, the two youngsters could be angels one minute and devils the next; there rarely seemed to be any middle ground with them. But

Ryan's company had definitely helped Lucy through the worst of her grief, and for that Jane was thankful.

Trying to avoid waking the two children, she crept downstairs and into the kitchen, and quietly closed the door behind her. She wanted Adam's opinion on something before he left for work, and it was something she'd been considering for the past few weeks. She wasn't asking for her man's approval, her days of needing to do that were thankfully behind her, but she did want to hear his thoughts. Slipping her arms around his waist, she looked up into his eyes and spoke quietly. "I've been thinking about mum's life, and about how I knew so little of what she did when I wasn't around."

"It's called a private life," he smiled at her, "and everyone's entitled to one."

"All right," she smiled back at him, "so I'm just being nosy, but hear me out, please."

"I'm sorry. Go on."

"Mum sometimes mentioned a women's group and I know she regularly attended their meetings for many years. I was in my early teens when I first heard about it, and I'm ashamed to say that at that time I found it quite strange. I actually made fun of her for a while." Feeling slightly awkward, she looked away from him. "I'm feeling rather guilty now."

She felt him squeezing her into his firm chest. "Your mother loved you. She would never have worried about something as trivial as that. She brought you up to think for yourself, and to make your own decisions, didn't she?"

"And my own mistakes... yes, I know... but now I feel I'd like to see for myself what it was that she found so intriguing about that group. I think visiting them might help me to feel closer to her, and I'd enjoy talking to different people who'd known her over many years." She laughed nervously. "And maybe I'd find out what she told them about me."

Adam reached for the mug of tea that he'd obviously been intending to take upstairs to her. "Here, drink this. If you feel strongly enough about it, then you should go. When and where do these women meet up?"

"They have an organised gathering most afternoons at a large private property just outside Carlton. It's called Oakwell Grange. I've driven past it a couple of times, but that's as close as I've come to visiting the place. It's apparently owned by two middle-aged sisters who occasionally take in women who are homeless or in trouble. And they run various groups: a book club, a writing group, a candle making and herbalist class of some sort which sells its products on the local market stalls. And they also have regular spiritualist meetings." She took a large gulp of the hot tea. "They never allow any men to attend any of their meetings."

"None of that sounds like your kind of thing. Are you sure about this? Sometimes it's best to leave the past alone, and not risk spoiling the existing memories we have of our loved ones."

"I never told you this, but mum always believed she had something of a sixth sense. I used to laugh at her, but I believe that could be why she regularly attended their spiritualist meetings. I just want to see what the women there are all about, and to hear what mum did when she attended their gatherings."

"All women did you say? Are you sure you know what you could be letting yourself in for?"

"Don't laugh, it's nothing like that. Anyway, I'm not planning on joining anything. I just want to satisfy my curiosity. I telephoned the Grange yesterday and they invited me over this afternoon. I'll tell you all about it tonight."

"I can't wait," he glanced sideways at her as he turned away, an amused expression still lighting up his rugged face.

*

DCI Michael Forbes had been in his office since five a.m. Two major incidents were too much for him to handle efficiently. He was going to have to delegate.

At the Wednesday, eight a.m. briefing, he was facing a packed incident room. The larger, more modern stations had air conditioned conference rooms, but there were no suggestions of Leaburn being upgraded any time soon. If nothing else, it always felt cosy.

He began by announcing his decision. "Operation Lupin, the investigation of the unidentified woman's body discovered on Hawthorn Lane on Monday, will from today be headed up by DI Lang. The response from yesterday's television appeal was disappointing. If, as the post-mortem suggests from her dental work, the woman came from a Middle Eastern country and entered the United Kingdom legally at any time during the last ten years, then her fingerprints should have been on file, but they weren't. Without either a name or a crime scene, our best leads may still come from the public so I've arranged for a second television appeal to be broadcast on the six o'clock news tonight. You can handle that, can't you DI Lang?"

"Yes sir," DI Robert Lang was a thirty-five year old divorcee who'd recently been transferred from London after being caught up in two separate terrorist incidents, the second of which had landed him in intensive care with life threatening injuries. He had family in Derbyshire, and on the recommendation of the Met's psychiatrist, his request for a transfer had been fast-tracked.

Lang had been at Leaburn for six weeks, but the scars on his face and neck were still noticeable, and a visual reminder to everyone, Forbes especially, that both mentally and physically, DI Lang was still in recovery. He wanted his new detective to feel as though he was a valued member of his team. "Finding that baby alive will be your priority, DI Lang, but its mother's death may hold the key to where it is. Don't be afraid to ask for help if you need it, and keep pushing for national media coverage. And I want updates from you at least three times daily."

"Yes sir."

"So on to Operation Bluebell, and the attempted murder of Simon Carter and the hit-and-run killings of John Lewis and Philip Booth. We're assuming for the moment that the same vehicle was involved in both incidents. Simon Carter and the two witnesses to the hit-and-run have described a Land Rover type of vehicle, either navy blue or dark green, and with possibly only one occupant. In Ashtown, the street lamps on that stretch of road are orange, which may account for the colour confusion. Some flakes of blue paint have been found on one of the victim's clothing and with any luck we'll get a make, model, and a year from the paint reference databases. However, one of the witnesses is still insisting that at least some of the vehicle was dark green, so we can't rule out the possibility that it's multi-coloured. While we wait for that, I need some of you working on the list we've just received from the DVLA of all known Land Rovers in this area. Up to now, we've found no working CCTV cameras anywhere close to either incident and no similar vehicles have shown up on any cameras in the nearby towns around those times. Someone deliberately set out to kill John Lewis and Philip Booth on Monday night, and probably Simon Carter as well. Until we know why, we won't rule out the possibility of more attacks on the youngsters in this area. We need the public to be aware and to report anything suspicious. Families of the victims were interviewed yesterday, so today it's the turn of friends, work colleagues, and college associates. Someone may have had a grudge against these young men, and we need to know of anything they might have been involved with that none of their immediate families were aware of. You've all got your actions for the day, now bring me some names."

"What about Simon Carter's statement, sir?" DC Emily Jackson spoke out. "Are we taking his claims about those women seriously?"

"You told us he didn't seem confused when you spoke with him at the hospital yesterday. Use your loaf DC Jackson – add those names to the board."

6

The ten-bedroomed, grit-stone property was well over two hundred years old. Jane Goodwin had read that on their website, but she was still taken aback by the imposing, austere appearance of the place as she approached it. Old properties had always interested her, and like her mother she regarded most modern buildings as soulless. But even as she looked for a space to park, she couldn't imagine her mother regularly coming to this massive property to meet up with a group of superstitious women.

There were eight cars already parked on the weed free, gravelled parking area along the side of the house. She'd asked to visit on a day when there was a meeting of some sort in progress. When she'd phoned, a woman had told her she was welcome to visit on any afternoon after one o'clock, as there was usually a group meeting of some kind. Even so, she felt relieved to see so many vehicles. The trembling in her stomach was spreading upwards into her chest as she squeezed her little car into the only available space.

She wiped away an unexpected tear and tried to concentrate on the exterior of the building. It looked reasonably well maintained, with clean, fresh, black paintwork on the door and the windows. And considering its age, it had an amazingly straight, black slate roof, with black, cast-iron guttering and ornate rainwater hoppers. Decorative metal brackets held the painted downspouts tightly against the neatly pointed stone walls. It looked tidy.

The grounds were just as impressive as the house, both in size and overall layout. Weed free lawns and carefully trimmed bushes lined the driveway to the front of the house, and mature, deciduous trees flanked the boundaries against the fields. Behind the house she could see one small section of what she presumed was the vegetable garden. She decided to delay knocking on the door for a few minutes by taking a look.

She'd expected to see rows of winter greens: sprouts, cabbages, leeks and kale, all standing proud and protected from the worst of the weather by barriers of clear plastic and white fleece, just as she'd seen in the pictures on their website. But most of the area looked as though everything in it had been planted just a little too late in the season, with the remainder being freshly dug ground, presumably ready for the spring planting.

About fifty metres into the grounds was a large, plastic covered polytunnel, which was in turn flanked by a pair of matching greenhouses, and beyond that lay an area of grassland which was dotted with small trees. Presumably that was their orchard. The whole thing made her attempts at a salad and herb garden look extremely pathetic.

She walked back to the front of the house.

At least as old as the house, the massive stone doorstep was well-worn, with a dished-out area on its front edge where thousands of feet must have trodden. She studied the stone slab for a few moments before grasping the ice-cold, iron door knocker. No wireless doorbells here. And from the outside at least, everything appeared to be authentic to the property, just as the website had described it.

Almost instantly she heard women's voices, followed by footsteps on bare floorboards, and then a loud creak as the heavy wooden door swung open. The muscles of her right leg automatically flexed, ready to take a step back, but she managed to check the impulse. Instead, she blinked.

"Welcome, my dear, welcome, we've been expecting you." A tall, white-robed woman stood in the doorway, her slender shape framed by the darkness of the wide entrance hall behind her. It took Jane a few seconds to realise the woman was speaking unnaturally slowly and sympathetically to her.

The smiling woman didn't look too many years younger than her late mother had been, with a similarly shaped round face, and with naturally greying hair swept up into a neat bun on the top of her head. But there the similarities ended. Swirls of purple and red face paint covered most of the woman's forehead and continued on down the left side of her face. Jane tried to concentrate on the woman's eyes, but even those seemed to sparkle unnaturally.

"Jane... Jane... please... won't you come inside? We've been expecting you for so many months – ever since your dear mother left us for the other side. And I can see your mother in your eyes, my dear. I can see her soul pulsating within you. She is delighted that you have finally decided to join us. She was, and she still is, so very proud of you, her only daughter. She wants you to know that."

Jane felt a tingle running from the top of her head down to her feet. "I wasn't sure whether to come..." The urge to run back to her car was so close to winning at that moment.

"Don't look so worried, my child, this is only face-paint. A splash of soap and water and it will all disappear down the sink... the paint that is... not my face," she laughed, a warm, genuine laugh, and then reached out to take hold of Jane's arm. "I realise this must be very difficult for you, but do please come inside and meet our ladies."

She allowed herself to be guided through the dark hallway and into a large, poorly-lit and over-furnished room. She'd come this far. She didn't want them to see that when the door closed behind her she was trembling slightly. "My mother didn't tell me very much about your group."

"We get that a lot. Our next of kin don't always understand what we do here. It's difficult to explain to those who aren't genuinely interested. But rest assured that everyone here today was very well acquainted with your dear mother, indeed, we were all just talking about her and remembering what a lovely lady she was, when you knocked on our door. She allowed us to sense you were on your way here. I know everyone in this room will miss her for a long time to come, but our losses are nothing compared to yours. You have our most sincere condolences."

It wasn't only Jane's nerves churning up the remains of a late breakfast in her stomach. The air in the large room was saturated with a sickly-sweet aroma of wax, wood smoke, scented candles, and several other odours she couldn't isolate. What the hell had her mother been thinking of when she came here? More to the point, what was she realistically hoping to achieve now by following in her mother's footsteps?

Six flickering candles were the only light source in the cluttered room, and the shadows made her unsure of exactly what she was seeing. She squinted, blinked, and then squinted again. Through the gloom she counted ten figures standing in a row against a wall, all except one dressed in a floor length black robe, and all looking at her.

"Allow us to introduce ourselves."

She drew in a quick breath. She'd almost forgotten the white robed woman standing immediately behind her.

"I'm Sheila Hall, and the other lady dressed in white is my slightly older sister, Hannah Hall. This is our jointly owned property, and since our grandmother passed to the other side a few years ago, we have been maintaining the Oakwell traditions of charity and organised gatherings for the females of this district. The ladies you see here are some of our most loyal members."

What Jane wanted to say was, *'quite honestly ladies, I don't give a toss, open that door, I'm out of here,'* but her mouth felt dry and instead she politely replied, "I'm Jane Goodwin... I was hoping someone might be able to shed some light on the reasons for my mother's visits here." A poor choice of words, she thought, but what the heck.

She didn't hear anyone making a sound, but as if on some sort of a cue, the dark-robed women all stepped forward, but not equally. They formed a semi-circle. When she looked down she saw a circular black cloth on the centre of the dark, wooden floor. It wasn't thick enough to be a carpet, and she guessed it was about ten feet in diameter. None of the women's feet were touching it, but peeping from below the hems of their black robes, their bare toes were close to its edge.

Her heart pounded. She felt trapped, but didn't dare move as one by one the women announced their names. They weren't names that she could instantly put any faces to, but most of them sounded strangely familiar. Perhaps her mother had talked about them after all, and she'd just not been listening.

"Now that's over with ladies, and before we all go into the kitchen where we can be less formal, we'll give our guest a glimpse of our precious Alter." Hannah's voice came from the shadows behind her and Jane turned to look.

She realised she hadn't noticed the white-robed woman move. When her personal space was invaded she always felt uncomfortable, but this experience was taking her discomfort to a whole new level.

The sisters stepped away from her and moved towards the wall, but her sense of relief lasted for barely a second. They were now standing with their backs to the wall, one at each side of a coffin-sized, narrow, cloth-covered table which didn't have one square inch of space left on its surface. Just like the cloth on the floor, this cloth was black, and on it were four, black, unlit candles, several silver dishes containing mounds of dried flowers and foliage, and scattered along its length were various, unrecognisable lumps of dried and wizened fruits. She'd found the source of at least some of the more unpleasant odours in the room.

"Isn't it beautiful?" Hannah spread out her arms, seemingly expecting confirmation of some sort.

"Now then Hannah," Sheila took a step forward and linked her arm into Jane's elbow again, "we can't expect our new visitor to appreciate our artefacts until we've had a chance to explain them to her. But perhaps we'll save that for another day. There should be drinks ready for us in the kitchen by now."

Jane wouldn't have thought it possible a few minutes earlier, but the air in the kitchen was even more pungent than in the room she'd been guided out of. The larger space was at least bathed in a more natural light from the afternoon's winter sun, which streamed in through the leaded windows, but everywhere she looked, on the work surfaces and even on the kitchen table, the room resembled a busy production line. On one side of the room, antique brass Post Office scales were being used to weigh out tiny quantities of what she hoped were dried herbs, and on the other side, dozens of small packages were piled high, presumably ready to be labelled and packed into the cardboard trays stacked at the side of them.

Obediently, she sat in the kitchen chair offered to her. There wasn't enough seating in the room for everyone, and as each of the women found their own place to sit or to lean, she looked around the room at the faces. She realised she did know a few of the women by sight, but that knowledge made her feel only slightly less uneasy, and very glad she'd told Adam where she'd intended to be for part of her afternoon.

The women began chatting among themselves, while a slim girl who hadn't been introduced, and who looked no more than fifteen or sixteen, walked around the room offering cups of herbal tea. Jane felt as though conversations were being held over her head, almost as if she wasn't a part of the proceedings. This wasn't why she'd come here. She'd come to find out more about her mother's life, not to sit politely drinking stewed tea.

She looked around the group of women again. Was it just that she was seeing the women out of context? She realised at least two of them had children attending the same school as her daughter, and while she couldn't say that she knew them, they were on polite nodding terms. And she'd seen Sheila and Hannah and at least three of the others working in the school kitchens at lunchtimes. That must be why their meetings were held in the afternoons.

Just recently, she'd been thinking she ought to make more of an effort to make new friends. Since her split with her husband she'd lost touch with all of their mutual friends and hadn't felt inclined to make any attempts to mix with new people. Her ex was a well-known figure in the world of local business, and after being a special constable for several years, she could understand why some people felt reluctant to get close to her. But still, that was no excuse.

Maybe this was as good a place as any to start making new friends. After all, these women had been a part of her mother's life for many years. She took a deep breath, willed herself to relax, and then asked the woman closest to her just how well she'd known her mother.

7

DS Adam Ross was standing with the team of uniformed and plain clothed officers assigned to Operation Bluebell while they waited for DCI Forbes to complete his Wednesday afternoon briefing on Operation Lupin with DI Lang.

He'd been busy with the hit-and-run incident and only just read the summary of Simon Carter's statement from Tuesday afternoon. Could the women Simon was accusing of murdering his friends be the same women Jane had been telling him about only a few hours earlier? Were they the ones she'd been intending to visit today? DCI Forbes appeared to be in deep conversation with DI Lang and his team, so he stepped out of the incident room into the corridor and jabbed at his phone. "Jane, where are you?"

She'd already left Oakwell Grange and that was all he needed to know. He made an excuse about Ryan misplacing one of his favourite toy cars, told her not to worry, and then switched off his phone. Even though Simon's accusations seemed unlikely, he hesitated before returning his phone to his jacket pocket. Jane's voice had sounded strained. He understood how finding a hidden part of her mother's life could be important to her, and could be a part of her natural grieving process. Maybe that was why she'd sounded so distant.

He would have to tell her about the investigation, of course, but it wasn't something he could do over the phone.

Forbes turned his attention to the team working on Operation Bluebell. "The fragments of rust and blue paint recovered from the clothing of John Lewis and Philip Booth have been identified. Unfortunately, the paint was touch-up paint, sold in small quantities, available in most auto shops, and widely used for covering rust on thousands of vehicles. So for now we have to put our trust in the two witness statements and continue checking the list of Land Rovers. In view of Simon Carter's statement yesterday afternoon, Adam and I will begin by taking a look at all of the vehicles on the grounds of Oakwell Grange."

*

One hour after entering Oakwell Grange, and five minutes after leaving it, Jane drove her car into the first empty layby she could find, rested her hands on the top of her steering wheel, and gazed out across the patchwork of limestone walls and green fields. Daylight was fading fast and the air temperature had already fallen enough to be barely above freezing, but she couldn't resist opening the car window as far as it would go and breathing in the cleansing air.

The mental image of her mother, dressed only in a floor-length black robe, standing in a candle-lit room and chanting to the earth mother, or whoever the hell they were trying to communicate with, was one she would have found hilarious only a few months earlier. The women obviously weren't good at reading her body-language because they'd invited her back. They had even offered to initiate her into one of their groups. Not the fortnightly writing group which they seemed so proud of, nor the monthly candle-making group which was apparently making a modest profit these days, but the same group that her mother had been a part of, and with the same long black robe that her mother had worn.

"Your mother was a valued member of our group even before you were born, Jane," at least three of the women had told her while she'd been sitting at that cluttered kitchen table politely sipping at the revolting liquid.

She shuddered.

She'd tried hard not to look shocked when Sheila had gently lifted that black robe and its hanger from the back of the kitchen door. Hadn't they realised how distressing it was going to be for her just to see that single item of unwashed clothing?

Her eyes watered and now there was no reason not to let the tears flow. How could she not have known that her mother had belonged to some sort of weird cult? What kind of a daughter did that make her?

She leaned back into the driving seat and pressed a handkerchief against her eyes. Surely, somewhere deep in her memories, there must be some long forgotten snippets of conversations which might hold clues as to why her mother had gone to that place. But however far back her memories drifted, nothing clicked, not even vaguely. There was an important chunk of her mother's life that she knew almost nothing about, and the one person she really wanted to talk it through with was gone forever.

She wiped her face, tucked her handkerchief back into her trouser pocket, and was about to turn the ignition key when her phone rang.

No, she hadn't come across Ryan's favourite toy car.

Coming to terms with her feelings was going to take time, and she was even less sure now about talking it over with Adam. She would have to tell him something about her visit today, but it would be an edited version, and definitely minus the part about being invited back to follow in her mother's footsteps. She wasn't even sure she wanted to set foot in Oakwell Grange ever again, but she knew it was a decision she had to make alone.

*

Within minutes of leaving Leaburn station, Forbes and Adam were on the outskirts of the market town, on a road lined with reasonably well-built 1960's council houses, most of which had long since been purchased by their occupants and appeared to be well maintained. Beyond them, built on what only a couple of years earlier had been a green field, was a small housing estate that the council had optimistically dubbed, *'affordable housing'*. Forbes's father would have called them *'rabbit hutches with a college education'*, but they were all now occupied by locally born young families, and toys and trampolines decorated the small lawns. Neither Forbes nor Adam spoke as they drove through the two distinct areas.

Two miles further on, and immediately opposite the small but neatly kept graveyard fronting the Saxon church of Saint Michael, Forbes took the turn which his satellite navigation system cheerfully informed him would take him to the post code area which included Oakwell Grange. He was hoping a search warrant wouldn't be necessary, but he was aware of the rumours of the Oakwell women refusing to allow men onto their property uninvited.

A muffled female voice came through the closed door. "Oakwell Grange is not open to visitors. We don't welcome strangers. Please state your business and then leave."

"This is the police. I am DCI Forbes and with me is DS Ross. We are from Leaburn station and we need to speak to Sheila and Hannah Hall who we understand both live here. We are not going to go away. Open this door please so that you can check our IDs."

They were shown into a large and gloomy room by the woman who'd introduced herself as Sheila Hall. Forbes looked around the walls and saw that Adam was doing the same. A huge number of old fashioned landscape paintings, some with unrecognisable figures in the foreground, along with framed and faded sepia photographs, were covering almost every square inch of space on every wall of the room.

There were at least a dozen mismatched armchairs, two of which contained a middle-aged lady clutching a cup and saucer. He had the feeling that neither he nor his DS were about to be invited to sit down, or offered refreshments of any kind. Not that they would have accepted.

"Let me guess," Sheila added after introducing her sister, Hannah Hall, and their good friend, Prunella Leath. "We've all seen the local news, and sad though it is for their families, those boys were nothing but trouble to us here at the Grange. I don't mind stating that this area will be a safer and a calmer place without them, and I for one wouldn't have minded seeing all three of them..."

"Sheila..." Hannah stood up, and balancing her empty cup and saucer in her right hand, walked to her sister's side, "you can't go around saying things like that. The police will begin to think we had something to do with their deaths."

"Oh do wake up, Hannah, and use your brains for once. Why do you think they are here so soon after the incidents? Someone has already pointed the finger of suspicion in our direction, and we can all take a pretty good guess at who that person might be."

"Well... pardon me for speaking... I was only trying to help."

"Help... why would I need your help? If I need it, I'll ask for it."

The bickering sisters suddenly stopped talking and turned to face him.

Forbes felt disappointed. He'd been hoping for something unintentionally disclosed in the heat of the moment. He continued to quietly look at each of them in turn for several seconds, but his tactic failed.

"We are here as part of our investigations into the deaths of John Lewis and Philip Booth, and the attempted murder of Simon Carter. We will be interviewing a large number of people in the area, but your names have been suggested to us."

Sheila raised her arms towards her sister in a gesture of mock surprise. "What did I just say... that the police already believe it was us... unbelievable or what?"

The third woman, Prunella Leath, spoke from her seated position. "Sheila, do be quiet. I'm quite sure that they don't. These officers are just doing their jobs. Everyone from Oakwell has had conflicts with those three boys in the past, that's no secret to anyone living around here, but why would we want to harm them now, after all this time? Besides, we were all here on Monday evening."

"Do you live here, Mrs Leath?" He was well aware that she was the gamekeeper's wife, and as far as he knew still living with her husband in a tied cottage on the Samson Estate. For years their marriage had been a very turbulent one. On four occasions his officers had been called out to a domestic dispute at the gamekeeper's home, and each time the presence of firearms had been a huge concern. It could potentially save his officers many hours of paperwork if the marriage was over.

"No, of course not; I live at the Keeper's Cottage on the Samson Estate with my husband, as you know. I left here some time before one a.m. on Tuesday morning and was home by about quarter-past, as my husband will confirm."

"And until then you were all here together... none of you left the property... can anyone else corroborate that?"

"We have a couple of young, troubled girls living here at the moment, but they were both in their rooms, so no, I guess not."

"Could we look around your vehicles, and your garages and outbuildings while we're here? We're looking for a blue or a green Land Rover with possible bodywork and paintwork damage. We're checking all the farms and smallholdings in the area. Do you own anything like that?" He didn't want to threaten them with a search warrant yet.

"You can look, can't he Hannah," Sheila smiled at her sister, "but you won't find any. We can't afford more than one small car each."

Forbes never ceased to be amazed at the things people stored in their garages, in most instances almost everything except their expensive vehicles, but it didn't stop him feeling increasingly disappointed as they moved from one junk-filled outbuilding to another. It would have been too easy to find what they were looking for at their first attempt, but they had to start somewhere.

Those women were hiding something. The way they'd referred to the victims, and their complete lack of empathy or concern for the sole survivor of Monday night's incidents, seemed unnatural for women who had worked for years in school kitchens. He'd withheld the fact that it had been Simon who'd pointed the finger at them, but he'd be willing to bet a month's salary that they already knew.

Adam opened the double doors to the last of the garages on the property.

"Sir...? From the license plate, this dark blue Isuzu Trooper looks to be about twenty-five years old."

"Squeeze around to the front and check for signs of recent damage."

"It isn't covered in dust or cobwebs. I'd say it's been driven not too long ago." Adam ducked below the wing mirror, and in the process brushed his clean jacket against the cobweb-covered timber wall of the building. "There's been some damage to the front, sir, but it doesn't appear to be recent."

"Nevertheless," Forbes felt the butterflies in his stomach settling down very slightly, "we'll get scenes of crimes officers out here straight away to take samples. Why didn't the women mention this, I wonder? Let's go back inside and ask them."

Adam squeezed back out of the building, removed his jacket, shook it, and then brushed it with his hand. "Simon confessed that he'd been dazzled by sleet and headlights." He was sounding hopeful. "And could an elderly man who'd just come from the pub, and a woman who'd admittedly only witnessed the hit-and-run through net curtains and a wet window, have all been mistaken? There aren't too many Isuzu Troopers still on the roads these days so it isn't a make and model which easily springs to the minds of most people, especially at night and in poor visibility."

Sheila opened the door, let out an exaggerated sigh, and then directed them into a different room. They waited while she called upstairs to Hannah and Prunella. The even larger room had fewer pictures on the walls but was crammed with old, decent-looking, dark furniture. Two matching sideboards gleamed as if freshly polished, an identical pair of brown leather Chesterfield sofas flanked a stone fireplace large enough to stand half a dozen people inside its opening, and there were four narrow tables, one pressed up against each of the walls with at least a dozen ladder-backed chairs scattered among them. Adam raised his eyebrows but remained silent. Forbes knew his colleague was totting up the values. Adam's father had been an antique dealer and a lot of his knowledge had rubbed off onto his son.

The only sound in the room came from the large grandfather clock. Forbes's knowledge of antiques was very limited, but his own father had sold one far less grand than this one only a few years ago, and that had fetched a couple of thousand pounds at auction. There was money in this room – old money.

"We'd like to know who owns the blue Isuzu Trooper in the end garage, and when it was last driven." Forbes addressed all three women. "It doesn't quite match the descriptions we've been given but there is some damage to the front offside wing. How and when did that damage occur?"

Prunella looked amused, almost as though she'd been waiting for their questions. "That old Isuzu Trooper is mine, Inspector. We use her for travelling to Buxton in the winter for the weekly grocery shop. She's better than any of our other cars in icy conditions, and we have to go out early, sometimes before the roads are gritted, because Sheila and Hannah need to be at work for ten. The three litre petrol engine is far too greedy with fuel for her to be used any more frequently than that, but she holds a full week's groceries quite easily and she's very reliable. On the way to Buxton about two months ago, a deer jumped into the road and there was nothing I could do to avoid hitting it. That was the cause of the damage, officer, but she's such an old girl that as long as the lights were still working I didn't see any point in getting it fixed. Does that answer your questions satisfactorily?"

"Did you report the incident?" Accidents involving wildlife were a regular occurrence on many of the Peak District roads, but unless the driver intended to make an insurance claim, most of them went unreported.

"No, I phoned my husband and told him where to find the carcass. It kept the dogs fed for several weeks."

"So the vehicle was here until what time on Monday?"

"It never left these premises that day. I arrived here in my Golf and left in the same vehicle well after midnight, as I've already told you. The Isuzu is often left here for months at a time."

"We're going to have to examine the tyres and take paint samples from the Isuzu today. Officers are already on their way here. I take it you'll have no objections."

"None at all," Prunella actually smiled at him.

"What about the other residents here? Could any of them have driven it that night without you realising?"

"No, I have the only set of keys and I keep them in my bag. And I'm not sure that either of the girls we have staying with us at the moment is licensed to drive. It's a tight squeeze getting it in and out of that garage. It takes practice. No, the old Isuzu never moved that night. I can guarantee you that."

"Back to the three victims," Adam took over. "We're aware of the long-running feud between them and the ladies here at Oakwell Grange. While we're here would you care to tell us about it?"

"We've had run-ins with the local children for as long as we can remember," Hannah broke her silence, "and some of them have been worse than others. Our grandmother suffered similarly for years. We took jobs in the local school's kitchens to allow us to interact with some of the more sensible local children, and to show them that we're just ordinary women here at Oakwell Grange."

"And boys will be boys," Sheila added. "We've never had any great success with them. We think that's possibly because we don't normally allow males onto this property, not uninvited anyway. We've been the victims of many childish pranks over the years, some of which occasionally got out of hand, but we like to think we've done nothing wrong. That really should be an end to the matter."

"Is there any wonder the local youngsters find those women to be a source of entertainment?" Forbes was enjoying the drive back to Leaburn and the male companionship of his DS.

"Not really sir, no. I should mention though, Jane called in at Oakwell Grange earlier this afternoon – something to do with her late mother, I believe. She's never been there before but her mother was a regular visitor. I'll ask her not to call again until we've eliminated everyone involved in Oakwell from our enquiries."

"If she's any sense she'll keep well away without having to be asked. What's your opinion of their set-up?"

"The whole place needs a good clear out, and those paintings and sepia photographs in that first room, all those eyes watching our every move from behind a layer of dust, I've experienced some things over the years but I don't remember ever being in a room which felt quite as creepy as that. And did you notice that despite the breeze outside, there seemed to be no air movement in either of the rooms we were in? The two rooms and the hallway each had their own distinctive odour. If those women are brewing up their own herbal concoctions, there could be drugs involved. Even if the Isuzu is clean, I don't think we should eliminate them as suspects.

"I wasn't intending to."

8

Simon had been wallowing in self-pity, convinced his life was going from bad to worse and unable to see any future for himself and the love of his life, his beautiful Arianne, until two things happened.

The first was that the hospital had released him, so that finally, in his own room and alone, he could lie back on his bed and have a good cry. He gingerly turned onto his side, drew up his knees, and wrapped his arms across his sore ribs. He sobbed for a full five minutes before sitting up and taking in a few deep and painful breaths. After wiping his eyes he felt empty, but ready to look to the future.

The second was the news that his insurance company was going to pay the full market value of his bike. His dad had taken care of all that for him.

Within half an hour of arriving home, his dad had acted very predictably and resorted to the old emotional blackmail. "Your mother's nerves won't stand it if you get another bike," he'd said. But he needn't have wasted his breath. He had no intentions of buying a replacement. He'd never really been that keen on risking his neck in the rush hour traffic around the college, and Monday's brush with death had ended his brief affair with motorbikes for good.

He couldn't imagine anyone ever replacing his true, lifelong friends, John and Philip. They were the real cause of his hot tears and the empty feeling in his chest. They'd been a huge part of his life and it had taken their deaths for him to realise that. He almost wished he'd died that night too, his loss felt so unbearable. But he hadn't, he was alive – battered but very much alive, and now he had Arianne to consider. Sooner or later his injuries would heal, but however much he was hurting, he wasn't going to rest until someone had paid for his friends' deaths.

The bedroom door creaked open and Simon lifted his head from the pillow.

"The police have just phoned," his father poked his head around the bedroom door. "They wanted to let you know that they've visited Oakwell Grange, and that under no circumstances are any of us to contact any of the women from there. Your mother will bring your food to your room in about an hour."

Simon simply nodded, balling the damp tissue in his fist.

The door closed and a wave of realisation hit him. The police hadn't even bothered to tell him personally, let alone offer him any kind of protection. It was obvious that they actually believed he'd sent them there on a wild goose chase.

John and Philip were no longer headline news and the next attempt on his life could come from absolutely anywhere. While he was under his parent's roof he might even be placing them in danger.

All of them deserved better.

He desperately wished he hadn't promised to keep Arianne's presence in that place a secret. Maybe if he'd broken that promise and told them about Arianne's situation, told them her story and how frightened he was for her, maybe then the police would have looked more closely at Oakwell Grange and its crazy occupants. But then they might think that his infatuation with a girl was motive enough for sending them there in the first place.

No, he had to keep his promise – he wouldn't risk making things worse for her.

He'd never been in love before – if that was what this really was. "The girl I love and would like to spend the rest of my life with." He whispered it over and over again into his damp pillow. It sounded so unrealistic for a boy of his age, but it was how he'd felt since he'd first met her on that fateful, moonlit night. She was so rarely out of his thoughts that it had to be love he was feeling.

He guessed that being an only child and growing up in a rural area was the reason he'd always had imaginary friends and heard voices inside his head, but since that first meeting with Arianne, her soft, fearful voice had haunted him to the point where all those he'd grown up with had been silenced.

He'd slept with a girl from college a couple of times. Half the youths in his year had been there, he'd learned with disgust after the event, but he'd just wanted to know what sex was really like. It wasn't as if she'd been a proper girlfriend. Only his male pride had been hurt when she'd dumped him after he'd refused to buy her a second Big Mac. He'd put that liaison down to experience.

He stretched out on his bed, determined not to waste time on meaningless memories. They were nothing when compared to the intimacy he'd experienced over the past few months with Arianne. He would concentrate his thoughts on her.

The day that he'd kept his promise, bought Arianne a very basic pay-as-you-go phone and patiently shown her how to use it, had proved to him how vulnerable she was. He'd never seen anyone so grateful to receive something valued at less than ten pounds. That anyone could have stumbled across her and bought her devotion for a tenner, had to be wrong. But he'd been the one who'd found her, and for as long as he possibly could, he intended to keep her safe from harm.

He never contacted her. He'd explained how she had to keep it switched off unless she was calling out, to save the battery and to prevent anyone from hearing it if the network or anyone else tried to contact her. Whenever she felt it was safe to leave Oakwell she would send him a text, and if he could get to her, he would.

Philip and John had gone with him to Oakwell on a few of his visits. John had got his kicks by placing nails under car tyres, while Philip had released crickets and large spiders, bought for him by a friend from the local pet shop, into the garages. And any road kill that they'd found had always ended up one of the three stone doorsteps of Oakwell Grange.

Those times had ended.

He whispered into his pillow again, "Arianne, I've loved since that very first night. I will get you out of there, I promise."

He pictured her shaking her head in despair, as she so often did. He knew she felt a weight of the responsibility on her fragile shoulders that he could do nothing about. She'd never doubted that the men who'd organised her passage into Britain had enough far reaching thugs in their employ to hurt her family. "This is my burden, Simon," she'd told him. "This isn't one of your computer games where you can alter things to control the outcome. I am a realist and you have to be too."

He'd wanted to make rash promises to show her how strongly he felt. "I'll get some cash from somewhere. I'll get a job. I'll buy your freedom," he'd said the last time they'd met. "However large their organisation, they're not going to turn down money, surely?"

She'd refused his offer. "I appreciate it, really I do, but I can't let you do that. You need to finish college to find a decent job. And I'm not sure that my contract is about money any more. I was traded. I don't know what for, but I do know I belong to the women of Oakwell Grange for as long as they need me. They have my passport and my papers. I'm sure it will all be all right. I will get my freedom eventually and living here isn't so bad. But it makes me sad to think you might not want to wait for me. I would understand if you didn't."

"I'll wait. Never doubt that fact," he'd reassured her.

One way or another, he was going to get her out of that place.

9

Prunella Leath quietly studied her brood of cackling females as they took their places around the kitchen table for the Thursday afternoon book club meeting, and she politely listened and nodded as they gossiped over the grisly fate of the two dead youths. She displayed no emotion and not one of the group looked at her with the slightest hint of suspicion.

The Gods, as always, were on her side.

She was aware that many of the women who met here were now calling her 'the new dragon'. That was fine with her, just as long as they remembered to show her the respect that her position demanded.

It was ten years since the original old dragon, old grandma Hall, had passed away peacefully in her sleep, and since Prunella had met only a token resistance from the sisters, Sheila and Hannah, as she'd taken control of the day-to-day running of the businesses and finances of Oakwell Grange. Twenty years before that, Sheila and Hannah had lost both parents in a traffic accident, and after that sad day their grandmother had controlled Oakwell. But during the last few years of her life she'd allowed the legitimate side of the businesses to slide. To be fair, the woman had been in declining health for a couple of years before her death, but long before that it had been Prunella who had kept all their heads above water, financially speaking. She'd even invested the last of her savings in the businesses. It was only right and proper that she'd been allowed to take charge, and the sisters had quickly been persuaded of that fact.

The herbal soaps and scented candles were selling particularly well, and more to the point, they were now making a healthy profit. "*A consistently good range of products, available when and where our customers want them, and all at profitable but competitive prices,*" she'd drilled her mantra into the sisters until they'd finally taken it on board. Not that they often remembered to thank her for her efforts.

She closed the kitchen door on the book club meeting and headed up the stairs to her room. She couldn't be bothered with their mind-numbing chatter today. A few hours from now it would be exactly three days since she'd disposed of two of the boys. Now she needed to think. She needed to plan. She'd worked too hard and sacrificed too much to allow Simon or Arianne to ruin everything.

The future of Oakwell Grange was at stake.

And like so many other things in Prunella's life, it was a future inextricably linked to the past.

The Grange had always been known for taking in females who'd found themselves in desperate, and sometimes life-threatening, situations. It had been used as a refuge for as long as anyone had been able to research. Built in the early eighteen-hundreds, the generally accepted story was that it had been built to house orphans who were too young or too weak to be sent into the workhouses, but that the son of the original benefactor, on inheriting his late father's estate, had installed a dozen or more young women in the property and subsequently produced so many children of his own that there were no places left for the waifs and strays that the church continued to bring to his door.

His long-suffering wife had just happened to have tenuous links with the Devonshire dynasty, claiming to be a descendant of the dynasty's original founding mother, Bess of Hardwick, and very wealthy in her own right. The philanderer's sudden and unidentified illness, followed by a fatal fall from his favourite horse, was rumoured to have been treated as suspicious for a while, but as so often happened with the wealthier aristocracy in centuries past, no charges were ever brought.

The Grange had belonged to the Hall family since the middle of the eighteenth century after it had been given away by the widow on the condition that it was always used as a refuge for girls and young women under the age of twenty-two. The deeds to the property stated that while any of the seven top-floor bedrooms were unoccupied, no female child or young woman in distress was ever to be turned away.

That had been all well and good while the Hall family had had the finances and the standing in the community to meet the unusual condition, but since the middle of the twentieth century, when inheritance tax had drained most of the family's accessible money, it had been a huge drain on the Oakwell purse. The Hall family hadn't even had the finances to hire a good lawyer to attempt to get the deeds altered and the clause removed. But it was a clause that Prunella had been able to take advantage of and a drain on funds that she alone had been able to turn around. And despite never living at the Grange, her schemes had cemented her position as head of the female household.

More importantly, her successes with money had meant that the sisters had listened to her, and had been easily persuaded to unwittingly fall in with her long-term plans.

Prunella had lived and worked on the wrong side of the law for all of her adult life, and ten years earlier, after months of planning, and meetings with people who spoke very poor English and whom she would normally have crossed the road to avoid rubbing shoulders with, she had made a deal. Since then, she'd regularly sat at the kitchen table of Oakwell Grange with a smile on her face and a huge wad of used twenty-pound and fifty-pound notes in front of her. There were more lines on her face now, and more money to reflect the increased risk they were all taking, but she still always waited for Hannah and Sheila to shower her with praise before she locked the money away in the vast cellar below the kitchen.

They could never bank it, of course, but it was there to be used for the improvement and the upkeep of Oakwell Grange, and for any unseen emergency. Both sisters shared her commitment to preserving the Grange for the future generations – that was the single most important thing she'd drilled into them from the day she'd first stepped over the worn, granite doorstep. They were all determined not to leave the massive debts and repair bills that the old lady had saddled them with. And it felt good to be able to maintain the old place without having to go grovelling to a bank manager who was still complaining about the size of the Oakwell overdraft, despite it being halved over the last ten years.

The next generation of Oakwell women, Hannah's daughter, Acacia, and Sheila's daughter, Jasmine, were both twenty and living and running a business in Manchester. They too were very well aware of their responsibilities towards Oakwell Grange, and when the time was right they would return. She'd made sure of that.

And Simon Carter would return to Oakwell Grange at some point. She was equally certain of that. She'd seen Arianne sneaking out and climbing over the wall beyond the orchard. If she knew anything about boys of his age, it was that any brains they had turned to mush at the sight of a defenceless, beautiful young girl. The lure that would ensure his return was skivvying away somewhere in the house, just as she did every day of the week. Simon had to be disposed of first, and as quickly as possible, but she couldn't risk suspicion falling onto the household for a second time.

She was going to have to plan carefully.

*

Forbes stood at the front of the packed, and unusually quiet, incident room. "This is the Thursday afternoon briefing of Operation Bluebell, which is now two and a half days old but not making much meaningful progress. The initial persons of interest named in Simon Carter's statement have been interviewed, and their registered vehicles examined and samples taken to the forensics lab. Those of you continuing to check the vehicles on the list from the DVLA, I want to keep your eyes open for any old, unregistered vehicles. Many of the hill farmers out there would prefer to let an old workhorse of a vehicle rot away in a barn, or simply keep it for getting around on their own land, rather than obtain a SORN document for it, or even sell it for scrap. There are more than a few out there without the necessary, up to date, paperwork – remember that."

He took a step away from Operation Bluebell's whiteboard. "DI Lang, I'm sure we'd all like to hear the latest on Operation Lupin." He was assuming the similar lack of progress in finding the missing baby was the cause of the sombre atmosphere in the room.

"We had a reasonable response from the public following yesterday's television and radio appeals, sir, but as yet, no solid leads. None of the local maternity hospitals or midwives could provide a name for our victim. I'm extending that search out of our area via e-mails. The carpet and clothing from the body had been submerged in slow-running, muddy water for too long for any complete DNA samples to be retrieved, other than that of the victim. The forensics lab is working on some partials. The carpet was made in Britain; most probably manufactured in the late nineteen forties or fifties, certainly post-war, and had been used on a timber floor prior to being cleaned several years ago and then stored in an attic or a shed before being used as a body-bag. We're following that up, but most of the factories and department stores from that era have long since closed, and even if they haven't, their records aren't likely to go back that far. We are checking all the 'mispers' in the UK, but if she is an illegal, unless her family are making enquiries about her disappearance, or unless she has a friend in this country who is missing her, it may be impossible to ever put a name to her."

"Keep your main focus on that missing baby." Forbes didn't like that his DI was already sounding defeated. He felt his brow wrinkling. He'd put Lang in charge of the investigation, rather than one of his own longer-standing detectives, because he believed that the officer needed to feel useful after his long recuperation. He suspected that one or two in the station weren't happy about his decision, not that they would ever have voiced their grievances directly to him.

"General hospitals, GPs, health service workers, social workers and even pharmacists need to be on the lookout for anyone with a new-born baby; anyone who doesn't quite fit the bill, or who makes them even remotely suspicious or uncomfortable. Make them aware that we would rather check out a hundred innocent families than miss the guilty person. Our best hope is that the baby is out there, is healthy, and is being well taken care of until we find it. Put whatever pressure you have to onto the media to keep the story in the headlines. The public are invaluable in cases such as these."

"Yes sir."

"Adam, did you want to add something?"

DS Adam Ross had been studying the DVLA printouts. "Sir, back to Operation Bluebell, I recognise one of the names on this list. Mr Leath, the husband of Prunella Leath who we've already met, is the registered keeper of two blue Land Rovers. He hasn't had a visit from us yet."

"Then first thing tomorrow, Adam, you and I will check the gamekeeper's land, followed by the Samson Estate and all its employees. On an old estate like that there are likely to be more than a few old vehicles knocking about, wouldn't you think?"

10

His Mercedes had gone in for repairs, and at six feet and ten inches tall, DCI Forbes had difficulty hauling his frame in or out of the small, unmarked Ford. He eventually squeezed out onto the yard and looked around at the detritus of what he considered to be a very unsavoury occupation. He was surprised that the manager of the Samson Estate didn't force his gamekeeper to have a good old tidy up. About fifty metres to their right were three black and white collies, all bouncing their well-toned bodies off the chain-link fence which was preventing them from charging at the intruders. A half-grown rabbit ran for the safety of an ancient, rusting, and presumably broken down tractor. The dogs merely glanced at it before returning their attentions back to their two visitors.

Forbes followed Adam to the front door of the two-bedroomed, ivy-covered cottage, praying that a forth collie wasn't about to charge at them from one of the many crumbling sheds, or from behind the mound of rubble, or even from underneath one of the piles of rotting timbers and rusting metal sheets. Orange shotgun cartridges littered one side of the yard. Six decomposing jackdaws, presumably victims of the contents of those cartridges, were hanging from a rope suspended between two of the sheds, just high enough to be out of reach of the dogs but high enough for any returning jackdaws to see, and to act as a warning to them to keep well away. Forbes could think of no other purpose for the display.

Thick grey smoke billowed from one of the two, cracked chimney pots which all appeared to be only balancing on the summit of the grit-stone chimney stack.

"There's someone home, sir." Adam stepped back from the door to look up at the bedroom windows. "I heard a door being slammed, and unless they're totally deaf they must have been alerted by the dogs."

He signalled to Adam to knock again while he stepped further back to watch for any loose dogs. He'd been fooled by a working farm dog once before and still bore the scars on his left ankle.

When the door was opened the space was completely filled by a middle-aged man in clean blue jeans and a white, bulging tee-shirt. He was a couple of inches shorter than Forbes but with the muscular build and broken-veined face of someone who had worked outdoors for much of his life.

"If it's religion or politics that you're peddling, you can both sod off now."

He was also a man who didn't like to have his time wasted.

Before they could respond, the man took a step towards them, ducking slightly to avoid losing his cap against the top of the door frame, and then tilted his head at an angle that from one of his dogs would have looked quite cute, but from him only served to reinforce his aggression. Forbes had learned not to be fooled by first impressions, and thought that if he'd lived out here, doing the kind of work that this man did for the wealthy owners of the Samson Estate, then he would probably have developed the same sort of attitude towards uninvited strangers.

"Police, Mr Leath," they held up their IDs. "Nothing to worry about, this is a routine visit. We are looking for a blue, or blue and green Land Rover type of vehicle in relation to a serious traffic incident on Monday night. Our records show that you own two. May we take a look at them?"

Forbes saw a flicker of disgust on the man's face.

"Come on through while I get my boots and jacket on. I heard about what happened to those poor boys. Is that what this is about, because if it is you're wasting your time with me? Would either of you care for a drink? I was just about to have a coffee."

"Thanks, but no; we've a lot to get through. Are all your vehicles on these premises at the moment?" He watched Leath putting on a freshly ironed, checked shirt, and noted how clean and tidy the kitchen was. If Prunella spent so much time at the Grange, he wondered if perhaps Mr Leath was the house-proud half of the partnership. Given his profession, he could understand that Mr Leath would never have had women flocking around him, but why would anyone put up with a wife who was so rarely at home? He made a mental note to check on the explanations the police had been given for being called out to the previous domestic disputes at this property.

"Aye, they are, and they're both in the barn." Leath eventually answered after he'd unhooked the vehicle's keys. "And I've got another one I've been meaning to do up for years. She's in pieces and practically a vintage machine. She hasn't been on the road for years but you're welcome to take a look at her as well, if you like. The other two are my workhorses. They've both got more than a few dents and scrapes on them, and one of them hit a deer a while back, but neither of them has ever struck a human, I can assure you of that. I'll drive them out into the daylight for you."

A few dents and scrapes was a polite way of describing Mr Leath's 'workhorses'. Both had front bumpers and running boards held in place by lengths of fraying, orange string, presumably baler twine which itself looked almost as old as the vehicles, and therefore, thankfully, not bio-degradable. The wing mirrors were all either missing their glass completely or were badly cracked, and large areas of the blue paintwork were flaking off. Some of the exposed metalwork appeared white.

"MOT's...?" Forbes felt he had to enquire while Adam was taking a closer look.

"Oh aye, everything has to be above board for the estate manager, though it might be expensive to get them both through the test again this year. I'm trying to get a new one out of them, or at least, a newer one."

"Japanese frostbite," Forbes pointed to the white metal. "I remember my father announcing that after I'd brought home my first, and last, motorbike." That had been his father's explanation for the exposed patches of bare, white metal. Forbes had originally bought the bike for getting home from university for the weekends, but the episode had turned out better than he could ever have expected when his father had immediately paid for an intensive course of driving lessons, and then allowed him to use his late mother's little car. He'd taken exceptionally good care of that car, to the point that the journey to and from university had taken almost twice as long as it had done on his motorbike. Once he'd saved enough money for a car of his own, he'd returned his mother's car to the family garage, where it still remained today.

Adam's voice cut into his memories.

"...twelve and eighteen years old. I can see that the damages aren't recent, but with your permission, Mr Leath, we'd like to take paint samples from both vehicles. We'll do that now, if that's all right, and then we won't have to bother you again. And we may as well take a small sample from the one you're restoring, just to rule it out."

"As you please, but like I said, but you'll find nothing useful on any of them."

"Could anyone else have driven either of them on Monday night, your wife for example?" Adam continued.

"No, why would she, she has her own car? Prunella has a little blue Ford Mondeo, which incidentally I have nothing at all to do with. She paid for it with her own money from her part-time work in the kitchens of Uppertown Junior School and she won't let me near it."

"We've already seen that," Adam said. "We may need to check other makes of vehicles as well as Land Rovers, but at the moment we're acting on eye-witness statements. Thank you for your co-operation, Mr Leath. We'll be in touch if we think you can help us further."

Forbes was beginning to wonder how many blue vehicles there could be in this area. He'd thought red and silver had been the most popular colours for the last few years, but then cars were just a means of getting from one place to another for him. He was fond of his Mercedes, but he'd never been a car enthusiast. "Do you or Prunella have any children, Mr Leath?" Forbes hadn't quite finished with the interview.

"No, we were never blessed that way, or hampered, depending on your viewpoint. Prunella spends most of her time at Oakwell Grange, on the opposite side of the village. The women living there are continually taking in and looking after vulnerable young women and I think she regards them as her substitute family. She certainly does if the hours she spends there are anything to go by. I have my dogs, of course. They're only in those pens till they've had their breakfasts. I'd be lost without their company."

"Does Prunella ever talk to you about what goes on at the Grange?"

"She used to tell me stuff when we were first married, until I told her exactly what I thought about that superstitious Goddess worshiping crap that they all seem so wrapped up in. That didn't go down too well," he laughed. "I mean, I'm all for helping the less fortunate in society, but how can all that pagan stuff really help anyone? It's all too way out for my liking."

Adam smiled at the gamekeeper. "I'd be interested to hear some of what you know, Mr Leath, if only from a personal perspective. My partner recently visited the Grange and I got the feeling she'd like to go there again, despite being unnerved by the women, because her late mother had been associated with the place. She's reluctant to talk it over with me, but even if she did, I don't know how best to advise her."

"Bloody hell mate. You want to nip that in the bud if you possibly can. Making smelly things to sell on a market stall is one thing, but dressing up in robes, creeping around stone circles, and wandering the hills under a full moon with nothing but old fashioned lanterns and candles, just ain't healthy. Prunella had been taking part in all sorts of pagan rituals, inside and outside Oakwell Grange, before I ever met her. I had no chance of stopping her, but you must stop your young lady. Take a bit of advice from a down-to-earth old gamekeeper and put your foot down with her, be subtle but firm, and do whatever it takes to stop her before she gets in too deep. You look a bright enough bloke, use a bit of kidology if you have to, but do your damnedest to stop her from ever becoming involved with that crowd of weirdoes."

*

Simon was managing the pain from his cracked ribs, with some chemical assistance from his mother's well stocked bathroom cabinet, and was feeling slightly more like his old self. He'd showered before going downstairs for his breakfast. It had been memories from Monday night that had kept him awake for most of the previous night, rather than the pain, but he'd used those long hours of darkness to begin making plans.

Most of his memories felt real, but others were still jumbled and vague. He had taken a whack to his head at some point, the doctors had told him, and maybe his brain was still playing tricks on him. Sounds coming and going, pain, smells, numbness from the sheer cold of the river, lights and people lifting him, were all stuck in a loop inside his head and playing over and over again. He wasn't even sure about what he'd seen in those moments before he'd landed in the swollen river.

Despite that, he'd given the police a clear statement. He knew exactly who was responsible for his injuries, and for the deaths of his friends, and in the early hours of the morning he'd resolved to overcome his fears and, sooner rather than later, make those women pay.

On some nights he would have been on his pushbike, on that narrow stretch of road with his friends, but on that particular evening he'd stayed at home because it was his mother's birthday. There had been moments during the night when he'd thought the pain killers were messing with his thoughts. Was it possible after all, that he'd been involved in a genuine accident? Or did someone try to kill him on his way home from college because they knew he wouldn't be going out that night? His mother had loads of friends, and dozens of people were aware of her birthday, but he wasn't a child. How many people would be expecting him to be staying at home? He couldn't even remember who he'd told, let alone come up with a plausible explanation for why they'd been attacked on that particular night.

If John or Philip had been in any kind of trouble, or made an enemy other than the Oakwell women, he would have known about it, he felt sure. They'd always worked together to sort out whatever problems any of them had, and they'd always supported each other.

For the first time in his life he felt truly alone.

"Trust your own gut instincts," John had so often said to him.

That was exactly what he was doing now by dismissing his doubts.

He checked his phone again. It was switched on and the battery was well charged.

While Arianne remained tied to that house, he would have to be careful. One day soon the two of them would be together, properly together. He had nothing to offer her except his life, but if he was stupid enough to lose that, then she would be lost too. He wasn't going to let that happen, but he was going to send them a message – he was very much alive, and he was going nowhere.

11

Eleven-year-old Eric Shutter had helped his mother and his sister to move into their new council house just six weeks earlier. They'd been allocated a three-bedroomed terraced house with a back garden, and happily left the damp, one-bedroomed flat for some other poor unfortunate soul to try to make a home of.

Eric's blind sister, Martha, shared the largest bedroom with their mother, a fact they hadn't revealed to the housing department for fear they would be offered only a two-bedroomed property. And so Simon had claimed the second largest bedroom, the one which faced north, but with views over open fields. Once he'd unpacked his games and his books, he stood by the window and watched a flock of sheep nibbling at the wet grass. He didn't think he'd ever felt quite so happy.

Martha had been born with cerebral palsy and needed constant attention. She was just two years younger than him, and Eric had always loved and fiercely protected her. Most evenings now, while his mother was busy cooking in her new, spotlessly clean kitchen, he would be brushing Martha's long, dark hair, while doing his best to describe what was happening on the television screen in their spacious living room. He could never keep pace with the characters or the story lines and his sister's fits of giggles invariably took over. He knew he would always do anything for her.

They had just had the most magical Christmas imaginable. He'd been able to spread his new Lego toys out across his bedroom floor and leave them there for days without fear of anyone treading on them or complaining.

The only thing spoiling the holiday season had been the absence of a card or a present from his father.

"He loved you both," his mother had tried to comfort him, "but when baby Martha needed surgery, and he thought she might be suffering, he just fell apart. He was a weak man who loved his children too much. Leaving us was his way of coping."

His sister needed love just as much as every other child, maybe even more than most, and she returned so much love to those around her. If only his father would visit them for just one Christmas, with or without presents, he didn't mind, Eric felt sure he would only have to share a few hours in Martha's company to convince him to return to his family for good.

He knew his mother worried about him as well. He'd told her about his inability to make friends at his new school, and about the class bullies. She'd offered to talk to his teachers, but that would only have made matters worse. And things were gradually improving; before Christmas a few of the boys had begun involving him in their conversations. But still the best part of every school day was coming home to Martha.

So just like every other morning, Eric waved to them both and then walked to his school alone. When a soft drizzle settled on his plastic-framed glasses, he removed them and stuffed them into the top pocket of his jacket. Where the stranger came from, he had no idea, but as he slung his school bag back over his shoulder, the man fell into step beside him.

"It's Eric, isn't it?"

Eric paused and squinted. He couldn't recognise the face peering down at him.

"Yes... but I haven't lived around here for long. I'm sorry but I don't know your name."

"Don't look so worried, lad. I'm a supply teacher at your school so you probably won't have noticed me. I saw your family waving you off and thought you might like some company on your way to school."

"You're a teacher...?" He didn't look old enough.

"Maths and science, and I bet those are your two favourite subjects. I'm right aren't I?"

The stranger still looked too young to be a proper teacher, but his eyes were smiling. Eric recognised that he was being teased. Who enjoyed maths lessons? The soft voice, together with the distinct Derbyshire accent, reminded Eric of the way his father used to speak to him. He decided he liked everything about this man and he smiled back at him before confidently striding out in the direction of his school.

"Is that a kitten behind those dustbins?" The unnamed man asked.

Eric peered into the only alleyway on the estate, but he couldn't see what the man was looking at.

"It won't last long on such a cold, damp morning, not when it's so tiny. I think we should take a look, don't you? There could be a whole litter of them back there."

Too late, Eric realised his mistake.

His right arm was in a vice-like grip. He felt his bones being squeezed against the sleeve of his jacket. The high brick wall rushed towards the back of his head and his breath was forced from his chest.

He was in trouble. And he was too terrified to even try to defend himself.

A cold hand was clamped across his mouth and for several long seconds he couldn't breathe.

"Don't make a sound and I promise I won't hurt you," the man growled.

This man wasn't one of his teachers.

Hot liquid trickled down the inside of his left leg. He was powerless to stop it. He wanted to be sick, his heart pounded and his legs felt like two sticks of wobbling jelly.

"I need you to do something for me, Eric, that's all, just a little job that I can't do myself. Do you promise not to scream if I loosen my grip a little?"

With the hand still clamped across his mouth it took real effort to force his neck muscles into nodding his head. When he finally managed, he felt warm blood trickling down inside his collar.

The stranger's face was so close now that he could taste the man's breath in his own open mouth.

"Good boy. Now I know you don't know me, but I've known your father for years. He's a proper little sleazebag and you're better off without him in your life, trust me. It's your mother who you wouldn't want to lose, or that pathetic specimen of a sister that you have. It would be so easy for me to get into your house, and no one would know until you came home from school. And can you guess what I'd like to do to them both? I bet you can if you really try. All boys have dirty books hidden away somewhere don't they? You know what I'm talking about, right?"

"Please don't hurt them," he forced a whisper.

"I could show that helpless sister of yours what a real man is all about. Or perhaps I might just allow her to remain sitting in her chair, listening while I'm screwing her mother and wondering when it will be her turn. I can't quite decide about that. She is a bit young, even for me. What do you think, Eric? Can you imagine walking in and finding them both tied up and both as naked as the day they were born?"

"What do you want...? I'll do anything... please..."

"Now you're getting the idea. Carry on with that attitude and I'll be very happy. And no one will have to get hurt."

Eric watched him reaching inside his jacket. He could only stare as the man slowly opened a supermarket carrier bag.

"You need to be very careful with these, my little friend. Can I trust you to be careful?"

Eric nodded and saw a slight smile, but not the kind that reached as far as the man's eyes.

"I'm sure a bright lad like you knows how to light a fire. I saw smoke this morning coming from the chimney of your house. You first screw up this paper, one sheet at a time, and then very carefully pour this lighter fluid onto it, and then you simply strike a match and set the whole thing alight."

Eric nodded again. "I can do that... I sometimes light the fire for mum." That wasn't true but he'd watched her doing it in their new house. "But where... why...?"

"I'm coming to that. I want you to light it inside your school, as close to the kitchens as you possibly can without getting caught. I don't want any children to get hurt, so you must wait till school has finished for the day. It must be today, and remember, I'll be outside watching. You won't see me, but trust me, I will be there. And if you can do enough damage to the place, then I promise that you'll never see me or hear from me ever again. Do we have a deal, young Eric?"

Everyone in his classroom was already in their own seat. His leg itched, but at least his trousers looked dry, even though they weren't. Mrs Heller, his form teacher, glared at him but didn't speak. He felt like an intruder as he muttered a few words of apology and hurried to his desk. He needed a few moments to adjust. He hoped no one would notice he'd been crying, or see his blood stained collar, or even ask him whether he was all right. Today he wanted to be left alone.

He prayed that they couldn't smell the lighter fluid, and that it wouldn't leak out into his bag. And then he wondered whether they could smell that he'd wet himself. His cheeks burned and he stared down at his desk.

The white tiles of the toilet cubicle merged together. Eric knelt forward and wretched into the toilet bowl again, but again only produced the same foul-tasting froth. He'd been too terrified of this moment to eat any lunch. Rocking back onto his heels, he pressed his back against the locked cubicle door.

He had to keep listening. Muffled voices, footsteps, and the slamming of doors in different areas of the school building, were all becoming less frequent. For the last ten minutes, no one had entered the toilet block where he was hiding, and the cloakroom next to it was deathly quiet.

Cramp threatened both of his legs.

It was time to move. Another terror that had shaken him while he'd been crouched in the cubicle was the thought of setting the fire and then finding that he'd been locked in the building alone.

After slowly sliding his back upwards against the door until he was standing straight, he wiped his mouth against the sleeve of his jumper. Then he picked up his jacket and schoolbag.

He opened his bag for at least the tenth time since the end of lessons, checked that all the items he was going to need were on the top of his books and ready for him to use, and then unlocked the cubicle door. He opened it, and peered out.

He'd used his lunch break to find what he hoped was a suitable spot.

The school had sprinklers in every room. He knew that because he'd heard how last year the place had been closed for a week when they'd come on during the night without being triggered by a fire. Since then the system had been updated, and the original fault attributed to rodents.

Apart from his shallow, rapid breaths, the whole building was deathly quiet now.

"I only need to make lots of smoke," he whispered, trying to build his confidence.

The cloakroom was only two doors away from the kitchens. It was as close as he dared to get.

Two coats had been left behind – that wasn't unusual. He hung them onto pegs next to each other, fell to his knees below them, and began crumpling the paper into a pile. His hands trembled and he blinked when fumes from the bottle stung his eyes and his nose. He wiped his nose on the back of his sleeve again and took a deep breath from the cleaner air over his shoulder. There was no going back now.

"This is for you mum... this is to keep you and Martha safe." He struck the match and quickly shoved it into the crumpled pile. The tiny flame spluttered and died. He really, really wanted to cry, but he stopped himself. Another deep breath and another match, more slowly and deliberately this time, allowed the flame to touch the edge of the pile and grow. He waited for the single flame to spread. It seemed to be taking forever. The paper had felt damp from the morning's rain and the lighter fluid wasn't burning. He could see only the tiniest of flames, one wisp of grey smoke, and one orange speck glowing on the edge of the paper. He remembered watching his mother leaning into their hearth and gently blowing on some smouldering paper very similar to this. He'd no idea why it had worked, but for her it had, so he ought to at least give it a try.

Heat blasted his face. It forced him onto his backside, his legs instinctively pushing him backwards, and within seconds both coats were hidden by a swirling trail of black smoke. Seconds later flames leapt past them onto the wooden panelling. He watched without moving as the woodwork erupted with loud crackles.

The thickening smoke had reached the ceiling and coiled over above his head. He felt an overwhelming sense of guilt. He should have reached out to one of his teachers and asked for help. Anything had to better than this.

The smoke and heat stung his eyes. He blinked hard. It was a simple movement but it jolted him out of his mesmerised state. He reached towards the flames for his school bag.

As he scrambled to his feet the fire alarms exploded into life.

Fresh air rushed into his lungs and his feet slapped against the pavement.

The sound of the alarms was fading.

Dogs barked and people rushed towards him, and then rushed on past him.

"It's the school," a woman shouted.

"Are all the children out?"

"It's not a drill. I can see smoke. God help anyone in there."

"Call the fire brigade."

Eric Shutter had intended to casually walk outside, looking for the unnamed man so he could explain that he'd done the best he could. Instead, tears streamed unchecked down his cheeks and his legs had taken on a life of their own as they propelled him homewards. He had to see for himself that his precious family was unharmed.

Little Eric Shutter never saw the car. It was approaching the only junction that Eric had to cross before he reached his new home.

He saw the woman's face, her mouth opening as if she was saying something to him, but he had no idea what it might have been.

He felt the heat of the car's engine through the metal bodywork, and then the cold glass of the windscreen against his face.

12

That shouldn't have happened. It absolutely, bloody well, should not have happened.

Simon sat on the edge of his bed and stared at the Friday night's Facebook posting by the local newspaper. A muscle twitched at the side of his mouth and he clenched his fists. He wasn't sure which emotion came first, anger or sadness, but both raged through him until he could barely breathe. The lad wasn't meant to die. Hell, no one was meant to get hurt. If it hadn't been for those bitches... if they hadn't been employed in those school kitchens... if he hadn't wanted to send them the clear message that he wasn't intending to go away, he would never, ever, have targeted a school. Eric's blood was on their hands far more than it was on his.

He pressed his fists against his temples. His ribs were hurting. He reached for his painkillers, washed them down with the remains of last night's tin of coke, and then stared at the half-empty cardboard packet. It must have been the damn painkillers. They must have addled his brain. He would never have bullied a vulnerable young boy like that – not before his friends' deaths.

Then he remembered – he'd only needed a couple of painkillers yesterday. His gut reaction had been the correct one after all; it had been those women who had worked their evil way into his brain. They were responsible for everything bad in his life.

He felt sick.

Again, he ran through the previous day's events. He'd made sure everything he'd given the boy had been wiped clean, and that the street had at least looked deserted. The light rain should have hidden him from anyone peering through a window, and anyway he'd made sure his face was well hidden by his hood. And no one had come to the boy's rescue at the time. He was as certain as he could be that he hadn't been seen.

And he'd been casually strolling past the school when Eric had come running out.

"Slow down lad, slow down," he'd muttered, not loud enough for anyone but himself to hear. The fire alarms had been triggered and he hadn't risked hanging around because nearly everyone had a camera phone at the ready. He'd retrieved his pushbike from the alleyway and pedalled home. And he'd slept soundly.

There were familiar sounds coming from the kitchen. His father always teased his mother about the amount of noise she made when preparing a meal. "It's only me," she would cheerfully shout after dropping yet another pan lid, or another item of cutlery. Had he stupidly placed his own family in even more danger now? He was sure that the bitches would rightly assume he was responsible for the school fire, whether the police suspected that Eric had been coerced or not.

He had to move out. It was no longer a matter of choice, it was survival, the survival of his family, and he already had a vehicle in mind. A college friend whose father owned a garage had e-mailed him yesterday with the details of a cheap van. It was a small, white Ford Transit, fifteen years old, without any distinguishing logos, and the right price for him to purchase with the insurance money from his motorbike. If he could beg for an advance of cash from his father, he could use the money to pay for the van and then register it under a false name and address. He had to assume the bitches had connections in the local police force, and he had to remain one step ahead of them.

Then all he would need would be a mattress, a good thick sleeping bag, a camping stove and a few implements from his mother's kitchen, and some basic provisions. There were always vacancies at the chicken processing plant on the outskirts of Buxton, everyone knew that. They were soul destroying jobs with a high turnover of staff, but in a white hat, white overalls, and white wellington boots, he would be as good as invisible.

*

DI Lang was handling Operation Lupin very competently, and slightly more positively now. Forbes indicated to Lang to begin the Saturday morning briefing in the incident room.

"It's been five days since our unidentified body was discovered and I don't have much to add to what most of you already know. There are a handful of leads coming in from the public and we are following all of them up, and the missing baby remains our greatest concern. We have no idea how long the woman may have been in this country. No one has reported her missing, but we know she died sometime in mid-December. If her baby is alive, we still hope to find it." Lang looked around the room. "I'd welcome any suggestions."

"Ports and airports," DC Rawlings suggested. "Someone may be intending to take the baby out of the country — if they haven't already done so."

"Good point," Forbes added. "Have you notified customs?"

"I'll do that this morning, sir. I still have a feeling that we're going to need a huge chunk of luck on this case."

"You make your own luck, DI Lang, you know that. Now, if no one has any more suggestions we'll move on to Operation Bluebell. So far, there are no matches to any of the paint samples we've taken, but that side of the investigation is on-going. All three youths," Forbes pointed to the pictures on the board, "had previously been given cautions for their behaviour towards the residents of Oakwell Grange after numerous complaints of trespassing and vandalism, but the last of those incidents happened three years ago, and none of the boys have been brought to our attention since then. However, interviews with their families and peers have given us a clearer picture of their characters. All agreed that John Lewis liked to play the fool; he liked to make people laugh, but never seemed to realise when he'd taken a joke too far. He seemed to lack a basic sense of self-control, and although no one could recall him acting aggressively, he very quickly alienated most of the people around him. He didn't make friends easily."

"Hardly a motive for mowing him down," DC Emily Jackson added from the back of the room.

"No, and Philip Booth was one of few people who could calm John. Philip had a more serious attitude to life. Some people have described Phillip as boring, but others who perhaps knew him better have described him as quietly manipulative and devious. Simon Carter displayed behavioural problems from an early age. At the age of three he was diagnosed as possibly mildly autistic, but that diagnosis was overturned when he started school. There he was pronounced dyslexic and given extra lessons which improved his behaviour. He had an IQ of almost one hundred and twenty, so he was an intelligent child, but his inability to read or write well was thought to be the cause of his frustration and his frequent outbursts of anger. When he wasn't with the other two, he was also frequently bullied. On one occasion, when he was fourteen, he shoved a classmate down a flight of stairs causing a broken arm and a fractured skull. Onlookers stated that Simon was being bullied by the youth at the time and so no action was taken. But the headmaster had added a footnote to the school's report of the incident, stating that in his opinion it showed that Simon was capable of extreme acts of violence."

"So the three were drawn together and found their amusement at Oakwell Grange," Adam was thinking of Jane as he spoke. "But how many other people did they annoy, and what about the boy who was shoved down the stairs?"

"He made a full recovery and the family moved to New Zealand. We're widening the search of their friends, beginning with names taken from their social media sites. Because of the large number of local women involved with the Grange, Adam, you and I are going back there this morning."

*

An unfamiliar car was drawing up alongside the others in the yard. Prunella squinted through the tiny, leaded panes of the upstairs window and scowled. She'd expected them to return with more questions, but if there had been fewer people in the building the situation would have been easier to control. At least they hadn't arrived in the middle of one of her afternoon spiritualist meetings, and all the women downstairs this morning knew better than to speak out of turn. All that the police would see was local women packing dried herbs ready for selling on the market stalls and the online shop. Nothing wrong with that, she told herself as she clattered down the uncarpeted stairs to take up her special place in the living room; the place where she could hear everything that was being said in the kitchen, without being seen.

*

Forbes and Adam followed Hannah Hall through the dark hallway towards the kitchen of Oakwell Grange. They both automatically cleared their throats. There was that same smell, but far stronger than on their last visit, of earthy, stale foliage and rotting vegetation. He knew why it almost made the pair of them gag. It wasn't too dissimilar to the odour from a rotted human corpse, one which was being dug out of the ground after being there for more than a few years.

Four women were sitting at the table, sorting through dried leaves and flowers, and Sheila was standing behind them. "You didn't find any matches to the paint samples you took the last time you were here, did you?" Sheila Hall smirked as she spoke. She followed up the question with a wink at Hannah who'd quietly gone to stand beside her.

Forbes didn't humour them by answering. Instead, he slowly scanned the room. There were heaps, bowls, and packets of dried vegetation on every available surface. If cannabis or any other illegal drug was amongst this lot, then his nose couldn't isolate it from the other stronger odours.

"Ladies, we know you're not denying your on and off, long term conflicts with John Lewis, Philip Booth, and Simon Carter, but as a part of our investigations we will need the names and addresses of all the people who have been involved in your various groups over the past five years, just in case one of them has taken it upon themselves to seek some kind of retribution."

"Really Inspector..." Sheila's smile faded.

"I can do that," Hannah added.

"Since the weekend, how many people have stayed here at the Grange?" Adam asked.

"Just my sister and I," Hannah answered, "and a Polish girl who likes to be known as Arianne, but don't ask us why. Her real name is Olesia Brodzki. She works for us in the house and the gardens, in return for meals and a room. Oh, and one young woman who only stayed on Sunday and Monday night, and whose name we never asked for. The four of us were here on Monday night, along with Prunella, of course, who left around midnight, but we've told you all that. Arianne is upstairs cleaning at the moment, but if you need to speak with her I can call her down."

"Please... if you wouldn't mind fetching her."

Hannah left the room and Forbes looked at the other four, as yet unidentified females.

"These ladies help out with our little dried herbs business, don't you girls?" Sheila informed him.

Girls they definitely weren't. They all showed off their wrinkles when they looked up and smiled at him.

"And in return, they benefit from our meditation and relaxation classes, and our holistic healing sessions, and of course the company of like-minded friends. But these ladies are only daytime visitors."

Forbes watched Sheila's hands. He was sure they hadn't been trembling while Hannah had been speaking, but they certainly were now. And she seemed to be studying his face. "Is there anything you'd like to tell me, Sheila, anything at all?"

"Hannah and I were friends of your mother, did you know that? It all seems such a long time ago now. What happened was so sad, and so many years have passed since she last stood in this room, all smiles, and desperate to tell us all about her new baby daughter."

He felt as though his vocal chords had been cut.

It was all he could do to remain standing.

His mother, had she lived, would have been a similar age to the women working in this room now. For a few seconds he pictured her, but exactly as he remembered her, without wrinkles or greying hair, bending over the worktop and diligently packaging a mound of stinking, dried, brown leaves.

"In this light," Sheila broke the silence, "I can see an incredibly strong resemblance. I'm sorry, I didn't intend to shock you, but you are Donna Forbes's son, aren't you? She was such a lovely lady, and so young to be taken like that. I distinctly remember her, in this very room in fact, proudly telling us all how her boy Michael wanted to be a policeman someday. And how is little Louise? Not so little, I suspect. She must be a grown woman by now."

On the journey from the station, Adam had reaffirmed his concerns about Jane. Forbes felt he'd had a sudden insight into how Jane must be feeling. "I wasn't aware my mother ever came here."

"There was no reason why you should. You were wrapped up in your academic studies, and our work here doesn't involve men. And I'm afraid your father never approved of us. She used to tell him she was visiting friends, which wasn't actually a lie, but I believe she ceased telling him her friends were based here in this building. She so wanted another baby to maintain the sounds of a youngster in her home. It was such a tragedy. We all went to her funeral, of course, but there were so many people there that your father didn't notice us."

Hannah returned to the kitchen and both men turned to look. She was being followed by a beautiful young girl, with dark eyes and thick, dark brown hair.

"This is Arianne, and she'll tell you herself that we were all here together on Monday night."

Of course she will, he thought, with the two of you standing here... but my mother?

Without prompting Adam took over the questioning. "Could you e-mail that list to us today? The names of the members of all the groups you run, as well as any regular visitors to Oakwell, all need to be on it. You understand we have to follow whatever leads we're given."

"We can do that," Sheila answered, "although I'm sure no one from here could be responsible for such a crime. We're a peaceful community, and we believe in trying to live in harmony with the natural world. The act of murder would fly in the face of our beliefs."

"We've been hearing about some of your nocturnal activities...," Adam hesitated, "your rambling in the woods, and full moon processions to the stone-age burial mounds up on the moor, and the stone circles in the woods. Those are things which might cause alarm to some of the more impressionable youngsters in the area. We're not condoning it, but you couldn't have been too surprised when the Grange became a target for vandalism."

"That doesn't make it right." Sheila snapped. "I can only repeat that we are a peaceful group, trying our best to live in harmony with Mother Earth and the old Gods and Goddesses."

Forbes sensed Adam looking for his cue to leave the building. He wasn't quite ready.

"Exactly what was my mother involved with when she came here?"

"Involved with...?" Sheila's sympathetic tone had slipped. "She was a friend of Oakwell. She took a great interest in the vegetable plot, the herb gardens especially, and she attended our reading group whenever she could. She liked to help with some of the unfortunate girls who passed through our doors. She was a good woman."

"How long...?"

"When your mother passed, Hannah and I would have been in our early twenties, but we both remember her. Your mother was a lot older than us, of course, and she'd been visiting about once a week for as long as I can recall. She enjoyed our activities, and I think she would have attended more meetings if it hadn't been for your father's disapproval."

He tried to control his frustration. "But what exactly did she do here, and what generated my father's disapproval?"

Sheila laughed. "This is an all-female establishment, Inspector Forbes. If I give away too many of our secrets, then I'll have to kill you." She hesitated. "Please excuse my sense of humour. I can see this has come as something of a shock to you. Take a look at our website and I'm sure it will help put your mind at rest." She picked up a business card from the kitchen window and handed it to him.

"You look like shit," Adam's voice jolted him into starting the engine. "What was all that about your mother?"

At that moment he needed to be as far away from Oakwell Grange as he possibly could. "It was nothing." He slammed his car into gear. "I think they were attempting to shock me."

He could almost feel the waves of sympathy coming across from Adam as they re-joined the narrow road. Until quite recently, it had been the other way around. Almost five years earlier, Adam had lost his wife within minutes of their son's birth, and he'd once confided in Forbes how only the needs of baby Ryan had pulled him back from the brink of suicide.

His own grief was so much further into the past.

"You look as though they succeeded." Adam said quietly.

"I can't have feelings one way or another for anyone involved in this case. That part of the interview doesn't go on record, understood?"

"It never happened, sir."

The smell of dead foliage lingered on his cloths and the warmth of the car wasn't helping.

Had his mother crafted wax candles, or chopped and bagged herbs, while she'd been pregnant, or even shortly after Louise's birth? Had she even used some of those herbs medicinally? It wasn't a subject he was knowledgeable about, but he did know certain things were best avoided at that time in a woman's life.

Ever since her death, his father had maintained that someone should be held responsible, that his wife's death had not been looked into properly, and that there had to have been more to her sudden demise than a brain aneurism. She had been so fit, and so recently subjected to all the usual hospital tests leading up to the birth of their daughter. His father had campaigned hard for answers, but never received anything like enough to satisfy him.

As his son, he felt guilty now for the times he'd done his best to ignore the bereaved man's obsession.

Was it possible that his father had been right all along, and did the answers to the questions he'd asked at the time lie in the room that Forbes had just been standing in?

13

Jane Goodwin looked out onto her back garden and sighed. The sky had been a tombstone grey all day, and if the weather forecast was right a scattering of snow was on its way. Thanks to the fire at Lucy's school, at least her daughter would be at home to enjoy it for the first few days of the following week.

For three days, she'd been preparing herself for her second visit to Oakwell. It had been an emotional struggle, and now the visit would now have to wait for a few more days. Not being able to discuss her worries with Adam had made her feel even more alone in the busy household. She'd never kept anything from him before, but she knew how he felt about revisiting the past; the ghost of his first wife still occasionally followed him around, and anyway he was busy with a murder investigation.

They would be her excuses if the time ever came for explanations.

She turned her attention back to preparing the Saturday evening meal.

For better or for worse, she felt compelled to visit the Grange one last time. She had to know more about her mother's role in that place.

*

Prunella Leath stood beside the kitchen door and watched as Arianne struggled past her with a large plastic tub of roughly chopped firewood. For three-quarters of the year, the old place needed four of those tubs every day to maintain a half-decent temperature. And that was only in the rooms that were actually used. Without Donald Muir's constant supply of free firewood from his parent's farm, the Oakwell heating bills would be astronomical.

Poor, pathetic Donald, even after so many years Sheila still had him at her beck and call, and Prunella had to admire her for that. At the age of nineteen, and after some gentle encouragement from her, Sheila had been persuaded that she needed a child to complete her lifestyle and had been easily steered towards Donald as a suitable sperm donor. Donald had fitted Sheila's requirements perfectly. He was healthy, reasonably good looking, intelligent, and entering into a profession with a steady salary and a pension.

Six months after Sheila and Donald married, their daughter Jasmine was born, and six months after that happy event, Donald had been shown the door and served with divorce papers.

"I simply don't love him anymore," she'd explained to everyone except Prunella and Hannah.

The sisters had always shared everything, and the truth was much more in the historical tradition of Oakwell Grange.

Hannah's daughter, Acacia, was born just eight weeks after Jasmine, and Donald was hit with double maintenance payments. The fact that the baby girls were so closely related was kept a secret from the outside world until both youngsters grew to resemble their father.

Since then, Donald's career had blossomed, and he'd become the headmaster of the local Uppertown Junior School. His pride had never totally recovered, but he'd been besotted with his daughters since their births, and they were the reasons that Sheila and Hannah had been able to maintain their hold over him. He'd recommended the young mothers for employment in his school's kitchens, falling nicely into Sheila's trap of maintaining regular contact with Donald once his daughters reached adulthood. And he paid for the lease on a flat in Manchester, complete with a shop below it, to allow the two girls to set up a health food store almost in the centre of the city.

Prunella considered her plans to be coming along very nicely.

She wrinkled her nose as Arianne carried the forth tub of logs through the kitchen towards the range. "Is there something wrong with you, girl? Can you not smell rotting wood when it's only inches from your face? Some of those logs need a lot longer to dry. Take them back and bring in more dry ones."

The simpering girl had gained a mobile phone, and obviously still believed that no one in the household knew anything about it. She hadn't even put a password on it – that's how stupid she was. And the message log showed that she'd only been in contact with one person – another mistake.

Simon Carter and Arianne were in love. That was something she planned to use to her advantage, so for now at least, the love-struck Arianne could keep her precious phone.

Back at home, with her husband slumped on the living room sofa, Prunella sat quietly at her kitchen table, listening through the open door for the local Saturday evening news. Brian always watched it, though she never knew why because the news rarely affected either of them way out here in the middle of nowhere.

"Come and see this," he shouted through to her, "the news is all about yesterday afternoon's fire at the school where you work. They're now saying that it's arson, and started by one of the pupils."

"Quiet, I'm listening." She walked to the back of the sofa.

"...an eleven year old boy, killed instantly when he ran across the road... believed to have been fleeing from the scene of the fire."

"Can you believe that any child of that age would do that?" he interrupted again.

"...neighbours said the family was new to the area and the boy had always seemed quiet and well behaved. Rumours of an unnamed male, seen talking to the boy as he walked to the school on Friday morning have so far not been confirmed by police."

The reporter then turned to a group of people on the familiar street beside the school. "Mrs Ball, you witnessed Simon with a man earlier that day. Can you describe him...?"

Prunella clapped both hands to her chest as she peered over her husband's shoulder. Then she slipped back out of the living room and closed the door behind her. She reached for the kitchen sink, turned on the cold tap, and splashed her cheeks with ice-cold water. The e-mails she'd received from Donald this morning had confirmed the fire had started in the junior's cloakroom, beside the school's kitchens.

They'd said nothing about an unknown male.

A child experimenting with a cigarette had been the explanation Donald had favoured.

The school should have provided more supervision; she'd heard other people saying.

After listening to Mrs Ball's description of the youth seen with Eric Shutter only hours before the fire, she knew they were all wrong.

It wasn't many years ago that the three boys had deliberately set fire to one of the Oakwell sheds, destroying their beloved vintage tractor and much of their antique furniture. Once an arsonist, always an arsonist, she believed.

Well Simon Carter had really excelled himself this time. A schoolboy lay on a mortuary slab, and that was down to him. She knew she was right. Why else would young Eric do something like that when everyone who knew him was saying it was so out of character for the boy? The child must have been in a state of absolute terror.

Simon had somehow forced the boy to light the fire next to the kitchens. Had he hoped that Sheila and Hannah would still be working there? They did work late on occasions, but only a few times each month. Or was Simon Carter sending a confrontational message to her?

'Hey, I'm still here! You failed to kill me and I'm not going anywhere.'

Either way, Simon Carter had just made his last mistake.

She intended to respond to his challenge all right. She already had plans, and the icing on the cake was that Arianne would unwittingly play a part in his destruction.

He obviously hadn't told the police anything too damning, but just how much did he really know about Oakwell, and how much had Arianne confided in him? The girl wasn't a problem as long as she was under the Oakwell roof, and as long as she believed her family would be in danger if she didn't cooperate. She would be easy enough to dispose of once she'd outlived her usefulness.

She smiled. Or had the three troublemakers had been bluffing all along?

Now wouldn't that be a sweet irony?

It certainly would, but she couldn't take that risk.

*

Michael Forbes was feeling his age. It was late on Saturday afternoon, and after a full week of investigations his team had made little progress. As the Senior Investigating Officer he needed to maintain contact with them over the weekend, but he also needed a little relaxation time with his family.

His father, Andrew, had thrown himself into the domestic chores of the family home as a means of coping with his wife's death, and as far as Michael was aware, had never even considered bringing another woman into the house. Andrew's trademark lasagne was prepared and ready to place into the oven, and Alison had called to say that she was on her way over to help them eat it. With Michael's sister, Louise, who had been such a mixed blessing over the years, and her baby daughter, the family group would be complete.

Louise, and Gemma who was now approaching her first birthday, had settled back unexpectedly well into the family home. She seemed to be enjoying her return to college life, and had even sworn to remain celibate until she had established herself in a worthwhile career and made her father proud of her again.

That left Michael, and his long-term girlfriend, Alison Ransom, as the only source of romance in the large Victorian family home. They'd been in a relationship since their early twenties, but both had been dedicated to their chosen careers and agreed that marriage wasn't something that either of them desired. Michael had remained in his family home and Alison had her own flat, part of a converted mill, on the outskirts of Leaburn.

Alison was five years his junior, and enjoyed her career as a forensic pathologist. Yesterday, somehow, she'd discovered her male colleagues' carefully whispered plans for her surprise fortieth birthday bash. She'd been less than pleased, threatening to castrate anyone who dared to follow through with the plans.

She was highly skilled with a sharpened scalpel, and had never been fond of children.

The party had quickly been cancelled.

Michael wasn't surprised at her reaction; Alison had never been a party animal. But it was time he booked a family meal in one of their favourite country pubs, because despite all of her protests, he knew she'd want to mark the milestone somehow.

*

The glare from Prunella's headlights illuminated the flattened area of crushed foliage at the roadside close to where Simon Carter's bike had been pulled from the River Lathkill. It was as if the dead grass was mocking her failure. The scene made her angry. It should have been that boy's useless, lifeless body that they'd dragged from the river, not his bike.

She stopped the car, blocking the narrow road, and thumped her fists on the steering wheel. Why had that boy been allowed to live? Things like that didn't happen without a good reason – not for her, at least.

There was nothing else to do except drive on.

She'd already passed several lengths of blue and white police incident tape, still hanging from the tree trunks. Why did no one ever bother to remove them? Wasn't it still an offence to leave litter?

The river was still running high. She could hear the constant rumble through her car's closed window. Even the water seemed to be laughing at her.

Barely another quarter of a mile on, the road forked, and on one side stood a painted wooden sign.

Mr and Mrs Carter welcome you to their bed and breakfast establishment. Hikers, bikers, and dogs all catered for.

This hadn't been a part of her plans, but she wasn't above sending messages if that was how Simon wanted to play it.

14

DC Green had taken his turn to be on duty on Sunday. "Sir, there's been a development of sorts over the weekend involving Simon Carter's family."

"And you didn't think to call me?"

"Sir, it happened during the early hours of Sunday morning, before I came in. Uniformed officers were called out to the scene of a fire at his parent's property. It wasn't until late Sunday afternoon that anyone connected a possible arson attack on the Carter's home, with Simon Carter, our attempted murder victim."

"Where is Simon now?"

"I'm not sure, sir."

"Give me the whole story."

"According to the Fire Investigation Officer, petrol was used to start a fire in the Carter's garden shed sometime between two a.m. and three a.m. There were several motorized garden implements and a can of petrol inside the shed. That resulted in an explosion at three-fifteen a.m. which woke Mr and Mrs Carter. The fire department was called at three-nineteen. No one in the house saw anyone outside."

"What's going on? Two arson attacks in our area in under two days...? I don't believe in coincidences. Who's in charge of the arson attack on the Uppertown Junior School?"

"Sergeant Thorpe, sir. I'd literally just put the phone down from speaking to him when you walked in."

"Does he think the two incidents could be connected?"

"Possibly; and there's been a more recent development. Just a few minutes before your arrival, the front desk took an anonymous call from a muffled, but definitely male caller claiming that the person seen talking to Eric Shutter on the morning of the school fire was in fact a woman, dressed to mislead anyone who might see her. The recording is being sent for analysis. I don't want to influence you, sir, and I've only listened to it once, but I think the caller could be Simon Carter."

"I'll listen to it now. I suppose it was from a pay-as-you-go phone?"

"Yes, it could be anyone's."

"And then I'll look over the files concerning the fire at the school. If there is any possibility of a link to our hit-and-run enquiries, then we'll take over that investigation from Sergeant Thorpe."

"I looked at those files yesterday, sir, after the fire at the Carter's property was brought to my attention. There was only one female eye-witness to the potential bullying of Eric in the street that morning, and she wasn't very clear about exactly what she'd seen. She was looking out of her bedroom window, down onto the street, but at that time there was a light drizzle making visibility poor. She could only confirm that the person with Eric was wearing dark jeans and a dark jacket, with a hood pulled up over their head. At the time, despite seeing Eric walking to and from school by himself on every other occasion, she assumed that it must have been the boy's father. Also, Eric's mother swears there was no lighter fluid in her house, and that the matches found in the boy's school bag were not the brand that she used to light her fire."

"The fire was set quite close to the school kitchens, wasn't it?"

"That's right, sir, and the kitchens are where the Oakwell sister work part-time."

"Was the school's headmaster interviewed?"

"That's where I think it gets weirder still. The headmaster's name is Donald Muir and he was once married to Sheila Hall of Oakwell Grange. Last night I discussed him with my family. I have cousins who attended his school and I remembered them gossiping about him. It seems he and Sheila had a daughter not long after they were married, and Hannah gave birth to a daughter very soon afterwards. Donald, despite very publicly declaring his undying love for

Sheila and the baby, was booted out of the Grange soon after the births. There was gossip at the time, but Hannah maintained that she had met a wonderful man, the father of her child, but that he'd been killed before she'd broken her news to him. As it turned out, the two girls could be mistaken for twins, and they've both inherited their father's features – they are both Donald's."

"He must see the sisters at his school most days, but do we know if he still goes to the Grange?"

"My cousins thought it highly amusing that he's the only man ever invited to set foot in the place, which despite being divorced from Sheila for almost twenty years, he apparently does quite regularly."

"These two cases are closing in on each other." If the last week was hectic, then this one was shaping up to be 'manic', as his father would put it. "Ask DS Ross to bring my car round to the front. I'd like another word with Simon Carter."

The smell of wood smoke and burning fuel still hung in the air.

"Simon hasn't been home since Friday afternoon." Mr Carter looked pale. "He phoned us on Saturday, and again on Sunday, just to let us know he's all right. His mother is distraught about his decision to leave home and live in a van, especially at this time of the year. It can be so cold at night."

"A van...? No one's mentioned that to us. Mr Carter, may we come in? Perhaps we can help find him for you."

"Don't you want to see the fire damage? We had uniformed officers all over the property yesterday."

"Another department is dealing with that side of the investigation at the moment. We're here to speak to Simon, but if he isn't here then perhaps you could provide us with some background information, and a few ideas as to where we might find him."

"My wife will be very relieved to know you're willing to look for Simon." He leaned towards them and whispered. "I loaned him the cash for the van while he waited for the insurance money for his bike to come through, so she's blaming me for his disappearance. Come on through to the kitchen."

Mrs Carter stepped towards her kettle and forced a smile. "Please sit down. Can I get you some tea or coffee?"

She'd been crying very recently and a damp-looking handkerchief remained tightly held in her left hand.

Her husband placed an arm around her shoulders. "The officers haven't come here on a social call, love. They're going to find our Simon for us and bring him back."

She brushed him away and ignored his words. "I'll make tea. Do you take milk and sugar? Humour me, will you? I'm used to catering for guests and it helps me to keep busy."

"Tea will be fine, Mrs Carter, thank you; milk with no sugar for both of us. Has Simon taken his mobile phone or any other electronic equipment with him?"

"He knows those modern things can be traced." She placed four mugs in a perfectly straight line and dropped a tea bag into each one. "My Simon is a bright boy. He said we would all be in danger if he stayed here, and that it would be better if we didn't know where he was. We don't understand what's going on..."

Her husband took over. "He's told us that he's bought a cheap mobile and intends to put a new sim card into it every few days. He told me that much because if I don't recognise a number on my phone, I usually reject the call."

"When he calls again, ask him to contact me directly. This is my number." Then he looked at Mrs Carter. "Could my DS take a quick look at Simon's room while we're here, and may we take his laptop, or tablet, or any other electronic equipment we find in his room? Any of those may hold a vital clue to his whereabouts."

He raised a hand to prevent Mr Carter from following his wife out of the kitchen, and then closed the kitchen door behind Adam.

"While your wife is out of the room, what can you tell me about Simon's emotional state?"

"He really is frightened, and so are we, now. We want you to find him, and quickly."

"Bearing in mind his long history of trouble, both with the police and the schools, would you ever consider him to be a danger to himself, or to others?"

"He's had more than his fair share of problems growing up, but I can't imagine him being suicidal, if that's what you're getting at. Like many teenagers he can be moody, and sometimes he has a quick temper, but he's a good lad at heart."

"Put bluntly, Mr Carter, would you say that your son is dangerous?"

"Why are you asking that? Has something else happened?"

"Do you think, for example, Simon could be an arsonist? He was involved in that fire at Oakwell Grange a few years ago."

"He would never set fire to our property. That's ridiculous."

"I was thinking more of the recent fire at Uppertown School. Someone phoned the station with information which we believe was a hoax. Do you know anything about that?"

"Of course not; and you seem to be forgetting we are the victims here." The man sunk into the nearest kitchen chair and looked totally stunned for a few moments.

Forbes waited for him to digest the idea.

"Are you suggesting it was our Simon who bullied that poor boy into setting fire to the school, and what has that got to do with our property being targeted? None of that makes any kind of sense. Anyway, why would he do that?"

"Your son, along with John Lewis and Philip Booth, appeared to have been obsessed, for a number of years, with some of the women who worked in the Uppertown School kitchens, and while we know the troubles took place when the boys were much younger, we all saw how distressed Simon became after the deaths of his friends. He was convinced that one of those women either killed them, or knew who was responsible. Is it possible that he could now be looking for some sort of revenge for their deaths?"

"How would I know?" Mr Carter placed his elbows onto the table and pressed his fists into his forehead. "But suppose for one second that my Simon is right? What if the Oakwell women are responsible for the horrors of last Monday night? You haven't caught anyone yet, have you? It could have been them, couldn't it?"

"This is why we need to find Simon. We don't believe he's told us everything he knows. For example, if he is right, and it's still a big if, why would those women launch an attack on the boys after years of relative calm? What triggered that level of violence, and why now?"

"I honestly don't know." He looked towards the door. Muffled sounds indicated his wife and DS Ross were returning to the kitchen. "We're very isolated down here. Is there any chance of us having some sort of police protection? We can't leave because of the livestock, and Simon needs to know we're here if he needs us."

"The best I can offer you is a police patrol car driving down here, past your drive entrance, a couple of times each night. If anyone is about, that should be enough to deter them. You have the direct line to the station, and you have my mobile number. I'll ensure that if you do call the station you're given top priority. If you're really concerned, I can arrange for a panic button to be installed and linked directly to the station, though that may take a few days to set up. But in return I expect you to let us know immediately if you see or hear from your son. And please ask him to come in to the station." That wasn't likely to happen, but he had to say it.

Only at the junction with the main road did Forbes decide where to go next. "Let's call on the Oakwell women before they go to work. I'd like to hear their thoughts on the fires. Let's see whether we can rattle them."

Adam responded to his boss's head movement by reaching into the glove box for the unopened, large bar of milk chocolate. He began to unwrap it.

"But sir, we don't know for certain that Simon bullied that boy into torching his school, and if he knows something damaging about those women, something damaging enough to get the three of them killed, why doesn't he just come forward and tell us? Did the boys do something we're not yet aware of?"

"Simon could be protecting someone, or we could have a case of blackmail. We need to look more closely at Simon's life, and his internet history. I want copies of his bank accounts, and also the bank accounts of the Oakwell Grange businesses and of the residents."

"Ladies, we have a few more questions. May we come in?"

"You really have to be joking." Hannah's eyes and cheeks looked set to explode. "It's that boy again, isn't it? Please don't tell us you're still taking his claims seriously."

They were reluctantly invited into the room they'd been shown into on their first visit, and when Adam asked Sheila and Hannah whether they were aware of the fire in the Carter's garden shed over the weekend, both women were speechless for a few seconds.

"Another fire...? Why, in heaven's name, would we want to damage a garden shed?" Sheila eventually spluttered.

"This is a return to the harassment we experienced when those horrible boys were pupils at Uppertown School." Hannah added. "If Prunella was here now she'd be absolutely furious. Look in your files if you don't believe us. We even tried to take out injunctions against them coming anywhere near Oakwell Grange, but the injunctions were refused. The police and the courts made us feel as though we were somehow responsible for the children's actions."

"We have looked, Miss Hall," Forbes said. "But there was never enough evidence to suggest that those three were responsible for all of the vandalism to your property, for an injunction to be issued. Are you both quite sure there isn't anything you think we might need to know? I must remind you that withholding evidence is a criminal offence. I'll give you the direct line to the station, and if either of you want to talk, ask for me, DCI Forbes, or for my sergeant here, DS Ross. If anyone here knows anything relevant to our enquiries, I promise you, I will find out."

"We've had just about enough of this." Hannah turned her back on them and was walking towards the front door as she spoke. "I think you should both leave now."

Forbes blinked at the winter sun, low in the sky and directly in his eye line, and as he turned in response to the heavy door being slammed behind them, he pictured a young woman on the doorstep; his own mother as he remembered her best, in the outfit she was wearing on the day she'd brought four-day-old Louise home from the hospital, and smiling with utter contentment.

"Where are we headed next, sir?"

He forced himself to turn away and blinked hard.

Uppertown School wasn't due to reopen until Wednesday morning, but the headmaster was there, overseeing the repairs and the arrival of a temporary cloakroom – he'd checked before leaving the station. "Mr Donald Muir is overdue a visit from us."

*

As they drove away from the school, Adam sounded sceptical. "Mr Muir was lying to us, don't you think?"

"I think that one of the sisters telephoned him as soon as we left the Grange. Some of his answers were almost too automatic and too brief. They'd warned him of exactly what not to say. I also think his name can be added to the bottom of the list of suspects for the attacks on the three boys. Which reminds me, that list from the Grange, their group members and visitors, have we run background checks on all of them yet?"

"Yes sir, there were a few misdemeanours by a couple of the women, shoplifting and prostitution, but nothing to set alarm bells ringing. And we've already interviewed about half of them in their own homes. None of them have offered up anything useful, and none so far have had anything other than praise for Sheila and Hannah Hall, or for Prunella Leath."

"Hmm, now that I find hard to believe; does that smack of brainwashing to you? That's how those religious cults operate, isn't it, by convincing people that their way is right and the rest of the world is wrong? Is Jane still considering joining one of their groups?"

"I don't think so. It's rather a touchy subject and I'm afraid I didn't take her seriously enough when she first mentioned it. I know that she feels the place holds a connection of some sort to her late mother, but I don't think she's any plans to go there on a regular basis."

"Do they know she's a special constable?"

"Not sure, sir, I suppose her mother may have told them."

"Well find out, will you? And ask her to come and have a word with me if she's thinking of returning to Oakwell in the near future."

"What about Simon Carter, sir, are we going ahead with the television appeal tonight? If it's a personal vendetta that he's conducting, he might not have strayed too far from this area."

"Simon's face will be all over the local early evening news. We can't risk there being another Eric Shutter incident, if indeed Simon was responsible."

15

Simon didn't think that his father was likely to miss one dusty old pair of binoculars. They were rarely used from one year to the next, and he was pleased now with his last minute decision to borrow them.

Last night's scattering of snow had melted away, and so he positioned the carrier bag containing the folded newspaper onto the wet grass and knelt on it. He'd found the ideal spot, approximately half way up the hillside on a little-used dirt track which led to an abandoned quarry, with the morning sun low in the sky behind him, and a dry-stone field wall in front of him. Resting his elbows gently on the rounded coping stones, he pointed the binoculars towards Oakwell Grange and adjusted the focus.

Four women, in long winter coats and woollen hats, were in the vegetable garden cutting kale leaves, but Arianne wasn't one of them. Disappointed, he lowered the glasses and rested his forearms on the top of the wall. She could be anywhere in that house.

The sun wasn't exactly warm, but it felt pleasant on the back of his neck. He would wait a while.

She hadn't sent him a text for almost thirty hours. When they met, he always gave her the phone number of his next sim card, but when he didn't have any contact with her for more than one day, he felt his heart was being ripped from his chest. He was hoping that if she would just look through one of those upstairs windows and see him, then she'd get back in touch.

He needed to be sure that she was all right.

Also, his new job was due to start at two o'clock that afternoon, and he wanted to let her know that he'd been offered afternoon shifts at the chicken processing plant, and would be working until ten o'clock each night.

The factory had reeked of chlorine and blood, and apart from the man who'd shown him around the place and the personnel officer, he hadn't heard one English speaking voice. But while he was working there he would be anonymous, and paid in cash. He considered it a bonus that there was a shower he could use at the end of each shift, a canteen where he could get a hot meal at either end of his shift, and clean taps where he could fill up his water bottles.

The stubble on his face was looking a bit ragged, and his designer haircut would very soon go the same way. He hoped Arianne wouldn't mind his appearance too much. For now, it was the best he could do by way of altering his appearance.

Next Monday, seven days from now, Arianne would be working on the market stall in Bakewell for the first time. Her last text had told him how thrilled she was to be allowed out to see new people. Her message had asked whether there was maybe some way they could see each other on that day, even if they couldn't get close enough to talk.

He fully intended be there.

Patience had never been one of his strengths and he needed to see her before then.

The begging nature of that text had made him throw his phone down onto his pillow. He was going to get her out of that place, he was going to set her free, and then he was going to make those women regret that they'd treated her as their personal slave.

It would be unbelievably satisfying to make them beg for Arianne's forgiveness, before he made them pay for everything they'd put him and his friends through.

He watched the women carrying their wicker baskets of leaves from the garden. He waited and watched for another few minutes before slowly pushing himself away from the wall, wincing at the pain from his ribs as he did so.

A full recovery was going to take longer than he'd thought, but the physical pain was nothing compared to the fear and the mental turmoil he'd endured over the past week.

The bitches were going to pay for every second of it.

His beard, if it could be described as such, should hopefully thicken during the coming days, and Monday's Bakewell market should be busy enough for him to be able to walk past the Oakwell stall without attracting the attention of anyone other than Arianne. Just a few seconds of eye-contact with the girl he'd so unexpectedly fallen in love with, would be better than nothing – and maybe, if he was lucky, she would give him enough of a smile to let him know that she was all right.

His father's shed being destroyed by fire over the weekend hadn't surprised him at all. He'd punched the air with delight when his father had finished telling him. It meant that the bitches had realised who had orchestrated the fire at their place of work. They'd received his message loud and clear, and they'd responded in kind. The shed was covered by insurance, his dad had said, but the stress he'd heard in his father's voice was something else the women would have to pay for.

And it meant that the next move was his to make.

It wouldn't hurt to leave the bitches wondering when and where he would strike next while he regained a little more of his strength.

He already had a few ideas.

Applying for work at the chicken processing plant had been a stroke of good fortune that he hadn't recognised until he'd been shown around the place.

Maybe it was because of the stink of death that hung over the factory, but there seemed to be almost a sub-culture of humans working there. Some of them looked like the dregs of society, too downtrodden to look up from their work stations when someone new walked past, and he'd had the impression that if one or two of them had looked up, their eyes would have been like those of a sleepwalker. He imagined them being close to the edge of sanity and willing to do anything, or get anything, for money.

He was fairly certain that somewhere in that building would be someone who could get him what he needed; a cheap weapon and a supply of ammunition.

He took one last look at the Oakwell gardens but no one had come back outside.

Placing one hand against his ribs and the other against the wall, he levered himself back onto his feet. He knew Arianne was in there. He could sense her. He wondered whether she was able to feel the power of his love from this distance.

They both had to remain patient just a little while longer.

16

Jane Goodwin stared at the open laptop on her kitchen table. In her hand was the list of women that Adam had asked her to look over. She felt the familiar thrill of helping with a police enquiry, but was still uncertain about officially returning to being a special constable with the Leaburn police. She was going to have to return to the world of work soon, but she wasn't sure that having two police officers in the house was such a good idea.

She wasn't sure about delving too deeply into her mother's private life, either.

Checking these associates of her late mother wasn't the same as enquiring into how such a gentle, mild-mannered lady had fitted into the odd group, was it? But the longer she looked at the list, the more unsettled she was feeling. "Sorry mum," she whispered, "but I think I ought to talk to someone."

In any case, she told herself, someone at the station would probably already have noticed the anomaly between the Oakwell Grange website and the list that the sisters had supplied to the police. It was only a copy that Adam had given to her, and she'd recognised his motive. He wanted her to keep well away from Oakwell, and he was hoping to achieve that by reminding her that these women might become part of a serious police investigation.

She jabbed his number into her phone. "It's most probably an oversight on the part of the sisters," she hesitated. It seemed so insignificant when she actually said it. "Prunella Leath's name features quite heavily on the website, but is missing from the list that you gave to me. She's practically the top dog at the Grange, and I know that you and DCI Forbes have already met her, but it seems odd, given that the sisters have both added their names to the list, that hers isn't there."

Her hand trembled as she gently placed the phone back into its holder. Why the hell had she allowed herself to get into such a state? She looked at the flowery cake tin on the top of one of the wall cupboards, the tin she'd bought for her mother out of her pocket money more than twenty years earlier.

For as long as she could remember, Tuesdays had been cake-baking days in this house. She closed her eyes and pictured her mother in her flour-spattered apron, busying herself over bowls, packets, and a cluttered worktop. And there hadn't been many Tuesdays when she hadn't been carried away with her passion and baked far too many cakes and buns for her family to eat in one week. On Wednesdays and Thursdays, her less able friends around the village had taken it in turns to welcome her into their homes and receive the home-baked offerings. For the first time, she thought that she and her daughter probably weren't the only people in the village who were missing her mother.

Then she looked at the list again. Her thoughts had gone full circle. Had some of her mum's wonderful cakes ended up with those creeps at Oakwell Grange? Even worse, had her mother deliberately over-baked in order to take some to that dreadful place? She looked up at the empty, battered cake tin once more and felt a tear roll down her cheek.

Her first visit to Oakwell had been so overwhelmingly emotional that her principle memories of that day were the mismatch of oil paintings and framed photographs on the living room walls, and the long robes being worn by the women. She felt a tingle along her spine. For a few seconds she was transported back into that room, and facing the line of women again. She remembered how some of them had seemed familiar to her, but now most of their faces were just a blur.

Prunella's was one of the faces she did remember. The dark haired, sour faced woman had been the one in control, ordering the sisters about in their own home, and everyone had willingly done her bidding.

Her laptop had returned itself to standby, and without thinking she closed the lid. Then she picked up her pen, and in capital letters added Prunella Leath's name to the space at the top of the sheet of lined A4 paper.

*

Prunella watched Arianne brushing the last of the dried leaves from the alter table. Her fancy, made-up name doesn't make her different to any of the other girls who've passed through here, she thought, or any more clever. The stupid girl will do anything I need her to do.

Sheila and Hannah had wanted an unpaid housemaid, and she'd kept them happy by providing them with one.

The girl had been useful already, helping to calm the new girls in the visitor's rooms. And she was going to be useful again soon, very soon, as bait for the love-struck Simon Carter. She'd laughed out loud when she'd come up with the brainwave of allowing Arianne to work on the Monday morning market stall in Bakewell. Just thinking about it now was making her chuckle.

And the girl was so predictable, sending that text, inviting Simon to walk through the stalls on Bakewell market.

'*Would you please come to see me? Xxx I love you and I miss you so much, xxx*'.

Of course he'll be there, why wouldn't he?

Manipulating people had always been easy for her, and she liked to think she'd become quite skilled at the art over the years. She believed she'd been helped by the old Gods and Goddesses, as a thank you for resurrecting them in this house. These days it took no effort at all for her to get people to do exactly what she wanted them to do, and she knew, without any shred of a doubt, that no matter how difficult any situation became, she would always end up as the winner.

*

Adam had been hoping that by involving Jane in the investigation, if the time ever came to tell her about his DCI's suggestion that she revisit Oakwell Grange, she'd be reluctant to go. After hearing the tension in her voice he was feeling uncomfortable, but he had to ignore his guilt and so he stood up from his desk.

Prunella Leath was already a person of interest, but as far as Adam was aware, no one on the team had noticed that her name was absent from the list that the officers were working through. Brian Leath had already been interviewed at the gamekeeper's cottage, but Prunella hadn't been there, and without looking at the file, he knew Prunella hadn't been officially interviewed yet.

Forbes placed his phone down on his desk and scowled at it. He'd just agreed to an 'off the record' deal with an old acquaintance, Bertram Cross, the manager of the bank used by the Oakwell women and their businesses. His team hadn't found enough evidence for a Production Order, but he'd gained information about the Oakwell finances in exchange for the promise of a meeting with Bertram at the golf club, and a full round of golf followed by a few rounds of drinks.

He enjoyed being in the company of the man, but it meant that he would have to use a taxi, something he avoided doing whenever possible because it left him feeling out of control. And he'd never been that keen on the game itself, but his main problem was that he knew he wasn't likely to have half a day to waste on socialising at any time in the near future.

He looked up as Adam walked into his office. "There have been no unusually large payments, in or out, of the Oakwell business accounts or the sisters' personal accounts. There's nothing on paper to suggest that they were blackmailing anyone, or that they were the victims of a blackmailer. Online sales, and cash sales from their market stalls, have shown a steady increase over the past ten years, and the women's wages have helped to boost their accounts. The overdrafts that the grandmother saddled the sisters with have all gradually been halved."

"So why would they risk everything over a feud with three spotty youths?" Adam asked.

"I don't know. But I still believe they're involved in the boy's deaths somehow. There has to be another aspect to this case – one we haven't uncovered yet."

"I came in to suggest that we interview Prunella Leath on her own, sir. Jane noticed her name was missing from the list already being used by the team."

"Sir," PC Philip Coates poked his head around the door and interrupted them. The constable's eyes betrayed him. He obviously believed he had something of interest. "Sir, we're working our way through that list of women's names and one couple, Mr and Mrs James, have voiced some concerns. They offered to come in and make a statement. They're in interview room two at the moment."

"What kind of concerns?" Forbes asked.

"Mrs James says that for many years, until quite recently in fact, she had been a regular member of the Oakwell writing group and that occasionally she'd been persuaded to take part in their 'superstitious nonsense'. Those are her words – not mine. She claims she'd only gone along with the nocturnal jaunts because her mother had been into all that stuff and she didn't like the idea of her going out into the night with those women."

Forbes thought of Jane, and then of his own mother. "Go on..."

"Her mother passed away a year ago, and because of that she's stopped visiting Oakwell altogether, but because of the family association, over the last ten years or so, Mr James has been offered occasional work at the Grange. He's done roofing repairs, exterior painting, repairs to the sheds and greenhouses, and so on. Apparently he was one of the few men ever invited onto the premises, but he was never allowed inside the house. He claims that the Oakwell finances were anything but regular. When urgent work was needed, the sisters would sometimes call him out on the understanding that they wouldn't be able to pay him straight away. Mr James referred to one example when a tree had been blown against the side of a barn and was at a precarious angle. He'd had to wait six months for payment for making it safe and sawing up the timber. At other times money was no problem, and when new greenhouses and fancy new sheds were delivered he was well-paid with cash to erect them. They never offered any explanations as to where the sudden glut of money had come from."

"And why would they?" Adam asked.

"Mr James is of the opinion that something illegal has been going on in the Grange for many years."

"Does he have any suggestions?" Forbes asked. A high proportion of cases were solved after a member of the public noticed something irregular and brought it to the attention of the police. He was suddenly hopeful that this might just be one of them.

"He thought of drugs at first, because of the comings and goings of so many different women, the weird behaviours that his wife had told him about, and the fact that they openly sold packets of dried herbs. He had previously thought the selling of herbs might have been a cover."

"But now...?"

"On several occasions, Mrs James noticed young, foreign-looking girls. On a couple of those occasions she'd been able to get close to them, but the girls were never allowed to speak to any of the visitors and they'd appeared subdued, and even frightened. It was enough to concern the couple. Mrs James mentioned it to some of the other group members but was told they were homeless girls in need of temporary accommodation and that in the Oakwell tradition the sisters were being charitable by taking them in. After watching a recent television documentary, Mr and Mrs James both began wondering whether the Grange was being used for human trafficking, or slavery."

Adam didn't look convinced. "No one else has had anything bad to report, and apart from the housekeeper, Arianne, we aren't aware of any young girls staying there."

Forbes dismissed PC Coates and thought for a moment. "If these young girls aren't illegals, who would send them to the Grange; Social Services maybe, or an agency, and isn't there somewhere in Leaburn where Eastern Europeans can go for help?"

"Yes sir, there's an advice centre above one of the Polish shops in the town centre. I'll get onto it."

"Do that, and then go back to the Grange and ask why the names of these girls, and the name of Prunella Leath, were omitted from that list. And while you're there, enquire about the dates when any major works and improvements were carried out on the property. Let's see if they tally with what Mr James is telling us."

He needed to think. It was his job to overview the case. If Mr and Mrs James were correct in thinking that some illegal money-making scheme was being conducted at the Grange, then was it just possible that three bored teenagers, with nothing more than mischief on their minds, had stumbled upon it? Whatever it was, it would have to be big and it would have to be illegal, to commit murder in order to keep it quiet. It would explain everything they'd uncovered so far, and for the first time they would have a motive for the deliberate hit-and-run killings.

Because of the huge amounts of money involved in drug dealing, people trafficking, and organised prostitution, large-scale, organised crime syndicates were often involved. And the people in charge of those didn't tolerate loose ends.

If he was right, it would mean that Simon Carter was still in serious danger, and until the youth was found there was no way of protecting him.

17

There was a loud hammering on the sturdy front door. The police were back. Prunella didn't need to see them, she could smell them. Within seconds of hearing the heavy door being opened, alien molecules of expensive aftershave were destroying her house's natural, plant-based perfumes. Then she heard her name.

"Prunella isn't here at the moment." Sheila was answering.

There was only one officer this time, and Sheila and Hannah knew better than to let him know that she was here. She listened as he was led into the kitchen, and then she slowly crept to where she was able to hear the conversation.

"Prunella was the one who compiled the final list of names," Sheila said.

"With help from me," Hannah added.

"I suppose she just forgot to add hers," Sheila continued. "You've already met her. She isn't hiding anything. And yes, we do occasionally have one or two non-English speaking girls staying with us for short periods of time. Word gets around that we take in people like that. They come knocking at our door and we give them food and shelter for as long as they need it, and we ask no questions. We have difficulty pronouncing some of their names, let alone spelling them, and we have no idea where they go to after they leave here. That's why they weren't on that list. It would have been pointless."

"You should have at least mentioned them. We will need to speak again with Prunella. Do you know where we might find her?"

She'd heard enough. She couldn't have them going to her home, not when her husband might be there. Quickly and silently she moved to the front door, opened and closed it, and then walked into the kitchen. "I thought we had visitors. I don't suppose this is a social call, officer. What has the rumour mill been saying about us now?"

"Mrs Leath, we've already asked Sheila and Hannah, but where were you during the early hours of Sunday morning, between midnight and three a.m.?" Adam looked directly at her.

"Is this to do with the fire at that boy's home? It is, isn't it? Unbelievable, really officer, do you think I would be so petty-minded? Now let me think. It wasn't the night of a full moon was it?" She smiled and casually made eye contact with Sheila. "Then I would have been safely tucked up in my bed, alone, and most probably fast asleep. I usually retire to bed with a book while my husband stays up to watch the sports channels. We have separate bedrooms, but unless he was asleep, I'm sure he would have heard me if I'd left at that sort of time. But I expect you'll be asking him."

"Could he have left the house without you hearing him?"

"If I was sound asleep, yes, so I guess neither of have an actual alibi."

Adam returned the false smile she was giving him. "The foreign girls who spent short periods of time here, have you any idea where any of them might be now?"

"No officer, no I don't, and quite frankly I'm beginning to find all your questions a bit too intrusive. What could our charity work possibly have to do with the deaths of two youths and a couple of small fires? Evidently you think someone from our small group of women is involved in some sort of strange vendetta. You'll most probably find that Mr Carter torched his own shed for the insurance because business is so slow at this time of the year. Now please go away and stop harassing us."

Her cheeks had flushed and her eyes sparkled.

He gave her his more genuine smile. "I'm impressed with your vegetable area. That tunnel must extend your growing season quite considerably. How long have you had it?"

"Almost five years," Hannah took a step towards him as she answered.

"I was thinking of investing in one. What time of the year did you erect yours?"

"Early in the year; March I think it was," Hannah was smiling at him. "It's been well worth the investment."

"I'm undecided whether to go for a tunnel or something more solid. How long have you had those glass greenhouses, and have you found they're worth the extra cost?"

"Three years in June and..." Hannah was suddenly shouldered to one side as Prunella stepped closer to him.

"What has this got to do with anything? Have I not already asked you to leave?"

"Thank you ladies, I'll bid you good day. We know where to find you if we have any more questions." He smiled at each of them in turn and then steadily walked towards the front door.

Once again, he'd rattled Prunella Leath.

*

DCI Forbes stood at the front of the packed incident room. "This Tuesday afternoon's briefing is to enable us to pull together all the various strands of these investigations, and for any of you to offer up any suggestions – anything you think we may have overlooked, or missed. Firstly, DI Lang, what progress is there on Operation Lupin?"

"Very little I'm afraid, sir; we've e-mailed the victim's details, together with her photo-shopped picture, to every hospital and health centre in the country, and to the European branch of Interpol in case they'd come into contact with her as she'd made her way across to Britain. There's been absolutely nothing back from Europe. The Asian and South Pacific branch of Interpol have a National Central Bureau at Kabul, in Afghanistan – I contacted them because Alison thinks that our victim may have come from that area, but they seem to be more interested in counter terrorism and border patrols at the moment. They made all the right noises, but I don't think they have the resources to be able to help us. The nationwide appeal for information on the baby produced several dozen calls, but so far none have led to anything useful. Without an identity or a murder scene, there's little else we can do except keep appealing to the public."

"Keep promoting the story for now. That woman and her baby deserve your best efforts, DI Lang. I realise it's frustrating for your team, but someone must be wondering what's happened to their friend, or their family member. And remember, that baby could be alive. We're a very long way from turning it into a cold case."

"Yes sir."

"On to Operation Bluebell, and DC Rawlings, has the lab finished analysing the paint samples from all the known Land Rovers in this area?"

"Yes sir, I spoke with them this morning and they'd just finished, but none of them matched anything SOCO removed from the clothing of the victims. I was thinking, sir, since the rust indicated an older type of vehicle, what about the scrapyards?"

"What about them, Rawlings?"

"My uncle has a small hill farm, and he owns a couple of really ancient Land Rovers that he only uses off-road. They've already been sampled. When he needs a part for either of them he always goes to one of the two scrapyards in his local area before he goes to a garage. Many of the hill farmers do the same. It's possible that the vehicle we're looking for is a marriage of different parts of old scrapped Land Rovers, and that it's unregistered. I've found three scrapyards within a ten mile radius of Leaburn. I think they might be worth checking out, sir. The owners of those yards might be able to suggest a few new names."

"Then consider that your action for tomorrow, Rawlings. Now, have any names on that list of Oakwell visitors produced anything more of interest?"

"Nothing of note, sir," DC Robert Bell answered. "Also, Brian Leath has a clean record. He has a firearms licence, being the gamekeeper for the Samson Estate, and he's considered by his employers to be an extremely responsible person, but other than the domestic incidents that we already know about, I couldn't find anything at all on Prunella Leath. It's almost as if she doesn't exist."

"Keep searching. What about known friends and associates of the three boys, have they all been questioned now?"

"We think we've contacted everyone who knew them," Bell answered, "and they've all said similar things – that the Oakwell women were the only people who disliked the boys enough to be behind the violence. It's starting to stir up some bad feelings locally. Some of the ladies who attend the group meetings at the Grange have claimed they are being victimised by us."

He noticed a few heads nodding and a couple of exchanged looks. The atmosphere in the incident room felt suddenly tense. "Is there something else I should know?"

DC Harry Green answered. "There's been increasing activity on Facebook, Instagram and Twitter, today, sir. Several local people have called for Sheila and Hannah Hall, and Prunella Leath, to be suspended from working in the school kitchens on the grounds that they could be killers. You can understand the concerns of the parents."

"Has anyone contacted the school?"

"No sir, we were only made aware of it a few minutes before you came in."

"Who made us aware?"

"Jane Goodwin called it in, sir. She has a daughter at Uppertown School and she thought we ought to know. It's due to reopen tomorrow."

"Adam, get on the phone to the head teacher, now. Find out whether he's aware of local feelings. And if he is, find out what he intends to do. We can't have this getting out of hand."

"Yes sir."

"That just leaves Simon Carter. Have there been any definite sightings of him?"

DC Emily Jackson answered that question. "We took six calls after last night's television appeal, but none of the callers knew Simon personally so they weren't positive identifications, and they were spread over quite a wide area. If he's changed his appearance and put false plates on the van that his father said he'd bought, then he could be anywhere."

18

Jane was beginning to wonder whether she needed a reality check. Noticing her mother's old cake tin hadn't been some sort of a sign to her, had it? It was something she'd done to herself. And she'd never believed in messages from the spirit world, even if her mother had.

She'd been on the verge of changing her mind about putting herself through an hour of potentially emotional torture when she'd taken the phone call from DCI Forbes asking her to call in at the station.

Now the huge front door of Oakwell Grange was swinging open in front of her.

"Jane, welcome, I'm so glad you could attend our little get-together." Sheila Hall was dressed in her long white robe, but this time thankfully, without the facial artwork.

In exactly the same manner as on her last visit, she found herself being steered through the dimly lit entrance hall. It was too late to go back now.

"Come and meet the other ladies again, my dear. We all feel your mother's presence at this special time. Her spirit surrounds you, Jane, never forget that. She is looking after you, protecting both you and your daughter, always and forever."

She forced a smile and peered around the large, candle-lit room. And just as on the last occasion, with the exception of Hannah who was dressed in white, the group of waiting women were all wearing black, floor-length robes. If they asked her to wear her mother's old robe, she knew she'd be tempted to run for the hills – DCI Forbes or no DCI Forbes. This time she wasn't here only to feel closer to her mother, and she still wasn't sure just how much they knew about her life. If they'd all known her mother as well as they claimed to, then they must be aware that a special constable with the Leaburn police force was now standing before them.

That thought frightened her as much as it reassured her.

Sheila was maintaining the grip on her arm and guiding her towards an impressive stone fireplace, and a smouldering log fire. Again, she was uncomfortably aware of Hannah following too closely behind her. She could hear the woman's breathing. By the time the three of them turned to face the line of black-robed women, she felt like a prize exhibit. Only then did Sheila release her grip.

She watched as Hannah took a piece of paper from the large pocket on the side of her white gown. Hannah carefully unfolded it and read off the names. After each name the silence was broken with the word, "Present". She'd seen at least two of the women in the line-up dropping their children off at the gates of Lucy's school, and she recognised each of the names from the list Adam had given her.

She wasn't given any extra time to think. Prunella Leath, also dressed in a floor-length white gown, flounced into the room, walked directly towards her, and ignoring the other women reached out to her with outstretched arms.

It wasn't the first time Jane had seen the woman, but this time her thoughts flashed to the pictures she'd seen in the incident room only an hour earlier – the pictures of the broken bodies of John Lewis and Philip Booth, and the pools and tyre tracks of congealing blood on wet tarmac.

She forced herself not to recoil from the firm embrace.

"You are so very, very welcome, my dear. My name, you may remember, is Prunella, and I'm here to help guide you along your path of enlightenment. Do you feel ready to share in something that your dear mother held very close to her heart?"

"I'll try," she swallowed back an unexpected tear.

"Put on your mother's gown, my dear, we've been airing it by the fire for you. You really should be naked underneath, but as it's your first time we'll overlook that small detail."

She looked to her left. Hannah's arm was already fully outstretched and draped over it was the long black garment. She stared at the skirt. There was grey dirt on the hem from the last time it had been worn.

"I'm sorry, but... I'm really not sure about that," she stammered.

"Then we won't force you. We don't want to make you do anything you're not comfortable with. Just remove your coat and follow us through. Sheila will talk you through the short ceremony and I will answer any questions you may have, after we've finished."

"Actually, I'm rather cold. Do you mind if I keep my coat on?" She resisted the temptation to reach into her coat pocket to touch her phone, just to check. It was set on speed dial.

"As you wish, my dear," Prunella purred at her.

She'd come this far – now she had to follow the women across the hallway into another large, candle-lit room.

She was the last to enter and the others had already positioned themselves in a semi-circle. In the centre of the room, on yet another wooden floor, she saw the same circular black cloth that she'd seen on her previous visit. It looked to be about nine or ten feet in diameter. A slight pressure in the small of her back guided her towards the space that the women had left for her and Sheila.

"This is our temple," Sheila whispered. "This room is always kept clean, fresh, and free from debris for our magical undertakings."

"What...?" She couldn't imagine her down-to-earth mother ever standing here, not in a million years, not like this. Were these ghastly women having fun at her expense? Was it all some sort of elaborate joke and was there a hidden camera somewhere? If so, it was a sick joke, making fun of her grief.

"Shush, questions are for later."

That hand was still resting on the small of her back. She straightened her body, leaning forward slightly and hoping that Sheila would get the message.

She did, but the woman tilted her head towards her and began to whisper. "Our circle is the ideal size, exactly nine feet in diameter. You must try to imagine it as a sphere, both above and below the floor."

Was this really happening on a regular basis, and just a few miles from her home? DCI Forbes had asked her to come here, but she'd only agreed to accept the invitation to the Grange when she'd thought the women would be sitting around talking and drinking coffee, or that dreadful herbal tea. This wasn't what she'd expected to be doing.

"The Alter is at the northern sector of our temple," Sheila gestured to where Hannah and Prunella were already standing. Both women had their backs turned to the circle and were facing a covered item of furniture. "The figures that you see on the Alter represent the Goddess and the Horned God."

She raised her hand to her mouth. *'You surely can't be serious*;' she had to force herself not to blurt out.

"Concentrate, Jane, concentrate, and you will begin to feel the power."

She looked at the shadowed faces, but no one was looking at her. They really were all concentrating on something. Despite the almost overpowering urge to run from the room, she was becoming intrigued.

"The two alter candlesticks are at the back corners, with the North candle between them. And at the front is the Pentacle; ours is made from copper. That is the symbol of the element of Earth and of magic, and items to be blessed are placed upon it."

She tried to memorise at least some of the details for the team, though she wasn't sure why. What Sheila was telling her was utter garbage.

"We'll explain the significance of the other sacred articles later. On the Alter there has to be salt and water, a chalice, a scourge, a Censer of Incense, a bell, a book of shadows, a wand, three cods, a sword, a white-handled knife and an athame – that is a black-handled, double-bladed knife. Our robes are blessed, and clothing and underwear from everyday life is never normally brought to the circle."

A double bladed knife...? She turned her head slightly and looked past Sheila, towards the closed door. One sudden step backwards, four or five steps at the most past the nearest three women, who appeared to be in some sort of a trance, and she could be through that door within seconds.

But what if they turned and grabbed her?

'Get a grip,' she almost said aloud. Why would they?

What if they wanted to teach her a lesson for snooping, or how about a sacrifice?

That was it – she didn't care what anyone here thought about her – she was getting out of this place.

She swallowed hard and took the initial step backwards.

*

"I'm sorry sir," twenty minutes later Jane's hands had almost stopped shaking and she was feeling foolish. "I feel really bad for letting you down like that. It was very unprofessional of me. I was feeling emotional when I arrived at Oakwell and I think I had some sort of panic attack."

Her legs still felt as though they might let her down, but she refused the seat offered to her by her DCI. She didn't want the more experienced officers to see how traumatised she was really feeling.

"I'm sorry, Jane," Forbes looked genuinely concerned. "I should never have asked you to go there alone, and I wouldn't have done so if you hadn't already been there, and if the women hadn't invited you back. Do you feel ready to tell us about it?"

She described what she'd seen in the second room.

"You were quite right to leave. I'm sure many of us here would have done the same."

"Unless it was one huge joke at my expense, and I don't believe that it was, the stories of white witches at Oakwell Grange appear to be true. But I can't see how that helps with the investigation, not unless the boys were blackmailing someone over their involvement."

"That isn't all they do though, is it?" Forbes was thinking of his mother. "The dried herbs and scented candles – did you get a chance to ask about that aspect of their business? And did you notice any young women who weren't a part of the proceedings?"

"No sir, nor did I see or smell anything suggesting the use of illegal drugs. There was an incense burner, but I didn't hang around long enough to notice whether it had an effect on those closest to it. It all got too much for me."

"Don't beat yourself up about today, Jane. I realise it must have been difficult for you, and thank you for agreeing to go there at all. Just one other thing – did you speak to Prunella?"

"Only briefly when she wanted me to wear my mother's gown," she shuddered again. "She was talking at me, if you know what I mean, and the others all followed her. They reminded me of sheep in an open field, all walking in the footsteps of one leader."

*

Simon was the middle of his eight-hour shift and he had a thirty minute break. He strolled into the car park hoping that he looked more composed than he felt. There was one floodlit area where the security cameras had apparently never worked, and in the centre of the illuminated space he saw a pick-up truck with two men leaning against it. He tried to walk casually as he approached them.

"This is the cheapest gun we can offer you today. It is a Webley MK VI service revolver." The tired looking, middle-aged man informed him. The man was from the packing department and he spoke English more fluently than most of those Simon had met on the factory floor. "It is one hundred and twenty pounds, but then five pounds for each of the bullets. The gun is clean."

"Clean...?"

"That means it has never been used in a crime."

He'd handled an air rifle and a twelve-bore shotgun often enough, and enjoyed shooting at clay pigeons and tin cans, but this gun wasn't for pleasure. This gun gave him a different feeling altogether – a feeling of regained control. The handle of the revolver felt strangely comforting.

He would buy four bullets for now, keeping his last thirty pounds back for food and diesel, and a roll of black tape, he decided.

"It has a squared-off, target-style grip," the man added, "which sits perfectly in the hand, and it has a one-hundred-and-fifty millimetre barrel. It isn't the most powerful weapon here on our tailboard, but it might be just what you're looking for."

The metal was tarnished and scuffed, but that was exactly as he'd expected.

"Production of this model ceased in nineteen-twenty-three," the man continued explaining. "It has been tested and is working fine. It will be effective over fifty yards."

"That should be more than enough for what I need."

"Whatever you want, my friend," the man smiled, "whatever you want, but if you need something more out of the ordinary it may take me a week or two."

"I need it now, and this one looks just fine."

"That's good, it'll see you right, but for a couple of hundred pounds I know someone who can get you a grenade. Now one of those will stop anyone. I once saw one used in America and it took the guy's head clean off."

"I'll keep that in mind," he replied.

19

After walking around three industrial estates and getting thoroughly frozen in the process, Simon had found a van of the same make and model as his own. He'd photographed the registration and then used the black tape he'd bought to copy it onto some white and then some yellow metal sheeting that he'd found lying around at the factory.

Luck was on his side for once. He felt confident and relaxed driving towards the Samson Estate. With the weight that he'd lost over the past eight days, due mainly to his sore ribs and his bruised jaw, and his patchy beard, his own mother would have had to look at him twice. Not that there were many people about to see him at six a.m. on a cold, dark, Wednesday morning.

He parked in the long, empty lay-by, about half a mile past the main entrance to the Samson Estate. In the summer, tourists frequently used this spot for free overnight parking, but in January you could normally rely on it being empty during the hours of darkness. He fastened up his makeshift curtains, making his van resemble one of hated travellers who in better weather camped in the area and left piles of rubbish behind them. He didn't think that anyone would want to look twice at his plain white van. Then he clambered out and hurried along the road.

The cold, damp air stung his face.

He felt calmer from the moment he stepped off the tarmac into the familiar wooded area hiding the gamekeeper's cottage from the road. The absence of moonlight and the uneven ground slowed him, but now he was out of sight of anyone travelling along the road he was in no rush. The winter stumps of perennial ferns twisted his ankles in unnatural directions, and the wiry bilberry bushes, persistent remnants of the days when this area had been open moorland, forced him to lift his knees higher than normal as he walked. With each exaggerated step, his ribs ached a little more. He felt the barrel of his newly-acquired gun pressing sharply into his right hip, and when his legs began to ache he stopped to slip his left hand into his coat pocket to check that all four of his precious bullets were safe.

The distance from the lay-by to the gamekeeper's cottage where Prunella and Brian Leath lived was about four hundred metres, an easy walk in daylight, even through the woods, but in the darkness he was beginning to wonder whether he wasn't walking in circles when through the trees ahead of him he saw the lights of two vehicles. He hadn't expected anyone other than Brian to be about before seven o'clock and thought about the dogs. Would they recognise and remember him? It had been a while. He bent over and peered into the undergrowth for a decent sized stick.

The two sets of lights bounced along the track towards the road, and as far as he knew, only two people still lived there. That meant the dogs would either be fastened up or in one of the vehicles, and the place would be empty.

He wasn't ready yet to confront Prunella Leath. It was Brian that he'd come to see.

The one person he felt he could go to for answers had been a school friend of his father, and Simon had known him and worked alongside him during the summer months since the age of twelve. And they'd all been particularly careful over the years to keep their close friendship a secret from Prunella.

"What she doesn't know doesn't hurt her," Brian had often said. "I tolerate Pru because she's a good cook, but I prefer the quiet life, if you know what I mean," he'd usually added with a wink. Simon hadn't known what he'd meant, but he'd played along.

Brian would understand that Simon hadn't meant for Eric Shutter to die.

He really had wanted to question the one person outside of his family who he knew he could trust. The gamekeeper detested the whole Oakwell Grange community, but being married to Prunella, he may be the one person who could make sense of what had happened. Until he knew the cause of the violence, until he had all the facts, how could he know which of the women to confront first? If he got his next move wrong, he could be putting Arianne in extreme danger, and that was the last thing he intended to do.

But it looked as though Brian had driven away and there was nothing he could do about that. He decided to continue walking and take a look around the property anyway. Maybe the gamekeeper was just off to check his mole traps and wouldn't be away for too long.

Brian had been the one who'd introduced him to guns, but killing dumb, defenceless animals, even for food, had never sat well with Simon.

People on the other hand, now they were a different matter.

How many people would be able to truthfully say that they'd never fantasised about killing someone they detested? Surely no one could go through life without making enemies, but thankfully very few of them ever did anything about it. Sure, they'd grumble and complain to their nearest and dearest who would nod their heads and then think nothing more about it. That was because they were normal, rational, human beings. But he'd been knocked off his 'normal' axis last Monday evening, and then knocked even further the following morning when he'd watched the news from his hospital bed.

He knew he couldn't kill just anyone in cold blood, but if the time came when he had to pull the trigger to save Arianne, or to avenge Philip and John, he was fairly sure that he wouldn't have to think twice.

Daylight was slowly breaking as he approached the Keepers Cottage.

It was a spur of the moment idea, a flash of divine inspiration almost, when the first thing he saw in the gamekeeper's yard was a stack of dismantled, large, metal dog crates. He lifted the top one and stood it against the house wall. It looked large enough for what, or who, he had in mind.

The dog pens were empty and so he slid open the door of the tractor shed and quickly stepped inside. He'd remembered the large assortment of ropes, hanging from row after row of rusty nails. Selecting what he thought was a pair of the longest skeins; he placed them over his head and onto one shoulder. It wasn't really stealing. He fully intended to either return them or pay Brian their full value.

And when Brian eventually learns what they've been used for he will most probably have a good laugh, he thought as he stepped out of the shed and picked up the crate.

Despite his awkward load he had to return to his van by the route he'd used to arrive at the gamekeeper's cottage. It was far too risky for him to walk down the potholed driveway. If anyone other than Brian was to see him with his haul, his plan would be dead in the water, so to speak.

*

DC Rawlings bounced up the stairs, two at a time, and burst into the incident room. Not one face in the busy room remained focused on its computer screen. "Sir, two acquaintances of the dead boys have come forward with new information."

"Well you've got the room's attention now, Rawlings." Forbes said. "So share your news with us all."

"Anthony Vale and Neil Smith knew John, Philip and Simon from when they were all at secondary school together. They hadn't thought it important enough to mention until they heard the talk about the Oakwell women, but a few days before the Christmas break they were all in the same café in town and overheard our victims talking about renewing their campaign of retaliation against some women. It seems Philip believed the women's influences were preventing any of them from getting into the colleges they'd applied for. They heard John and Philip discussing the contents of an anonymous letter they intended to send to Oakwell, and laughing about it."

"Get to the point, Rawlings. Do they know what the letter was about, and whether it was ever posted?"

He referred to his notebook. "They couldn't remember the exact wording but It went along the lines of; *'we know what you are doing and how you make your money... the truth is about to be revealed to the world... be prepared to be shamed...'* or words very similar to those, and as the boys had sounded so enthusiastic at the time, Anthony and Neil both assumed the letter would have been posted."

"Then we'll assume that it was received, but possibly not until early January. Ask your informants not to mention this to anyone else, will you?"

"Yes sir."

"Oh and Rawlings, have you visited the scrapyards yet?"

"On my way now, sir," his officer said as he left the room.

20

Despite his strong desire to question the Oakwell women about whether or not they'd received the letter, Forbes was driving Adam out towards the Samson Estate.

"If that letter was sent," Adam said, "the Oakwell women aren't likely to admit to receiving it, are they? They will know that they'd been handing us a motive. Whether they'd committed the crimes or not, they'll probably assume it would make them our prime suspects."

"At the moment, they are. Think about it for a few minutes. Is it just possible that those boys actually uncovered something too damning, or too dangerous, to be made public, and were they perhaps unwittingly poking the wasps' nest? If that letter does exist, then its contents give us our first plausible motive – money. We're back to what Mr and Mrs James were concerned about; an irregular source of finance.

We need to find out exactly when the polytunnel and greenhouses were purchased by the women, and whether they were paid for in one lump sum, or in instalments. Find someone to check with the local suppliers. Also double check the dates when Mr James claimed to have been paid for his services, and the amounts. Assure him we've no interest in his tax returns, and that anything he tells us will go no further. But first, I think we should have another word with Mr Leath."

He'd waited until he'd thought Prunella Leath would have left the cottage. He knew the couple spent as little time together as possible, but just to be sure of catching the gamekeeper alone, he'd phoned ahead.

"You were lucky to catch me." Brian Leath's frame filled the porch doorway. "I'd just popped back for another roll of wire when the phone went. I'm fixing up the pheasant pens ready for the first batch of chicks, but that job can easily wait for another day. The dogs won't bother you while I'm here. They've had their breakfasts. Come on in – I've been hoping you'd call back for a quick word while Pru was out."

Leath was a large man with a shaven head and a bulbous nose, he could have been a boxer or a night club bouncer in his earlier years, and still looked adequately built for the business of handling whole venison carcasses.

He liked to think that judging people's innermost feelings had become one of his stronger attributes over the years, and although he occasionally got it wrong, he felt confident that Mr Leath's hatred of his wife's friends was genuine. There were no pheasant carcasses hanging in the porch this time, only a neat row of clean wellington boots on the clean tiled floor, and a selection of polished walking sticks in a purpose-built, triangular wooden container in the corner.

The living room they were shown into still looked tidy and dust-free. They refused drinks, took their overcoats off, and sat on the beige leather sofa. Forbes looked around – there were no pictures in this room – the walls were painted in neutral tones of cream and beige, but were completely devoid of any other decoration. It was the complete opposite of the walls they'd seen in Oakwell Grange where there was hardly an inch of space to be seen. Perhaps Prunella spent so little of her time here with her husband that nest-building wouldn't concern her.

"Now then officers, how can I help you?"

"We're working on a few leads," Forbes began, "and we're collecting background information on Oakwell Grange as we go. Very few men ever seem to have been admitted into the Grange and most of the group members we've spoken to have nothing but praise for the two women who live there. Your wife is one of the main organisers of the group meetings and the businesses, and so we'd be interested in anything you can tell us about them, and about your wife's background and involvement in the place."

Brian slowly nodded. "I thought it'd be something like that. I don't pay much attention to what they get up to at Oakwell, but I can tell you plenty about Prunella. She was running that place long before I knew her, and I keep telling her she might as well go and live there. She's an exceptionally clever woman, my Pru, did you know that?"

"We could see that she's strong willed," Adam said tactfully.

"Before I met her she was a qualified solicitor who returned to college to train as an accountant. Three years into her training she says she found religion – not the normal kind, of course, because as you may have noticed, our Prunella doesn't do normal. Apparently she discovered some sort of pagan religion and turned her back on all her education and all her qualifications. She's very obsessive. I realised too late that she needs to control everyone around her. I guess she found a property full of weak-willed females and potential followers when in her mid-twenties she crossed the threshold of Oakwell Grange. We have a sham marriage, I don't mind admitting that, but I can't leave because this property comes with the job. I'm in charge of the venison larder and several other major sources of income for the Samson Estate. I enjoy my work and positions like this aren't too plentiful. Pru and I live pretty much separate lives. She occasionally cooks and I frequently clean. She claims to keep coming back here because she likes to see the dogs. Can you believe such a feeble excuse – it would be funny if it wasn't so pathetic."

"You need a good solicitor, Mr Leath," Forbes said. "How much do you know about the mental state of the sisters if they allowed your wife to dominate them and their businesses so easily?"

"Not much I'm afraid. I'd only known Prunella for a few months before we tied the knot. She made it clear from the start that that part of her life would never involve me."

"Do you know how or why she became involved with Oakwell in the first place?"

"Someone once told me that while she was studying for her 'A' levels she dated Donald Muir, then a student himself of course. I know it's a tenuous link, but maybe that's how she got to know the Hall sisters."

"Our Donald Muir, the local head teacher?" Forbes tried to keep his voice steady.

"The one and only; but then young Sheila Hall married him and produced a daughter, Jasmine, and a couple of months later Hannah gave birth to another female, Acacia. Both children were the products of Donald's brief stay at the Grange. I don't like to judge people – live and let live is my motto, but I can make an exception for those women. In my humble opinion, they should have both been shot at birth."

"Have you or your wife got any children?"

"I've none that I'm aware of. I was never a ladies man, if you know what I mean, and Prunella has always claimed to be far too selfish to devote the necessary time and energy to a child of her own. I've always thought it strange that there was nothing she wouldn't do for those two girls of Donald's."

"What can you tell us about the lodgers – the young homeless women that the sisters supposedly take in from time to time? How is that side financed?"

"I'd hardly call them lodgers, because from what I've heard the poor sods have to work hard for their keep. Several of them seem to pass through the place each year. According to Prunella many of them don't speak English and can't get help elsewhere, and I don't know that any money is involved. I was told the Grange is supposed to be run as a charity, and I know they rattle collection boxes in the town every few weeks."

"So you wouldn't know anything about any of the finances of the women or the businesses?"

"I neither know nor care."

"Can you think of anything at all that any of the women might be desperate to keep from becoming public knowledge?"

"People around here have always known about the weird spiritual stuff, but I suppose there might some from further afield who don't want their husbands to discover what they get up to on the nights of a full moon. Donald Muir's employers wouldn't care about his private life, especially from a couple of decades ago, would they? And I don't know how many people are aware that he's still screwing my wife, but if I don't care, why should anyone else?"

"Sorry... he's what? Are you certain about that?"

"They make no secret of it if he calls here to pick her up. They don't go snogging in front of me or anything like that, but they always hug when they meet and there's the odd peck on the cheek that they think I don't see. You're probably thinking I should break his jaw or something, but she really isn't worth the effort. You may already have noticed, Inspector, but my wife is an extremely arrogant woman who genuinely believes that she can get away with anything."

*

Jane Goodwin could have almost bitten off her own tongue. She hadn't intended for it to sound so clumsy and so cruel. It had been the result of an emotionally exhausting few days, but still she couldn't quite believe that Adam had taken it so badly. She hadn't imagined for one moment that he would ever storm out of her house, with his sleeping son in his arms, without talking things through with her. She wasn't breaking up with him – she needed a break – there was a world of difference.

After reporting back to DCI Forbes, yesterday afternoon, and having the ordeal on her mind all day today, all she'd wanted to do tonight was take a shower, read Lucy a bedtime story, and then curl up on the sofa with a duvet, a nice bottle of wine and a large glass, and to remain there all night if she felt like it. With two small children in the house, it perhaps wasn't the healthiest thing to do, as Adam had begun to point out at the exact moment that the top had come off the one litre bottle. Well she didn't need company, she'd decided on the spur of the moment, and she didn't need her mind distracting, or whatever it was that Adam thought he was doing for her. She needed time alone with her daughter, time for them to help each other, and time to think things through and to grieve for her mother in her own way.

Her glass was empty again and Adam had only been gone for one hour. She picked up the half empty bottle and examined its contents before placing it back on the floor and picking up her phone. They'd never had any kind of an argument before. She'd never raised her voice to him like that and so there was no precedent as to how or when they would sort this out. She desperately needed to feel his arms around her before she drifted off to sleep, but just as importantly, she wanted him to listen to her.

His phone rang until the voicemail cut in. At least he hadn't simply rejected her call. She needed him to know, although she hadn't told him for a few days, that she dearly loved both him and his son, but with almost half a bottle of wine in her stomach, she couldn't trust herself to speak to a machine.

*

One fire engine and two police cars screamed past his little white van. They weren't heading in the direction of anyone Simon cared about, so he pulled into the first available field entrance, switched off his engine, and reached into the glove box for the newspaper cutting. The grainy pictures of his two friends brought up unexpected tears. Angrily he brushed his sleeve across his face. Why was there still no news from the police of any arrests? It was unthinkable that anyone other than those bitches would want to harm them. Why hadn't the police been able to see that?

The dog cage was wrapped in his spare duvet, underneath his mattress. He climbed into the back to check that it hadn't moved as he'd been driving. Brian must have power-washed them. It didn't smell, as he'd anticipated it might, so it wouldn't hurt to leave it there until he was ready to use it. He washed another couple of painkillers down with a few gulps from a screw-topped bottle of wine he'd treated himself to, climbed back into the front of the van, and turned the engine back on. Then he turned the heater up and pulled back out onto the tarmac. He was looking for the junction which would take him down towards the familiar river.

Minutes later he pulled up again.

The faded white lettering on the wooden gate was just legible. *Private – no trespassing.* A rough track threaded between the trees, down to a gravelled area large enough to comfortably hold about half a dozen vehicles. He'd been here so many times with John and Philip that he knew every bend and every pot hole. There wouldn't be any fishermen using the private park at this time of the year. He lifted the loop of chain from around the strainer post, heaved the gate open, drove in, and heaved the gate shut again.

He was right – the park was empty.

The frame of the sluice gate which had once formed part of one of the eleven weirs on the River Lathkill was standing proudly in the centre of the river. During the long, hot, summer days of his childhood he'd walked along the man-made barrier more times than he could count, and fallen into the river on a good few occasions as well. Each summer since then the water level had fallen to lower than the previous year.

In the middle of the summer for the last few years, he and his father, and Brian, had helped out with the Environment Agency's annual fish rescue at the head of the river. Brown trout fry and yearling fish always needed to be rescued in their thousands as a direct result of the river water disappearing down into the Magpie mine, an ancient, and long-abandoned lead mine, and following an underground route. The problem was worsening, year by year, and many of the local residents were trying to find a way of diverting the water back to its original route and restoring River Lathkill to its natural splendour.

Even this far down from the source of the river, and after it had been topped up by several small streams, the tempting water was rarely more than a few inches deep in summer. But it looked at least knee deep now – and probably a lot deeper in places and very fast-flowing – this wasn't the weather for falling in. Besides, he could still taste the earthy water from nine days ago, and his ribs were still too sore to risk anything remotely dangerous.

He would just have to estimate the length of rope he was going to need.

It didn't take him long. It was too cold to bother about being too accurate.

He was as ready as he'd ever be.

He coiled the ropes back up, returned them to the passenger side of his van, and climbed back into the relative warmth. Then he moved onto his mattress, tucked the gun and the bullets under his pillow, and pulled the duvet over him.

Arianne had texted. She was missing him but they wouldn't be able to meet before Monday. He needed to make eye-contact with her once more before he put his plan into action, just in case anything went wrong, even if that contact was in the centre of a crowded market. He read her text half a dozen more times, then switched off his phone and closed his eyes. Thanks to the painkillers he could get some much needed sleep before his afternoon shift began.

He needed a few more days to allow his ribs to heal a little more, and then he would be good to go. The thought made him smile. He felt a calmness drifting over him. Normally he would be looking for a place in town to park and sleep, somewhere where people would be milling about, because the sounds of other humans usually made him feel safe enough to sleep soundly. Today though, with the muffled sounds from the river that had almost claimed him, he felt relaxed enough to sleep well. He pushed the loaded gun a few inches further underneath his pillow, pulled an extra duvet over the top of his other bedding, and listened to the familiar, twittering conversations of the blackbirds and finches in the trees around his van.

21

Jacob Muir quietly muttered what he considered to be a moderate swear word, pressed his right hand into the small of his back, and then exhaled noisily as he pushed himself away from the window and straightened up his creaking spine. The single-glazed living room window provided an excellent view of the lane leading up to their four-bedroomed farmhouse. He'd been watching Donald Muir driving away from his cottage at the bottom of the lane, on his way to his school. His wife, Dottie, was saying something, and these days if he couldn't see her lips moving, he couldn't always catch everything that she said. He turned to face her.

"Well I don't know why you're so upset, Jacob," she was saying. "I told you not to bother phoning him. Our Donald has always followed the money, and there's always been more of that in the teaching profession than in hill farming. He was never going to be the kind of person you and I wanted in order to keep this farm in the family. How many times has he helped you out in the past year? I bet you could count them on those old arthritic fingers of yours. You should be well used to his rejections by now. Go and put the kettle on. We'll have a nice cuppa together before I phone Robbie from Hill Top Farm. He'll be over here in a matter of minutes to help you with those ewes, but only as long as you give him a chance to eat his breakfast in peace."

"I was so proud of him, Dottie," Jacob Muir said as he shuffled into the kitchen, "when he first graduated, before we both realised just what a selfish oaf we'd raised. I only needed him for an hour or two after he'd finished at his school tonight, and then he could have eaten with us. It's not right, lass. I don't feel ready to be put out to pasture yet, but I don't know how much longer we can manage the livestock by ourselves. I don't like to keep asking Robbie because he never accepts proper payment for his labour."

"Rubbish, you never charged him for those six lambs I gave him a couple of months ago, and they'll all do well for him if he looks after them for another three or four months. We need a lad like Robbie because we both know what Donald has in mind. The less he helps out around here, the quicker he thinks he'll wear us down and have us out of this farmhouse. Well he's going to have a very long wait."

Jacob had spent his whole life working the three hundred acre hill farm, which last year had carried two dozen suckler cows and their calves, alongside the usual two hundred Blackface ewes and their respective lambs. At the age of ten months, the weaned calves were always taken to Bakewell and sold at the weekly auctions, and as soon as the lambs were ready they were dispersed to the usual neighbouring farmers. Mr Muir had never owned a bull; instead priding himself on his ability, by closely watching his cows, to detect the exact time to call on the services of Genus, the nationwide artificial insemination group. He rarely got his timings wrong, his calves were sired by prize-winning bulls from all around the country, and his calves regularly made top prices at the Bakewell cattle market.

After being in the Muir family for five generations, Dottie knew how acutely painful her husband felt the idea was, of the farm finally being placed on the open market. She sometimes hoped that Jacob could remain here for many more years, before finally passing away in his sleep just as his father had done, an old man in his own bed, rather than having to witness such a dreadful day.

Donald had his own cottage at the end of the farm track, in the two acre bottom paddock. Even excluding that, Dottie knew the farm would be snapped up at an asking price of well over a million pounds. She'd kept an eye on property and land prices and was all too aware that Donald had been doing the same.

But Dottie harboured a secret hope. "Our Acacia and Jasmine are coming to stay with us for the weekend, don't forget. I can't wait to meet Jasmine's boyfriend. She must be serious about him if she's bringing him to meet us. It would be such a blessing to have a young farmer in the family again."

"How could I forget that, woman, with you reminding me almost every hour since she phoned yesterday morning? And it's only Thursday morning now." His eyes creased with mirth as he placed the unopened packet of biscuits on the coffee table, just out of her reach.

"Put those biscuits back, you old rogue, those are Jasmine's favourites. Fetch the own brand digestives and be quick about it. I wonder who he is. She hinted that we might know him but she wouldn't say whose family he originated from. The Gordons at Pike Top Farm have three strapping sons who all want to be farmers. It could be one of them."

He knew better than to encourage her daydreams. "It's only three weeks till we begin the calving. I'll ask Robbie to give us a hand in cleaning out the byres next week. Then the main sheds will need mucking out as soon as the weather is decent enough."

Moving the cattle from one shed to another without getting knocked or trampled, lifting the gates and the feed barriers out of the way, ensuring the loader didn't damage the walls or the floor while it removed the tons of damp and soiled straw bedding, and then rolling out the clean straw, replacing the feeders and filling them with silage before allowing two dozen heavily pregnant cattle back in and closing and securing the gates on them, wasn't an old man's job. At one time Jacob would have done it single-handedly between breakfast and lunch, and thought nothing of it, but now his back ached at the thought of the job.

"Make that call now, lass, while I go and set up the foot bath. There looked to be at least four ewes in the bottom field with footrot last night so those four at least will need a shot of penicillin. You know how much I hate seeing them suffer. We'll get them all through the bath and onto the top field where it's a bit dryer. Let's hope that way we can prevent any of the others from catching it."

It was rarely silent on the sides of these hills, Jacob thought as he tugged at his zipper, trying to keep the wind away from his wheezing chest. He stepped away from the shelter of the farmhouse wall and glanced up at the grey skyline. There were two public footpaths crossing his land. There was nothing he could do about them and as long as people were responsible with their litter and their dogs, he didn't consider them too much of a problem. The footpath which eventually met the Tissington Trail was the one most frequently used. But that path couldn't be seen from the farmyard.

Jacob stared up at the solitary figure on the less-used path. From this distance, even with his glasses on, the figure could have been male or female, but why, in such a bitterly cold wind, would anyone be just standing there? He looked around for other walkers, perhaps the person was waiting for someone to catch up, and then he scanned his fields for a loose dog. Apart from his sheep, which were all contentedly grazing, there were no other signs of life. Jacob shrugged and walked towards the sheds.

When he looked back the figure had gone.

"Taking the bloody shotgun to bed tonight, that I am," he muttered as he scanned the horizon once more before opening the sliding door of the barn and quickly stepping inside to escape from the cold.

*

A two week long crackdown of illegal workers, across the Greater Manchester area, had come to an end the previous weekend. After twenty coordinated raids by Home Office immigration enforcement officers, twenty-four men and ten women had been arrested, forty residential properties had been raided, and dozens of boxes of documents had been seized. It was late on Thursday afternoon and most of the team working on Operation Lupin were about to leave when one of the immigration enforcement officers phoned the station and asked to be put in direct contact with DI Lang.

*

"Ryan is sleeping over at his gran's tonight." Adam stated. "They've been out together all day and he conked out on them. It seemed a shame to move him so I thought I'd take the opportunity to retrieve some of my toiletries from your bathroom."

Jane had been so pleased to see Adam's car pulling onto her drive that the formality of his short speech on her doorstep left her feeling breathless. She suddenly regretted having that extra glass of wine after Lucy had fallen asleep. "You don't have to…, please…, come inside. We need to talk."

"I understand that you need time alone to sort your life out. And if Ryan asks to come and visit, then I'll phone you."

"I want you both to feel free to come over at any time. I don't want it to be like this."

"Are you now saying that I don't need to make an appointment to check whether you're free?"

"Now you're being stupid, Adam. You know that isn't what I was saying."

"Stupid...? Things were going well between us until last Wednesday. I just wish you hadn't have accepted that misguided request from DCI Forbes to return to Oakwell Grange. From the day you first went to that place you've been distant with me, but after that second visit you shut me out completely. I do understand grief, you know that, and I want to help you, but I can only do that if you'll let me."

"Adam, I love you, really I do, both you and Ryan, but I feel that at the moment I need to be allowed a little more space to breath. What is so difficult to understand about that? Please, don't let's argue. Come in and share a glass of wine with me."

He pulled her towards him and wrapped his arms around her. "I get it that the idea of your mother being caught up in some sort of secret world must have come as a shock, and I know that the grieving process goes through several stages and is different for everyone. If it's space that you want, then space you shall have. I'm here for you when you're ready. But don't shut me out."

"Please don't take any of your things away."

"I won't, but I'll only respect your wishes if you'll promise not to return to Oakwell, not unless someone from the station authorises it and someone goes with you." He leaned back to look at her.

"I promise."

*

"You're not really worried, are you?" Dottie Muir had been enjoying her bedtime mug of cocoa until Jacob had mentioned the lone figure. She scowled at the shotgun as if it was somehow to blame. "Maybe it's time now for us to bring another dog into the house – a middle-aged one from the rescue centre to act as a deterrent and warn us if anyone is about at night."

"I'll think about it... maybe we'll do just that."

"Should we mention your lone figure to Duncan, or to the police? They've not got anyone for that hit-and-run in Ashtown and people are saying that those boys were deliberately targeted. I don't like to think there's a killer on the loose somewhere in our rural community. And then there's that other youth who they're all looking for. It could have been him, don't you think, looking for somewhere to hide out? I've heard that he believes someone is still trying to kill him. If that is the case, we don't want him anywhere near our property."

"I'm telling no one, and neither should you, at least not until our Jasmine and Acacia are safely back in Manchester. We don't want to worry them. Anyway, why would anyone want to bother with us, everyone knows there's nothing of value in this house? And if Duncan is in any kind of trouble, then it's of his own making, and don't you forget that, girl."

Dottie's hands trembled as she cradled the warm mug. "You don't think our Duncan could be in danger, do you? The reason for that fire at his school has never been fully explained to us."

"Trust me love, none of these goings-on have anything to do with us. This loaded shotgun underneath our bed is only to give us some peace of mind. We'll keep our doors locked and let the other daft buggers fight it out amongst themselves."

*

Prunella Leath slipped her phone back into her coat pocket and pulled her gloves back on. It was only a short distance from the shed where she'd gone to make the call, to the house where she'd left her husband asleep in front of his precious television, but it was damn cold.

She couldn't help smiling. Her Manchester contacts, the Gang Lords as they liked to call themselves these days, had come through for her. She'd known that they would. But then so they should after the years she'd spent tidying up their loose ends and ensuring that the main families had ready alibis for the police, whenever they were needed.

But that was in another lifetime. At least that was how it felt when she had to deal with the grandsons of the gangsters she'd known and worked for back then. She often wondered what her husband would do, and how he would react, if he ever discovered that when he did finally marry, he'd hitched himself to a female contract killer.

Killing had come remarkably easily to her.

She hadn't found life as a teenager much fun, and despite getting excellent grades at school, her uncle had thrown her out of his house on the day she'd secured her place at University. Friends had reluctantly taken her in, but without money her dreams of becoming a lawyer had for a while looked unobtainable. She hadn't had the figure or the face for prostitution, at least not for earning the serious amounts of money needed to pay for a flat and for tuition fees. In high school, her teachers had often told her to stop scowling, not that she had been, that was just the way that her face fell and there wasn't an awful lot she could do about it.

And so she'd taken a summer job, waitressing at a dockside cafe.

That was where she'd first met Johnny Bell, the charming, and dangerously handsome son of one of the two brothers who had then controlled most of the criminal activity on the southern side of the Manchester docks. At eighteen, she'd been savvy enough to know that he hadn't wanted her for her body, but when he asked her to sell drugs for him she'd actually told him that she would rather shoot someone stone dead than kill them slowly with their stinking chemicals.

Johnny Bell had never been known for his sense of humour, and that day he'd taken her statement quite literally.

Her busiest year, as she'd sailed through University, had involved fourteen fatal shootings. She'd been so efficient and so professional that the Bells had hired out her services to the gangs on the northern side of the docks, and beyond. She was earning more than even the most glamorous of her street sisters, and she'd enjoyed the sense of belonging, and the feeling of being protected and whispered about by so many strong, ruthless men and their families.

But like all good things, it had come to an end. The police had been closing in on her, Johnny had provided her with the new identity that he'd always promised her, and they'd parted amicably after their one and only night of love making. She hadn't seen him since, but several times each year, they spoke together on the phone. She liked to think that one long night of indiscretion with her had kindled a small torch somewhere inside Johnny's otherwise cold heart.

Behind closed doors, her escapades were still spoken about and her reputation lived on, he'd frequently told her that much, and when she spoke to the younger members of his family she could hear the respect in their voices.

Of course they were going to help her. This was one assassination that was too close to home for her to deal with herself. Someone else had to take out Simon Carter, and now everything was set for Monday.

She could hardly wait.

22

DCI Forbes poked his head into the incident room and then continued on to his office. Leaburn station was unusually quiet for Friday morning, but then it was barely seven a.m.

His office was even quieter. Instead of working on the case, his thoughts drifted to his family. He and his father had both been impressed by Louise's commitment to her studies. If her exam results proved good enough she still intended to apply for a job in the mortuary, and Alison Ransom, she'd informed them, had become her role model.

He wasn't supposed to discuss the details of any on-going cases with his family, but his sister's pleading usually wore him down. He hadn't been much of a big brother to her while she'd been growing up and he felt he owed it to her to encourage her now and to try and maintain her interest in her chosen career. And this time she'd been even more persistent because she'd known John Lewis, Philip Booth and Simon Carter.

He'd discussed certain aspects of the case with her, but he hadn't been able to put his own dark thoughts into words. The idea that their mother may have taken part in some of the weird group meetings at Oakwell Grange had even disrupted his dreams. His mind had repeatedly churned over the idea that maybe she'd been exposed to drugs of some sort – legal or otherwise, and that maybe they'd contributed to her death. Some roadside herbs were incredibly lethal, and her death within weeks of giving birth had never been fully explained. An aneurism, the doctors had said, nothing which could have been foreseen or prevented, they'd assured both him and his father, but his father had never accepted their platitudes.

What if the old man had been right all along?

In an unsolved murder case, samples of body tissues are stored away indefinitely, in case new technology can ever be used on them, or new information comes to light, but it was highly unlikely that anything like that would have happened with his mother's body. Would it be too distressing to enquire? When this case was over he would give it some serious consideration. But it was a complication that he didn't need at the moment, and if his superiors heard about it then they might consider that he had a personal involvement, however tenuous, in the case of the hit-and-run murders. Sometimes the past was best left alone – if only it would leave him alone.

He checked his e-mails, picked up his jacket, opened the door to the corridor and headed back towards the incident room.

"Adam, do you and I need to clear the air on the subject of Jane Goodwin's visit to Oakwell Grange?" His DS had barely made eye-contact with him as they'd prepared for the morning's briefing on adjacent tables.

"We're all feeling the pressure of this case, sir. Jane needs more space and more time to grieve for her mother, and although I still think it was wrong of you to ask her to return to the Grange, I realise you didn't understand the turmoil she's been going through this past week."

"Have I been the cause of a problem between the two of you?"

"Jane and I will come through this, sir, don't worry about us."

"I really hope you're right, because you make a lovely little family unit. If there's anything I can do to help, if you need me to talk with her again, to apologise...."

"Don't take this wrong, sir, but I think we both agree that Jane fixating on Oakwell Grange isn't healthy, also...," Adam hesitated.

"Spit it out."

"Well I was wondering whether perhaps we weren't doing the same. We haven't found any physical evidence to link anyone from the Grange to the boys' deaths. All we have pointing us in their direction is the word of a troubled teenage boy and some local gossip. Is it time to widen our search, sir?"

"Maybe, but you're forgetting that we now have a possible motive. The fluctuations in the Oakwell finances haven't been explained to my satisfaction. Savings from their wages at the school, as they tried to convince us, don't account for why they were too broke to pay for essential repairs one month, and then erecting fancy new greenhouses the next. Something about that whole set-up doesn't feel right. We need to dig a little deeper into the lives of everyone involved in that place. I'm becoming more convinced that those youths discovered something which got two of them killed and the third running for his life. What I don't understand is why Simon Carter hasn't come to us."

"Either he's protecting someone, or his family or other friends have been threatened. There was the incident of the fire at his parent's property. That could have been a warning to him, or a reprisal for the fire at the women's school."

"And there we have it, Adam. You've talked yourself round to my way of thinking. Until we either find the hit-and-run vehicle, or someone comes forward with some information which deflects suspicion away from those women, they'll remain our main suspects."

As he stepped up to the whiteboard he wondered whether Adam could be right. Had he been blinkered by thoughts of his mother's death? It was his job to overview the entire case, but had he been doing that as well as he ought to?

"Sir, I have news on Operation Lupin," DI Lang entered the incident room over half an hour late. That was very unlike him. "I have an unconfirmed name for my dead woman. Immigration officers contacted me late yesterday with some news. They'd recently raided businesses and private properties in and around Greater Manchester, and as well as illegal immigrants they found stacks of forged and genuine passports. Organized gangs have been smuggling people into this country and forcing them to work, promising them their documents back just as soon as they'd worked off the cost of their transport."

"I think we're all aware of how human trafficking works." Forbes said.

"One of the officers checking the genuine passports noticed a resemblance to the picture of the woman in the e-mails I've been sending out. He checked police records in case she'd passed through their hands, but he found nothing. We can't be certain it's her, not without a DNA comparison from a family member, but the woman's passport photo bears a strong resemblance to our unnamed victim, and so far, no one the immigration officers have spoken to have admitted to knowing where the owner of the passport can be found. I'd like to go to Manchester this weekend to try to find someone who either knew or worked with the woman. There's a slim chance they may be able to positively identify her, or even have an idea of where the baby is now."

23

This wasn't how Simon had imagined it. He'd never seen the Monday morning Bakewell outdoor market looking so deserted. At least half of the stalls were empty. The bitterly cold wind and the threat of snow had reduced the numbers of stallholders and customers alike. He checked his reflection in the window of the outdoor clothing shop on the edge of the market, but only a fragmented, dark silhouette stared back at him.

Was it too risky to go any further? He'd crossed the narrowest, least-used footbridge over the river to avoid being seen by too many people, but the crowds he'd expected to blend into between the stalls just weren't there. It was a risk worth taking, he suddenly decided, and besides, he was unlikely to be harmed in such an open and public place.

He took a deep breath and stepped towards one elderly couple who were having a deep discussion over something for sale at the end of the second row of stalls. As he stood beside them, the old man, who had a pipe hanging from the side of his mouth, a white cap perched at a jaunty angle on the top of his head, bulging eyes and broken-veined red cheeks, reminded him Popeye. The woman looked over her shoulder and Popeye placed his arm around her and gently pulled her closer to his side. He couldn't blame him. He hoped he would have done the same in a similar situation.

But then there she was – his beautiful Arianne.

She was standing half way down the very next row, with her woollen hat pulled down over her delicate ears and with her perfectly formed back turned towards him. His mouth felt dry. What if she didn't recognise him? Or worse still, what if today was the last time that he ever saw her?

Popeye was staring at him now.

A large woman waddled past the three of them and turned to walk between the rows of stalls. He stepped out and followed her, hoping her bulk and her tent-like coat would hide him from the two women standing closest to Arianne. He prayed she wouldn't think he was a purse snatcher and turn to hit him with her bag, or scream at him. She hadn't seemed to have noticed him. Instead, she paused to look at the price tags on some waxed coats and some leather bags, and then she stopped at a stall strewn with jumpers and cardigans. "None of those have a hope in hell of fitting you, lady. For Christ's sake just move along," he muttered. The fat lady looked up and her eyes met his. She gripped her bag in both hands and waddled away, obviously aiming to put as much distance as she could, as quickly as she could, between herself and her stalker. He looked around but there was no other obvious cover.

Head bowed, he casually walked towards the Oakwell stall.

Arianne's deep brown eyes looked up and straight into his. He watched them crease with her sweet smile of recognition and he opened his mouth to speak. He felt pathetic when he couldn't even manage a single word to her in the precious few moments it took to walk past the stall.

But he had to keep on walking.

One of the women, the one with her back towards him and apparently in conversation with a man, was Prunella Leath. Prunella seemed to stiffen as her meeting apparently ended and her head turned very slightly in Simon's direction. He daren't risk looking back at Arianne now. Head bowed again and feeling totally deflated, he marched away from the market.

He had begun to see the world through different eyes, he realised. That corny phrase from the old song his mother sometimes sang along to was true – love did hurt. With every step he took along the wet, tarmacked pavement, more anger surged through him, his chest pains returned and suddenly he was struggling to breathe. He stopped to lean on someone's neat, limestone, garden wall.

Rapid footsteps approached from behind. He steeled himself to turn his head and look, cursing himself for not putting the gun in his coat pocket.

But it was just a trim young woman, jogging along the pavement towards him, and as she drew level she smiled at him. Her whole face lit up.

"Morning..." she chirped at him in a shrill voice.

"Morning..." he could only croak back through the dryness in his throat. She was maybe ten years older than his Arianne, but her smile was, if anything, even brighter. It compelled him to smile back at her. She was small and skinny, and obviously fit, with a mountain of wavy, fair hair swept up into a ponytail on the top of her head. The mountain was being held aloft by a wide, black sweatband and a black ribbon, and it bounced with every step that she took. If that was the cartoon character Popeye that he'd seen in the market then this was Popeye's girlfriend – his fickle and disloyal, Olive Oyl.

Just seeing a smile which was so much like Arianne's had made him feel so much better, and he felt sure that this girl could be neither fickle nor disloyal. He stifled a laugh but couldn't resist muttering, "There goes Olive Oyl with a bird's nest on her head."

Two couples walked along the opposite pavement in the direction of the market. They looked straight ahead, probably thinking he was just another drunk, or at this time of the morning, high on drugs. Let them think what they liked. The deliberately deep breaths, followed by the sight of that young woman's incredibly infectious smile, had calmed him. He took one more deep breath, straightened himself up, and then continued along the deserted side of the road.

Olive Oyl was rapidly disappearing around the bend in the road, but his van was still there, a hundred metres beyond where the pavements ended. Parking there had enabled him to park with two wheels on the tarmac, two on the grass verge, and with the driver's door almost touching the thick hawthorn hedge. On the narrow road adjacent to the showground no parking ticket was needed and there were no cameras, and because of the weather his was the only vehicle parked there.

*

Prunella smiled as she watched the dejected figure walking away. She was in an ebullient mood. He'd come, just as she'd known he would, the poor love-struck sap whose life was about to end.

Only one part of the plan had messed with her mind. What kind of a dumb, unprofessional assassin sought out the person organising the hit to whinge about having to stand around in the cold? The idiot only needed to hang around on the market until she gave the signal. Once his target had returned to their vehicle, he was to take him at knifepoint, force him to drive to a quiet spot, and then shoot him. As long as the idiot kept the knife out of sight, even if anyone had recognised Simon, it wouldn't have mattered as long as her plans were followed.

Blacktop quarry was in the process of being filled in and the digger operator there was waiting to push the van, with Simon's body inside it, to where it would never be found. She'd even arranged for a lift back into town for the assassin.

She'd have killed for a hit as simple as that at one time. She smiled again. That was a really stupid thought, but men were such infuriating wimps. When he'd wanted to disappear into a café for a hot drink she'd been tempted to slap him, and she might have done if at that exact moment she hadn't seen Simon Carter approaching her stall.

Everyone had accepted that Simon had gone into hiding and sooner or later the police would stop looking for him.

He'd almost made it too easy for her to dispose of him

*

He climbed into the driver's side of his van, leaned across the seats, and began rummaging around in the glove box. The feel of cold steel was just what he needed to calm his racing heartbeat. The handle slipped so easily into his palm that he couldn't resist fingering the trigger, albeit very gently. He'd left it loaded, but he hadn't been able to afford enough ammunition to risk an accidental discharge.

Suddenly, instinctively, he pressed his body flat across the length of the van's two front seats.

His peripheral vision had picked up movement in the driver's side wing mirror. There was someone on the grass verge, in the narrow gap between his van and the hedge. Quickly and quietly, he pulled the gun clear of the hard plastic and pointed it at the driver's door. Several seconds passed. He counted them by the pounding of the blood vessels in his brain – two thumps to each second. Adrenaline, he'd read somewhere, prepares the body for the voluntary choice of 'fight or flight'. He was ready for the fight.

From deafening silence to deafening noise, in the fraction of a second that it took for the van door to be opened his brain had registered the flash of a blade. He saw the man's free hand grab at the steering wheel and he kicked out as hard as he could with both feet. As his knees straightened and his boots thudded, he squeezed the trigger.

A firework exploded inside his head and pain shot through his left leg and his chest.

What happened after that occurred in the same surreal slow motion that he'd experienced while in the icy river.

There might be more of them, he thought quite rationally. There was no time to reload the gun. He had to get away.

He grabbed hold of the steering wheel, roared from the combination of fear and pain, and hauled himself upright into the driving seat.

His fingers throbbed and he felt as though he might throw up, but he had to look.

Impaled on the fencepost and supported by the thorny hedge, was a man's twitching body, with its lower jaw barely hanging on and blood pumping from its open mouth. Its eyes were open, bulging but seeing nothing. They reminded him oddly of the Popeye look-alike's bulging eyes when they'd been warning him off.

The gun thudded onto the rubber mat in the passenger's foot well. He turned the key and then slammed his vehicle into gear. Without looking for other traffic he turned his van around in the road, reached out for the handle of the swinging door and then screeched his tyres on the wet tarmac.

Before she walked away from the stall, Prunella Leath flashed a genuine smile at Arianne. If the morning hadn't been so entertaining, she wouldn't now be feeling almost sorry for the smug little cow. "You thought you'd found your soul mate, didn't you," she muttered just quietly enough for the girl not to hear, "well you hadn't, you'd found yourself a teenage monster, a monster who tore other people's lives to shreds – yours included now."

She was too pleased with herself to be able to stand still. She marched to the end of the row of stalls.

A group of four women looked at her as she turned and walked back past them for a second time. She could see in their eyes what they thought of her, but she didn't care. She continued to mutter. "Did he whisper into your ear that he wanted to spend the rest of his life with you? I'll wager that while he was using you he did just that. Everyone has used you girl. Let fate have its way with you. Today I've used you as bait, and tomorrow, if I feel like it, I'll dispose of you without the slightest of qualms." She laughed out loud, and continued pacing.

The first siren she heard raised her heart beat even more. "It's all right," she told herself, "it could be going anywhere."

She turned and walked through the row of market stalls again. More people were staring at her so she flung her arms around her shoulders as though trying to keep herself warm.

All she could hear now were sirens. Some people were running into doorways and others were gathering in small groups. Had something gone wrong with her plan? Had the idiot defied her and killed Simon somewhere in the town? For the entire morning she'd been in public view in the centre of the market, and she'd made Sheila and Hannah volunteer for some early shifts in the school kitchens.

She'd made certain no one could ever connect Simon's permanent disappearance with Oakwell Grange. "It's all right," she told herself again, "even if things haven't gone to plan, the Gods are on your side. Everything is going to be all right."

"Someone's been shot near the showground," she heard a breathless woman yelling to a small gathering of concerned-looking pensioners.

"I've just come from there and I heard the shot," a man in green overalls and wellington boots, who'd obviously just come from the cattle market, said. "We all thought a car had backfired until a little girl let out the most blood curdling scream. It might not even be safe for us to be here. There could be a gunman on the loose in our town."

More people moved into shop doorways and a few scurried to the relative safety of the nearby co-op supermarket.

Prunella forced herself to look concerned. They've got it wrong, she thought. If he's dead, surely he's been stabbed and not shot. She dearly wanted to put them straight but instead pressed her lips together and concentrated on appearing as worried as the dozen or so men and women who'd congregated in the centre of the market around her stall. This nearest group appeared to be confused as to which direction would be safest for them to go.

"Shall we pack up now? The other stall holders are leaving." Arianne looked like a frightened bird, desperate to take flight but too scared to leave the ground.

"I think that would be wise," she tried to sound calm. She could guess why the girl was so agitated. "You can help us prepare for our visitors. Acacia and Jasmine are calling on their mothers this afternoon so you can clean their rooms in case they want to stay over."

All praise to the Gods and Goddesses; Simon was no longer a problem.

Even if things hadn't gone exactly to plan, it was turning into an excellent week.

*

"Well I suppose that's one less villain off the streets of Manchester," DS Adam Ross draped his coat over the back of his chair and sat down. "Though what Cokehead Colin was doing in Bakewell on a wintery Monday morning will have to be fully investigated, and I expect his shoes will soon be filled by another low-life. It's been a waste of a morning for us, traipsing all the way over there. The Bakewell and Buxton officers were quite capable of handling the situation, as it turned out, though I don't know how that constable from Buxton could so confidently recognise only half of a face. I'm glad I didn't have to look at it too closely."

Forbes felt the same way. "A turf-war between two drug-dealing criminals – let's hope that's all it turns out to be, but anything involving firearms in a public place has to be taken seriously. The public need to feel safe on our British streets, especially in a small market town in the centre of the Peak District where we've never needed to have armed officers on patrol. And the Good Lord permitting, we never will."

*

DI Lang had made some progress in Manchester, but not as much as he'd hoped. The photo in the seized passport was a close enough match to his victim to make him think he hadn't wasted his time, bearing in mind that she had been dead for about a fortnight before being found. He hadn't come away with anything conclusive, but from the photo and from what he'd been told, he felt sure he now had the right name for her.

Darya Jamal had come to Britain from Afghanistan, but neither her passport nor any of her other documents seized by customs officers had been through any of the legitimate channels. That meant that customs had no record of Darya's fingerprints. It was possible of course that her identity would never be conclusively proved, not unless her family could be contacted to provide a DNA sample. And coming from war-torn Afghanistan, how likely was that going to be? Also he hadn't realised until yesterday that most Afghanis don't have family names; instead they have two or more given names.

He'd spent the best part of his weekend in the interview rooms of an unfamiliar police station, in the company of both male and female illegal immigrants and interpreters, conducting painfully slow interviews. But he had gained what he hoped was some useable information.

He faced the packed incident room of Leaburn station. "I had mixed responses from the detainees," he began. "Of those I interviewed, only two women, both from Afghanistan, admitted to having known the missing owner of the passport. When shown the mortuary photograph they both thought it could have been Darya Jamal. They individually recounted a tale of how the friends had been promised their freedom and all the necessary papers to make a life here in Britain. But not before they'd worked off the cost of their safe passage to our shores. They realised too late that they'd unwittingly sold themselves into slavery. It's a story we are all too familiar with, but at the time of leaving their homeland these women were unaware of the dangers they were facing. Darya, Tarana and Chaman, all in their late teens, had fled from abusive situations in Afghanistan, and if the girl in our mortuary is the third member of the trio, then nineteen year old Darya Jamal lived a short and painful life." He paused as he remembered some of the horrors he'd heard being described to him.

"Manchester detectives will be investigating the people traffickers," Forbes added. "They might be able to establish a motive for her murder."

"I think I might have a motive, sir."

"Go on..."

"The women who knew her spoke very emotionally about one of the guards who'd repeatedly raped Darya. He was an English, middle-aged, dark haired and thick-set man. Most of the other guards seemed nervous when he was around, the women said, and everyone was wary of him. He was a guard – just one of the criminal gang's employees, the girls thought – but although the other guards knew what he was up to, no one ever tried to stop him. Darya confided in the two women that she was pregnant and one morning she picked up a shard of flint from the floor of the van that was used to transport the workers to and from the vegetable packing plant. As they arrived at the factory she told her two friends of her intention to take her own life by cutting her wrists. Once inside the works they weren't allowed to talk. About an hour after she'd spoken of suicide, she was pulled off the packing line and neither of the women saw Darya or the English guard again."

"And you think it's unlikely that they rode off into the sunset to live happily ever after?" Forbes's anomalous sense of humour was lost on the majority of his team, so after a second's pause he continued. "How far back did all this happen?"

"Darya was removed from the group just over six months ago. If she was three to four months…"

"I think we can all work that one out for ourselves. There weren't any signs of a suicide attempt anywhere on our victim, were there?"

"No sir."

"Share your information with the Greater Manchester detectives who have her passport and concentrate your efforts on locating that baby. I think that's the best way you can help her now, DI Lang. And well done."

For several days, nothing new had come in regarding the missing baby, and Forbes had agreed with him that if it was ever found it would most likely be as the result of something random that a member of the public had either heard or seen and thought relevant enough to report. It was a matter of maintaining public awareness.

In the days preceding the call from customs officers, DI Lang had had very little to work with. He'd been keeping himself occupied by trawling through old murder cases, looking for any which bore the slightest similarity to what little they knew about the death of Darya Jamal.

He had a new press release prepared and ready to go out, and while he waited he saw no reason not to extend the parameters of his search.

From what little he had learned in the Manchester interview rooms, it seemed Darya had been nothing more than a commodity, to be transported around the country and used, and in handing the case over entirely to another force he felt as though he would be treating her in the same way. Had she been worth more dead than alive, he wondered, and had she died because of her baby? Something his sister had once said to him had been rattling around in his head since he'd left Manchester.

He went onto the internet.

The sites he was looking for were surprisingly easy to find.

In the United Kingdom, a new-born baby could be worth as much as ten thousand pounds. If he was right, that would more than cover the cost of shipping a whole boatload of illegals into the country, or the cost of setting up a new cannabis farm in a rented property somewhere.

Back into police records, he widened his search to the whole of the United Kingdom and included missing babies and missing toddlers from the previous ten years.

After one hour he was surprised by the numbers he'd found.

Cases reported by concerned citizens or social workers were often never fully investigated. Drug addicted or alcoholic parents, most of whom had already been on one of the many long lists that the Social Services had of unfit parents, and non-English speaking new parents living in squats and communes, could disappear overnight with their young children and were almost impossible to trace. They weren't considered worth spending police man-hours on. But he had found a handful of higher profile cases, and one of those in particular stood out.

24

DC Gary Rawlings tried not to appear too smug as he entered his DCI's office. "You allowed me to follow up on my idea of visiting the scrap yards looking for Land Rover parts, sir, and the initial reports have just come through. The lab has confirmed a match between one of my samples and the paint fragments taken from the clothing of John Lewis."

Forbes felt a weight lifting from him. "Excellent news, Rawlings, which yard was the positive sample taken from?"

"Peak Auto Breakers, sir. Mr Tom Little is the owner and he was very helpful. His yard's only eight miles from here and quite close to where I was brought up. Tom remembered selling spare car parts to my father and my grandfather. I've already alerted scenes of crimes officers in case you want more samples. If I may, I'd like to be the one to go and take a look at his records, but I know first-hand what an incredible memory this man has for both names and faces. I wouldn't be surprised if he remembers to whom he sold the parts, and exactly when. He's a real character."

"Off you go then... but Rawlings..."

"Yes sir."

"Don't go turning it into a social event."

*

"Gary, lad, it's good to see you again so soon in my humble scrap emporium," Mr Tom Little beamed at him, showing off his row of six, twenty-four karat gold teeth. "But could you do me an enormous favour? If these visits of yours are going to be a regular thing, could you try and turn up in one of those unmarked police cars? A blue and white parked up in my yard isn't good for business. Not that I've anything illegal going on here, everything I do is legit, you know that, but a fair few of my regular customers would rather give your people a wide berth, if you know what I mean."

"Point taken, Tom, I'll remember that. But today we need your help."

"I didn't think for one moment you'd come for spare parts for that motor you're driving. Does this mean you found what you were looking for on your last visit, or have you come for more samples? I did exactly as you said and made sure no one touched any of those parts your lot were interested in, and I've mentioned your interest in them to no one at all."

"That's good Tom, thank you, and yes the lab did find something." He took out his notebook. "Shed two, shelf number three, and the first items on the right hand side as we walk in. I need to know who's been buying from there; as far back as you can tell me. Would your records show that?"

"I have detailed records for everything that's been moved on and off this site for the last twenty years, but you know me, Gary, for most of my stock I don't need to refer to a piece of paper. I can tell you straight off who's been buying from there because for the last ten years that area has been reserved for one person, and one person only. Anything I get that I think might be of use to him goes straight onto that shelf until he's seen it. Old Land Rover parts are always in demand around here. Can't you tell a curious old man what this is all about?"

"Just a name please, Tom."

"It's that randy old bugger of a head teacher from the Uppertown Junior School, Mr Donald Muir."

"You're quite sure he's the only one who's bought anything from there?"

"Quite sure, because he's restored several old Land Rovers over the years. He's a good customer. The one he's working on now required parts from that very shelf. May I ask if this is anything to do with the vehicle you're after for mowing down those two lads the other week? I won't tell anyone."

"I can't comment I'm afraid. I can only ask you again not to repeat any part of our conversations until we find the vehicle we're looking for. Does that answer your question, Tom?"

"Aye lad, it does, and you can trust me to keep quiet."

"And don't allow anyone near those shelves until scenes of crimes officers have been, although with what's happened in Bakewell this morning I can't give you any idea of when to expect them."

"No crimes have been committed here."

"No Tom, I know that. They'll probably only want to take a couple of parts away with them. You'll get a receipt and you'll eventually get them back. Do you know how far Donald Muir has got with his latest vehicle restoration, is it road worthy yet?"

"It wouldn't think it's too far away from being street legal, and I believe he's got the engine running smoothly."

"Can you remember how long it is since he last came into your yard?"

"Between three and four weeks; he came in for some trims. That's why I think he's nearly finished; that and the fact that each restoration he does normally takes him about two years to complete."

"Do you know what he does with the vehicles when he's finished them?"

"He sells them on. He doesn't make much of a profit, but on a headmaster's salary he doesn't need to, does he? He just enjoys tinkering with old motors. He never quibbles about the price of the parts, and that's good because some of the ones he asks me for are becoming difficult to get hold of now."

"You don't need to use your sales patter on me, Tom, I know you of old, don't forget."

"Aye, you're a good lad, despite being one of them. But tell me, if Donald Muir was to walk into my yard looking for a part before your SOCO boys have been, what should I say to him?"

"Treat him as you normally would. Sell him the part if you have it on the shelf, and then phone me directly. But he should be at work now, and with any luck we'll have found and checked out his vehicle before the end of the day."

*

The pain in Simon's ankle was spreading. Instead of stinging like crazy in one small area the whole of his lower leg was beginning to throb. He wasn't sure whether that was a good or a bad sign. He could only hope that the knife blade had been clean when it had sliced into him, and that the antiseptic liquid he'd bought would be powerful enough to sterilise the site. He'd received worse cuts on his parents' farm but as he looked at his ankle again he realised it ought to have at least a couple of stitches. Seeking medical attention was well and truly out of the question. And his parents' house was almost certainly being watched, if not by the police, then by whoever was still determined to kill him.

He'd have to rely on painkillers while his body hopefully healed itself.

He phoned in sick for his Monday afternoon shift at the factory, and found he was almost too shaken up to perform that simple task. Money was one thing he couldn't do without. He couldn't lose too many shifts.

He emptied another can of lager and it relaxed him a little more.

He was thinking more rationally now.

How did they know he'd be at the market on Monday? Arianne wouldn't have said anything to anyone, so either her phone had been discovered or someone had hacked into one or both of their phones. Those women weren't clever enough to intercept text messages, he thought, so Arianne's must have been discovered. By giving her that phone had he placed her in mortal danger? If she died because of him, he wouldn't be able to go on living.

He'd killed a man.

He ought to turn himself in, if only to get Arianne out of that place.

He'd acted in self-defence. He'd only bought the gun because someone was trying to kill him. Surely the police and the courts would understand that. And pulling the trigger had been the reflex action of someone in a desperate, life or death situation. He hadn't even taken the time to aim it properly. And if he did hand himself in, at least his ankle would receive the treatment it needed.

But supposing the police didn't believe him, and supposing they blamed him for Eric Shutter's death, where would that leave his claims that the Oakwell women were responsible for the deaths of John and Philip? No, he had to have proof of what he knew in his heart, he had to rescue Arianne himself, and if he could manage some barbaric revenge along the way, then so much the better. The bitches deserved it.

For the second time in less than a fortnight someone had died as a result of his actions, only this time the event had been so damn close he'd been able to smell the blood.

*

It was a cold, bright afternoon as DC Rawlings finally drew away from the scrapyard. He'd spent the last few minutes chatting over the radio to the new female officer on the front desk. Rachael had informed him that more officers from Leaburn station had been deployed to Bakewell, and now he was wondering why. But that thought hadn't occurred to him while he'd been trying to encourage her to come out for a drink with him. She'd turned him down, but not in such a way that she'd made him think she couldn't be persuaded. He looked in his rear view mirror, gave himself a broad smile that enabled him to check his front teeth as he drove, and made a determined effort to forget about the Bakewell shooting until he got back to the station.

He knew where Donald Muir lived, and taking a quick look would only mean a slight detour to his route. The headmaster shouldn't be leaving his school for at least a couple of hours yet.

From the recent checks on all the local farmer-owned Land Rovers, he knew that Donald Muir's parents were still living in the main farmhouse at the end of a long dirt track, half-way up a gently sloping hillside, while Donald was living in the much smaller, renovated farm cottage at the entrance to the farm. As far as he could recall, Donald's cottage had a double garage, was close to the public road, and had not been included in the search for the hit-and-run vehicle.

DC Rawlings pulled onto the driveway, noticing the small oil stain where Donald Muir's car was presumably parked when he didn't bother to use his garage, and turned off the car's engine. Both of the timber garage doors were closed, as he'd expect when the property owner was out, and the wooden entrance gate, which looked as though it had been intended for use as a field gate, was folded all the way back and leaning against a rotting fence post. Judging by the dead grasses entwined around the lower timber struts, it hadn't been moved from that position for several years.

The curtains were all open and all neatly held back by coloured ropes, and there were no lights on anywhere in the property. As far as he could tell there was no one home. He glanced at his watch in response to a rumble from his stomach, then stepped from his patrol car and walked towards the block-built garages. Normally there were windows down the sides of these types of buildings. It wouldn't hurt to take a look before he headed back to the station for his cheese and tomato sandwiches.

"Bloody hell, there's a car in there." Unreasonably startled, he stepped back. He would have been less alarmed if the Land Rover he'd been half-expecting to see had been sitting there. Through the cobwebs and dust he could see a small blue car.

*

Just as Adam was picking up his mobile phone to take a call, Forbes returned to the incident room. His mobile also began ringing and the two officers turned away from each other.

The calls ended simultaneously.

"Sir, it's about DC Rawlings," DS Ross sounded concerned as he placed his phone back into his jacket pocket. "DC Blake couldn't get through to your mobile and he thought we needed to know that when Rawlings left the scrapyard half an hour ago, he called in with a name we already have on our board, Mr Donald Muir."

"Half an hour ago...?"

"The message has only just come up from the front desk, sir. Don't ask."

"Did Rawlings provide any details?"

"Apparently Donald Muir has been buying parts to renovate a very old vehicle which he'd discovered in someone's barn. It won't be registered with the DVLA so we haven't come across it yet. Rawlings also said he intended taking a short detour on his way back to the station to take a quick look at Mr Muir's property while the head teacher is still in school."

"Bloody hell, Ross, didn't anyone have the sense to tell him not to do that?"

"Err... it seems not, sir."

"He should be on his way back here now, not out there trying to make a name for himself. Try his radio again. A lone officer shouldn't be following up a lead on a murder suspect. What was he thinking?"

"I don't know, sir."

Damn, he'd sent four uniformed offers to Bakewell in case there were any further developments, and to help to reassure the public. The last thing he needed was for one of his detectives to be in danger. "My call has just confirmed the news we were given an hour ago, that the driver of the white van seen speeding away from the area of the Bakewell shooting might have been recognised by a resident of the town. She'd had a good look when he'd had to brake for a lorry at the busy junction with the main road and is now willing to swear that she'd seen a scruffy-looking Simon Carter. If she's right, it means Simon is now in possession of a gun, and judging by the blood on the dead man's knife, he's injured."

"I'll alert the local hospitals, pharmacies, and health centres in case he turns up for treatment anywhere." Adam said.

"When Rawlings does return, make sure someone lets him know, in no uncertain terms, that he is not to leave this station again until I've had words with him. You and I need to bring Mr Muir into custody, for his sake as much as for ours. If we leave now we should be able to catch him at his school."

*

Clenching and unclenching her fists, Prunella crouched impatiently on the kitchen floor and listened for sounds of movement outside. What were the odds of a copper arriving at Donald's just as she'd closed the front door behind her? One interfering copper, what could he be doing here, anyway? Surely if they'd had any evidence against Donald then they would have sent more than one officer. Her car was tucked away in the garage, but if he'd seen it he wasn't approaching the door of the house.

She saw no reason to disclose her presence.

She'd heard the local news headlines on the car radio, given Arianne her instructions for the afternoon, and then, hardly able to look at the simpering girl, she'd come to Donald's for some peace and quiet. She wanted to think things through. Monday should have been her day of victory – her day of cleansing the world of the last of those toxic teenagers.

Only now there would be some seriously pissed-off people in Manchester who would be expecting a plausible explanation as to why she hadn't known that Monday's target might have been armed.

Once again, Simon had turned the aggravation back onto her, and that thought stung.

The gravel crunched. He was moving to the rear of the garages.

She reached for the handbag she'd dropped just inside the glass front door and slid her hand under the soft leather flap into the almost empty bag. Her breathing and her heart rate steadied. Since her late teens she'd never left home without the security of her special gun. It was the only thing she'd ever taken from a hit, and it was a memento of her first killing of a female. It was a beautifully engraved Colt handgun, the neatest and the prettiest gun she'd ever seen, and its pearl handle nestled perfectly into the palm of her hand. She'd been supplied with a different gun for each of her contracts and so never needed to use this one, but she liked to keep it loaded and close by.

She could take him out as he stepped into the open and he wouldn't know a thing about it. She could take his car and his body to the quarry which should have been Simon's last resting place. She could, but why create a problem for herself? She'd had enough drama for one day. As long as the officer didn't break into the house, she would spare him. The last thing she needed was the police looking for one of their own, most probably knowing that the last place the officer had visited had been her Donald's.

She was a strong woman, she assured herself, mentally strong enough to resist the urge to squeeze the comforting, smooth trigger. This time she would forego the incredible rush she always felt after a clean kill, and deny herself the old satisfaction of a job well done.

*

"Mr Donald Muir," the school secretary smiled sympathetically at Forbes and then at Adam, "I'm terribly sorry but you've literally just missed him by two minutes. I'm surprised you didn't see him as you came in. There was a call from his mother, something about a police car on his driveway, and he told me to cancel the remainder of his afternoon's meetings. That isn't like him at all because Mr Muir has a very busy schedule and he likes to keep to it." She paused and smiled at them again. "I expect he's eager to be helping the police with their enquiries in any way that he can. Would you like me to try his mobile, although he could be on the road by now? If it's important I'm sure no one would mind. Is this to do with the fire at our school?"

"Thank you, but no. Now we know where he's heading, I'm sure we'll find him."

"Helping the police with their enquiries," Forbes said as he secured his seatbelt. "Isn't that supposed to be our line? If he isn't in his cottage, we'll go up to his parent's house – the main farmhouse. I want to take another look in those sheds. Then maybe we'll find out why Mrs Muir thought it necessary to warn her son that a police car was parked in his drive. Call for some back-up, Adam. We may need it."

An elderly man in a thick, grey, padded jacket stood in the open doorway of the farmhouse. Neither of the two officers failed to notice the bright red, woollen hat of his wife as she peered over her husband's shoulder, or the broken, double-barrelled shotgun cradled over Jacob Muir's left elbow. From his expression as they drew closer, he was seriously considering using it.

Forbes suddenly regretted driving up the dirt track in his own Mercedes.

Something had already spooked this couple.

From experience he knew it took under a second for a loaded shotgun to be cocked, aimed and fired. "Warrant card Adam; show him your warrant card."

With both IDs pressed to the windscreen, Forbes slowly opened his door.

"Police, Mr Muir," he shouted in what he hoped sounded a calming manner, "please put the gun down on the ground now and step away from it. We're unarmed and here on police business. Firearms are never a good idea."

Mrs Muir broke the tense silence. "Do as they say, Jacob. What will become of me if you get yourself locked up?"

"How were we supposed to know who you were?" he growled. "You come tearing up our drive in that thing and expect us not to be nervous? A man's got a right to protect himself and his property, and people around here have been jumpy ever since the murders and the fires." As he spoke he tipped the cartridges out of the shotgun and pocketed them.

Forbes strode across the yard and gently took the gun from the man's firm grip.

"I've got a licence for that. You can't take it away from me."

"Calm down please, Mr Muir. We're looking for your son. He left the school about half an hour ago." He spoke softly, at the same time trying to calm his own pounding heart. On more than one occasion he'd stood in the mortuary across from Alison and witnessed the damage that shotgun pellets could inflict on the soft tissues of a human body. "Is Donald here?"

"No, and we've not spoken to him since this morning, have we love?"

"Let's all go inside and you can put this shotgun where it should be – in a locked cupboard. More officers are on their way. We'd like to conduct a thorough search of your farm sheds, but to save time can you tell us where we might find the Land Rover your son has been restoring?"

"Aye, you'd best follow me." The man's head dropped towards his chest, his cap slipped over his eyes and he removed it and reached for a woollen hat. He looked and sounded beaten. "Donald's been working on it down in his own garage for the last couple of years. It's almost finished. We had no idea at the time why he thought it necessary to bring it up here after you'd searched our farm sheds. Honestly we hadn't, had we love?"

Mrs Muir shook her head but didn't speak. She looked close to tears.

"You knew about the hit-and-run deaths, Mr Muir, so didn't his actions make you even a little bit suspicious? Didn't you think to look for any kind of damage?"

"I guess we did – but not straight away. And when we did, we didn't know how recently those dents had been made.

Donald was still painting it, and as far as we knew it hadn't been on the road, not without insurance and so on."

"And he's my son." Mrs Muir was trailing behind them across the yard. "He's my only child. How could we shop him to the police for something which might get him locked up for years? I might not live to see him released."

The group stopped at the double barn doors.

"So you were trying to warn him today when you telephoned his school, Mrs Muir?"

"Well yes, but we didn't really know what about... not really... not for sure." She looked up at her husband. "And even if Donald's car was involved in something so terrible, it doesn't mean that Donald was driving, does it? I mean, he could be protecting someone, couldn't he? Donald has an awful lot of friends."

Mr Muir took a firm grip of the large metal handle of one of the sliding doors and Adam did the same to the handle of the other. They pulled in opposite directions and the doors opened smoothly.

Forbes stared at the two dents on the otherwise undamaged front of the vehicle.

Then he looked up at Donald Muir.

The man was sitting in the driver's seat and staring straight ahead.

25

"Well, Monday was an eventful day," Adam's words broke into Forbes's thoughts and he looked away from the screen on his desk. He'd been reading about common, roadside herbs – both medicinal and toxic.

"And a night in the cells hasn't changed Donald Muir's attitude much." Adam continued. "He's still insisting that he doesn't know how his Land Rover came to be damaged."

"Give him another few hours." Forbes replied.

"Each new incident or development in this case has some kind of a link to Oakwell Grange. It can't be coincidence. By his own admission, Donald Muir visits the place every week. He's the ex-husband of Sheila Hall and he's confirmed to us that both Sheila's and Hannah's daughters are his. After the rumours we've been hearing, isn't it time we brought those women in for more formal questioning?"

"You're right," Forbes answered. "Maybe I've given them the benefit of the doubt for too long. Even if Donald Muir is telling the truth when he says he doesn't look inside his own garage every day, that the lock on the garage hasn't been operational for months, and that when he moved it he didn't notice the damage, how likely is it that joy-riders would know about the vehicle and the lock, steal his Land Rover, commit a serious crime with it, and then return it to his garage?"

"Someone could be trying to frame him, sir. I think it's unlikely but...."

"It's far more likely that he allowed someone to use it that night."

"He's denying that, sir."

"He's lying to us, Adam. Like he was lying when he said it had been a coincidence that he'd moved the vehicle the day after his parent's farm had been searched. And even if he wasn't lying about that, the damage to the front of his newly restored vehicle was the first thing we saw when the doors were opened. Let's see if we can obtain voluntary DNA samples from Sheila and Hannah and both of their daughters, and also from Prunella Leith, and anyone else living at the Grange at the time of the murders. If there is matching DNA evidence in that Land Rover, that will be soon enough to bring them in for questioning. None of them are likely to be going far."

Adam wasn't giving up. "But sir, if we can put out a press statement that the women are being held here for questioning, surely there's a chance that Simon Carter will come forward. We ought to be doing everything we can to find him before there's any more bloodshed. We know that he's armed but we don't know the extent of his injuries or his state of mind. He might respond to a television appeal from his parents."

"That's a good thought, but I'd still like to find some hard evidence against these women so we can hold them for longer."

*

Jane Goodwin's daughter was to spend almost a full week at her father's home for the first time since the divorce. It was Tuesday, he was collecting her from school later today, and Jane wouldn't see her again until they met at the school gates next Monday afternoon. The house felt eerily quiet, but she felt she'd been presented with the perfect opportunity to sort through her mother's clothes and personal papers. It was something she needed to do while she wasn't distracted, and it was time to begin the dreaded task. If she needed to stop and have a little cry, as she knew she almost certainly would, then she could indulge herself without having to reassure anyone that she was fine.

Once all her mother's clothes had been boxed up for the charity shops, she intended to open the bottle wine that had been languishing in the fridge for all of twenty-four hours.

Maybe, once the bottle was open, that would be the time to give Adam a call and invite him and Ryan over for their tea. She needed to hear his voice. She was missing him so much, and wondered whether he was feeling the same. Hopefully he was.

She opened the largest wardrobe first and began by gently running her fingers along a row of eight coats. She stopped at the sixth, the full-length, black, woollen winter coat that her mother had reserved for funerals.

She stepped back. The unexpected memory of her visit to the Grange, and of the floor-length, soiled, black gown worn by her mother, overpowered her. She wanted to cry but no tears came.

"Get a grip, girl," she whispered, "this is something you're just going to have to come to terms with." She reached out a hand but couldn't touch the coats again – not for a little while at least.

She gently closed the wardrobe door and took two more steps back. On the top of the wardrobe she saw a row of dusty, cardboard boxes. Maybe that would be a better place to begin the clear-out.

A folder of photographs almost fell into her hands and she laid it on the bed before carefully opening it. Stuffed amongst the old utility bills and property documents were her mother's copies of Jane's wedding photos. She placed her fingertips over her father's proud face. "Sorry dad," she whispered before kissing the picture and then holding it against her chest. "I know you liked him, but that marriage wasn't meant to last."

In the second and third boxes were even more photos, many of them of elderly people and babies she didn't recognise. She turned the unknown ones over but there were no names or dates to provide clues as to who they might have been, or still were. As she worked her way through them she was travelling back in time, each layer of pictures being more faded and more tattered than the last, but she wasn't achieving anything.

She touched the remaining box and then looked at her watch. Of the four that she'd lifted down, this was the largest and the heaviest, and the only one which was sealed with brown parcel tape. She'd been going to open this one first, but hesitated, and instead begun with the smallest. An hour had passed since she'd entered the room and at this rate she definitely wasn't going to achieve her goal in one week. Whatever it contained, she wouldn't spend more than a few minutes on it, she decided.

The tape came off easily and she opened the flaps. She pulled out one thick file after another – twenty-two of them altogether, and each one a dated, annual account, detailing the finances of Oakwell Grange.

26

Yesterday he'd been incredibly lucky, but even armed with a gun, how many attempts on his life could one person reasonably expect to survive?

Since his brush with death at Bakewell, Simon had returned to his original plan of spending his nights in the parking-lot of his employers. His wasn't the only white van in the yard, but it was the only one with an overnight occupant. The lame, white-haired night watchman was obliging enough and allowed Simon to remain parked in the shadows, in return for a shot of cheap whisky. The old man would no doubt be able to raise the alarm if anyone tried to break into the yard, but would be no match for a determined thief, or worse still, a contract killer.

A light swept across his curtains and he reached under his pillow.

"All clear, Simon, good night," a familiar voice croaked from somewhere close to his van.

He returned his arm to the warmth of his duvet, stared into the darkness, and concentrated on his breathing.

The female first-aider at work had patched up his ankle enough for him to complete his Tuesday afternoon shift. She'd done it without asking questions, the wound not being as bad as Simon had feared, and now, from the warmth of the duvet and the effect of the alcohol, the pain had eased considerably. But it was almost midnight, and it was two days since his phone had rung, or pinged with a text message. Only Arianne had this number and she'd never missed two consecutive days before. He must have guessed right. The women must have found her phone. That was the only explanation he allowed himself to even consider.

It was time for him to make a move – time that he found out what had turned his normal life onto its head and made him a killer? Once he knew that, he would be in a better position to deal with the fear which at times over the last fifteen days had almost paralyzed him. He couldn't go on blindly battling against unknown odds.

The women had made the last move, and what an unexpected move it had been.

But he'd survived it.

Tomorrow it would be his turn.

With his eyes closed he imagined the feel of Arianne's soft skin, the smell of her newly washed hair, and the gentleness of her voice. He was transported back into her arms.

A metallic sound woke him. He lay listening to the rhythmic padding of feline paws on the roof of his van, and then checked the time on his phone. With still a couple of hours to go until daybreak, he tossed the duvet to one side. He selected his brightest torch and picked up a piece of string. The bike store at the side of the factory held a selection of rusty pushbikes, bought as a job lot from the local auction rooms by the firm, to provide any worker who wanted to visit the local shops in their lunch breaks with a means of transport. It was the firm's token gesture towards reducing vehicle emissions, and helping to save the planet. Not one of the bikes was worth stealing, but he selected the one with the most reliable-looking tyres and tied his torch to the handlebar.

The night watchman waved him towards the main gates.

"Mind how you go lad. You ought to be wearing something white, you know. You'll get yourself knocked down going about like that, with no lights on the back."

"Don't worry about me. I'm going out in my van. I'm only testing the bike out. I'd like to borrow it for a job later today, if that's all right?"

"Aye, as long as you return it."

"I'll be back for my afternoon shift, with the bike. I'll see you tonight, Sid."

He parked in his favourite spot by the River Lathkill, well out of sight of the narrow, winding road. There was still almost an hour to go before daybreak. There was no rush. With the engine ticking over to keep him warm, he ran through his plan once more.

Ten minutes later he doubted himself. What if his plan went disastrously wrong? He still hadn't worked out every last detail or thought through every possible scenario.

He stared at his silent phone and tried to recall the voices of John and Philip.

"Go with your gut feelings," John would have said. And "today is as good a day as any to die."

Philip would most probably have been raging at Simon for taking so long.

The recent rains had maintained the river at a decent enough depth for what he had in mind. He listened to its low roar through his closed windows, and shivered. Memories of being dragged under the freezing water wiped out the last lingering prick of doubt. Now he couldn't wait to get started.

He began setting up his equipment.

Satisfied with it at last, he lifted the whisky bottle to his mouth, swallowed until his throat wouldn't take any more, coughed, and then wiped his mouth with the back of his sleeve. He hoped the fiery liquor would help to calm his impatience.

He lifted the bike from the rear of his van and began pedalling towards Oakwell Grange.

Almost within sight of the property, he squeezed the bike between a stone wall and a sprawling, spikey bush of some kind. The Grange, and within its walls the only girl he'd ever felt such an overwhelming passion for, was less than a hundred metres away from him. His heart thumped. He remembered how, a few metres from this very spot, they'd shared their first kiss, and how it had felt like to an electric charge surging through every vein in his young body, and how Arianne hadn't wanted to let him go.

He closed his eyes and ran through the first part of his plan.

It was almost nine o'clock. He had to get moving.

His ankle stung like hell and his boot felt tight. It wasn't going to be easy. He prayed his ankle wouldn't let him down, and that Arianne wouldn't see him in this sorry state.

The undergrowth in the woods around the Grange was soft and spongy from decades of fallen leaves. It wasn't helping his injury but it made it easy to move silently between the trees. Within minutes he was over the rotting fence and standing in the shadows against the wall of the garage where he knew the sisters parked their cars overnight. Prunella usually parked on the driveway when she arrived. Sheila and Hannah left for work before ten o'clock and each drove their own car. He was relying on that fact. He checked his watch. Not too long to wait now.

He checked his pockets again for the knife and the roll of tape, and he pulled out one of the three lengths of blue rope. He'd decided to leave his gun in the van. He only had three bullets left and it would have been an added complication. Anyone with any sense should be just as afraid of a knife at close quarters. And working at close quarters was exactly what he had in mind.

He wrapped the rope around the knuckles of his right hand.

Hannah was the first to get into her car and drive away. If they'd left together then he would have waited for Prunella, but the sisters seemed like easier targets, and he also thought they'd be quicker to break.

Sheila came out five minutes later, rushing towards her car and totally unaware of him as he moved from the shadows of the buildings into the daylight.

Then she saw him. He held the knife out in front of him and rushed towards her. He had to move quickly – he had to prevent her from opening her car door.

He'd expected her to scream, and to try to escape, but instead she just stood. He tilted his head and grinned at her. She'd obviously recognised him. Her mouth had fallen open and her eyes displayed the level of fear that he'd dreamed of inflicting on every single one of the Oakwell women.

"Hand over the keys, Sheila," he said in a friendly manner, "we're going to be taking a little ride together."

She didn't move. Was he imagining it or was her expression of fear turning into one of arrogance? The knuckles of her right hand were a bloodless white from the tight grip she had on her keys.

He didn't have time for this.

His rope-covered fist slammed into the left side of her jaw, she fell back against the side of her car and then rolled onto the dirt floor. She looked up at him and blood trickled from her open mouth. He'd never hit anyone before, at least not like that, not a woman, and not in anger. He was surprised at how much his knuckles stung but it was worth it to watch the bright red marks spreading across Sheila's face.

"Now you know that I mean business."

Now it was her turn to tremble and her turn to pant in terror. Whatever happened next, he wanted to remember these moments forever. Sheila Hall was in front of him, struggling to get onto her hands and knees and with blood dripping from her chin, while he was standing over her, smiling, and slowly unwinding a rope from around his fist.

It was almost a full, pleasure-filled minute before she managed to stagger to her feet. Then he watched as her wobbling legs buckled underneath her and sent her rolling onto her back. In her efforts to escape from him she rolled over onto her stomach, pathetically trying to squeeze her body underneath the car – she was almost helping him.

He had to get a move on – Prunella could arrive at any moment, and without the gun he was far too vulnerable.

He grabbed at Sheila's wrists and pulled them together behind her back, just as he'd seen the police doing with their handcuffs on the reality shows he used to enjoy watching. He bound her wrists together and then removed the second piece of rope from his pocket and grabbed at her ankles. She kicked furiously at him, landing one of her sturdy shoes on his injured ankle.

"That's the last time you're going to be able to do that, bitch."

He grabbed a handful of her short, bleached hair, and slammed the side of her head against the ground. She moaned, and he was about to slam her head down again, but instead he looked at her feet. They were still and so he quickly tied them together.

He picked up her keys and placed them in the ignition. Prunella's arrival now would force him to make a quick getaway. He had to be prepared for anything. He had to keep thinking clearly.

Her limp body repulsed him as he struggled to position her across the back seat and onto her stomach. He couldn't risk her choking on her own blood or vomit – not yet. Then he leaned in to check her breathing. It was steady and even.

Feeling calmer than when he'd arrived, he took one last look around the garage, picked up the leather handbag that he'd almost missed, and climbed into the driving seat.

He parked alongside his own van, which he'd left about twenty metres from the water, opened the driver's door of the car and listened. It was bitterly cold, but so peaceful. The uneven gurgles from the swirling eddies of deep water at the sides of the old sluice gate coaxed him from the car. Nothing else moved or made a sound, either inside or outside the car. Even the birds seemed to be taking a break from their usual twittering.   Maybe they were waiting for spring to arrive, or more likely there was a predator in the skies – a sparrow hawk or a goshawk. He'd seen both of them in this area.

And there was now a predator on the ground below them.

That was what these women had done to him.

Still feeling calmer than he'd expected to, he walked over to his van, inserted his key in the ignition, and then placed his knife onto the passenger seat and patted it. Hopefully he wouldn't need to use it until all his questions had been answered.

Another few gulps of whisky won't hurt, he thought, not too much though; he needed to keep thinking clearly. When he picked up his camera phone he felt strangely energised.

He strolled back to the car, and despite the pain in his ribs he breathed deeply, filling his lungs with the cold, clean-smelling air. "The time has come." He directed his words towards the river and watched his breath dispersing before he opened the rear door of Sheila's car.

"Remember me." He grabbed her ankles and pulled her half way out of the car. She let out a soft moan. He reached in with his right hand to support her head while he tugged her out. He wanted her awake.

Pain shot through his hand. The bitch had sunk her teeth into his hand and she wasn't letting go. She was biting down hard and shaking her head as if trying to separate his hand from his wrist. His left hand squeezed at the flesh of her throat, but it was making no difference. Her body writhed underneath him. He could only roar against the combination of pain, shock, and rage. Then he released her throat and dug his fingers into her wet eye sockets. She roared back at him and released his injured hand just enough for him to pull it free.

His pain suddenly didn't matter. He took two steps back and yanked her ankles so violently that she landed face-down onto the wet gravel with a satisfying thud. Still she writhed.

"What the hell's wrong with you, bitch? Don't you know when you're beaten?"

He knelt on her back and pulled at the ropes securing her ankles. They were good and tight. Then he did the same with the ropes on her wrists before retrieving the third length of rope from his jacket pocket. He could feel her fighting for each breath against the pressure from his knees, but he didn't ease up, instead he pulled her ankles back up towards her wrists and looped the length of rope around both ankles and wrists. She was hog-tied.

Fighting his pain, he dragged her across the wet ground towards the trees. She gasped and sobbed, and blood and mucous from her nose and mouth left a pink slime-trail along the gravel. Finally he rolled her onto her side, but still her reddened eyes glared up at him, showing him nothing but contempt. If she was trying to intimidate him, she was failing.

"I'm very glad to see I have your attention," he grinned down at her, "because I have a few questions buzzing around in my brain and I'd really like some answers from you."

"Go to hell, Simon Carter. You could have killed me. You should have killed me. Go to hell."

She wasn't going to be as easy to break as he'd thought.

He bent down towards her until his face was inches from her blood-streaked face. She might be acting tough, but if fear did have a smell, he was sure he could detect it coming from her now. "I want you to tell me which of you bitches was driving that Land Rover. Who was out on a killing spree the night my friends John Lewis and Philip Booth were mown down like vermin and I was very nearly drowned?"

"It wasn't... I don't... it wasn't me."

Her voice was starting to crack. That was good. She was struggling to maintain her act of defiance. He held eye contact with her as she began talking. "I went to my room after tea... I stayed there... I don't know who it was. The police have questioned us already, because of the lies you told them. If it had been any of us, don't you think they'd have arrested us by now? It could have been anyone. You're crazy. You have to let me go. The police know you're armed and they've started a manhunt. Even they now believe that you're off your trolley. You're beyond crazy, Simon Carter, you're completely delusional if you think that doing this to me is going to help your case." She stifled a sob. "My head and my shoulders hurt... please... just let me go."

He stepped back and continued to stare at her. "That was quite a speech for someone in your current predicament. I can see you're going to need a little extra persuasion before you begin to tell me the truth. Stay there a minute." He slapped his forehead with the palm of his good hand and smiled. "But you can't do any other, can you? Don't worry, I won't be long. I could turn you round so you could watch what I'm doing, but that would spoil the surprise."

He could have carried the dog cage, even with his injured hand, but dragging it along the ground caused the frames to rattle. He knew what the noise was, but even to his mind, against the quietness of the woods, it sounded intimidating.

Working quickly, he undid four bolts, removed one of the longer side panels, and then positioned the crate against the trunk of a pine tree with the open side facing Sheila's back. He'd guessed right, it did indeed look a perfect fit.

He moved closer to her and grabbed at her hair with his blood stained hand. "I will hurt you until you're begging to tell me everything I need to know. And I mean seriously hurt you."

"I don't know... honestly, I don't. It was neither me nor Hannah."

"We were three ordinary teenage boys with ordinary lives, but I'm the only one left alive and look at me now. I don't only want names – I want to know the reasons why. Why has this happened? Answer that at least and I might, I just might consider letting you go."

"You know we hated the three of you, but neither of us would do anything to harm any of you. That's the truth... I swear it."

"Not good enough... I don't believe you. You're a lying bitch." He slammed her head down onto the gravel but didn't release her.

Because of his damaged ribs his own breaths were short and shallow now. He needed a moment to clear his head in order to get this right. He might only have one shot at getting the truth from any of these women. He had to work more calmly. He had to maintain control.

Slowly he released his grip on her hair and her head turned upwards. She looked over her shoulder, and then with confusion etched across her face, she stared back up at him.

"Please... I can't tell you what I don't know. Let me go and I'll tell everyone you didn't really want to hurt me."

If she was hoping he might be relenting then she was in for one huge disappointment.

"Oh you're going to tell me all right – you're going to tell me everything. And do you know why; because if you don't, in one minute from now, you are going into this dog crate I prepared earlier."

"You can't do that."

He was back in control. She was whining like a whipped dog. He could see her waves of panic as she wriggled against the front edge of the cage, hopelessly trying to free herself from the ropes. He watched her useless struggles while she tired herself out. She should be making it easier for him to slide her body into the cage.

"Time's up," he suddenly announced. "In you go."

He didn't think it wasn't going to be an easy manoeuvre and he was right. Still she wriggled and squirmed, and bit at his coat sleeve. He had no choice but to slap her.

Finally she was in.

He fastened the bolts, securing the cage shut with her blood and mucous covered face pressed against the narrow, ice-cold metal bars, and then he tied the ends of the two separate ropes, one of which led directly back to his van and the other of which led to the river before it looped back to his van, to the top corners of the cage.

She was quietly whimpering as he stepped back to look at his work.

"I'd really like you to appreciate the work I've put into this," he smiled as he spoke. "If you could look up you'd see two ropes. Both of them are securely tied to my tow-bar. Movement on one rope, which you will see goes down to the water and is looped through the sluice gate in the centre of river, will result in the cage being pulled into the water, and a slow, but eventual death by drowning for you. And don't for one second think that I won't enjoy watching that. But movement on the second rope, which you will see is coiled up on the ground at the rear of my van to allow for plenty of movement on the first rope, will mean that you've answered all my questions satisfactorily, and that you are being pulled to safety."

"You're crazy."

"If I am, it's down to one of you. I know how it feels to be fighting for life in this river. Now it's your turn – this is payback time."

"You want locking up, you mad bastard. We didn't do anything to you. Let me go."

"That's the wrong answer, again. Are you really so stupid that you don't get it yet? When I ease my van forward you will be slowly dragged into the river. Only when you've told me everything I need to know, will I disconnect the rope leading into the water and pull you clear. Now do you get it?"

"Please Simon... no... your friends wouldn't have wanted this."

"I agree, but they didn't escalate the violence, did they? You did that – you and your weird group. And John and Philip certainly didn't want to end up as road kill. I intend to find out which one of you drove that vehicle into them that night, and why. And I intend to find out today."

"I keep telling you – I really don't know. You're making a dreadful mistake. Please don't put me into the water... please."

"That was another wrong answer."

She had to lying.

He hobbled to his van, clambered into it, and started the engine.

A couple of hours earlier, he'd been wondering whether he would actually have the guts to go through with his roughly-thought-out plan, but Sheila's defiance was making it easier for him than he'd expected. Now he was wondering whether he'd estimated the length of the rope correctly. If he drove as far as the third row of trees from where his van sat now, then the cage should just about be balancing on the muddy river bank. He slammed it into gear.

It was pointless being gentle with a bitch like that. He squeezed down on the accelerator, felt the wheels spin and then grip, and listened to her screams. The rope was doing an excellent job.

He hobbled the forty metres back down the bank towards the wriggling, screaming mess. Her knees were actually touching the icy water. "Are you ready to talk yet?"

"I'll tell you what bit I do know..." she sobbed. "I swear to you... I don't know much."

"Do you see this?" He showed her his phone camera. "I'm ready to record everything you tell me. And I should think very carefully unless you want me to be recording your last words. This is your final chance; the one and only chance that I'm going to give you. Now... who was it who mowed down my friends?"

"Prunella killed them...," she sobbed, "I swear... Hannah didn't... I didn't... we didn't know until days later... not for sure. You have to get me out of here. I've done nothing to hurt you."

"How do you know? Did she tell you?"

"Yes, she told us... she was proud of what she'd done. But she did it alone. You have to believe me."

"Then she must have told you why."

"You and your friends tormented us for years. You made our lives a misery and neither the police nor your parents seemed able to stop you."

"We were kids, for Christ's sake. We may have taken things a bit too far occasionally, but we never actually hurt anyone."

"Prunella told us about that letter. She said your persecution of us was starting all over again, but that this time it would have been so much worse for Oakwell Grange – for all of us. That's what she said."

"The letter...?" How could he have forgotten about that? He had some vague recollection of John and Philip laughing over a letter they'd sealed and posted with a second class stamp on it, just before Christmas. But they hadn't shown him its contents. He'd known it was destined for Oakwell Grange, but when they'd put their heads together and refused to share their joke, he'd stormed off. And he'd never given it another thought. "What did she mean, worse for Oakwell?"

"That's all I know. For pity's sake now, get me out of here... I'm in real pain." She whimpered again.

That last part at least was true. He could see the thin bars cutting into her face and her shoulder, and she had to be badly bruised. The noises she was making disgusted him. "Did you see what was in the letter?"

"No. Prunella opens the post most days, and anyway, it was addressed to her. But she told us about it. She said it was signed *'from the boys – who else?'*"

"Keep talking."

"Hannah and I tried to tell her... if it was from you boys then it must have been a lucky guess... a joke... a bluff... we tried to reassure her... we were certain that no one knew..." She stifled a scream. "I've got terrible cramp. At least untie my feet, please, I'm begging you."

"Not until you've told me everything. You're not making sense. No one knew what?"

"No one knew how we made most of our money. And I swear that I had no part in that girl's death. That was an accident, a dreadful accident. She fell backwards down the stairs, and it was Hannah who made Arianne dispose of the body."

He gasped. "Arianne...?"

"Yes, Prunella had told us she knew Arianne and you were seeing each other and were in love. She knew Arianne sneaked out of the house sometimes, but she didn't stop her. She said she'd seen you two together. If the girl's body was ever traced back to Oakwell, Hannah had planted evidence which would ensure that Arianne would be the one blamed for her murder, because that would hurt you. But that was before the letter came."

"Was that the body fished out of a ditch just before John and Philip died? I was in hospital when that was on the news. Wasn't there a missing baby?" His voice rose. He was trying to keep it steady.

"She lived at Oakwell for about two months – in the maternity rooms on the top floor. She was pregnant when she came to us. Please... I'm telling you everything... please help me... I'm hurting."

"What happened to the baby?"

"If I tell you that," she began sobbing but finally whispered, "Oakwell Grange will be finished for ever."

"And if you don't, your sad little life will be finished." He looked at his phone. It was still recording. But he still didn't understand. Until he'd heard Arianne's name he'd intended taking the recording to the police, but now...

She looked into his eyes, and in barely more than a whisper, she stammered, "Prunella sold it. She's sold them before... lots of them... for years now... to people who can't adopt through the proper channels... someone was going to do it... why not us, Prunella said... we were desperate for money for Oakwell."

"Keep talking."

"She has an agreement with a group of human traffickers. We take in and look after any women who fall pregnant. She sells the babies and then returns the women. The organisers get about half the money and we keep the rest, but Oakwell Grange has always taken in genuine hardship cases and our charity couldn't keep going without the extra income. And the women are well cared for while they're with us... Hannah and I always make sure of that."

"Where does Arianne fit into this?"

"She came from the traffickers. She miscarried and very nearly died. Prunella had to produce the foetus to prove she wasn't scamming her associates."

"So why is Arianne still with you?"

"Her legs were pretty much paralysed for weeks and they wrote her off. They ordered Prunella to dispose of her, but Hannah and I persuaded her to let us keep the girl to do the boring, sitting down jobs, such as packing the herbs for market. She grew stronger each day and now she does most of the housework."

"Arianne told me she was working off the cost of her passage into Britain. She said her family would be harmed if she didn't do exactly what you wanted."

"That's what Prunella told her in order to keep her working for us. It ensures she doesn't tell anyone what she knows, or run away. The people who brought her to this country believe she's dead. She doesn't have a bad life with us, and Hannah and I have become quite fond of the girl."

"So John and Philip must have written that they'd discovered how Oakwell made extra revenue. Then when that woman's body was found about ten miles from here, and she'd obviously just had a baby, Prunella must have thought that they'd go to the police. Prunella could have tried to blame Arianne for that woman's death, but not for years of sales of new-born babies once the story was out. I can't believe John or Philip actually knew any of that or they would have told me. That letter was just a prank. It was a shot in the dark. But Prunella couldn't take that risk, could she?"

"I'm so cold..."

He stopped the recording. "Let me put this safe and then I'll get you out. But you'd better have been telling me the truth, or I promise you, I will come back, and I will kill you – all of you."

He turned to scale the muddy bank, but slipped. As he looked up, his mouth fell open. How could he have been so stupid? He'd left his van keys in the ignition and someone was opening the driver's door. Underneath a dark winter coat, that someone looked like Prunella.

Then Prunella's voice projected down towards the river bank, "Hold on Sheila. I'll pull you out of there. Hold on girl."

Simon turned to look at Sheila. Was she actually smiling? "What...?"

"That phone in my bag – it has a tracker," Sheila spoke calmly. She believed she was being rescued.

"But don't you realise...?"

He launched his phone into the mass of brambles. If Prunella came at him with his own knife then he could jump into the river. He'd swum to safety once already. And if she found his gun and he was going to die here today, then at least someone would find the recording and know the truth of what had happened. And his Arianne could be rescued.

But as much as he hated all of the women, he couldn't allow Sheila to die. He yelled as loudly as he could, but the van's cold engine was already firing water vapour from its exhaust pipe into the cold air. "Stop, Prunella stop, don't drive forwards, the rope, for God's sake, untie that rope." There was too much distance for him to cover to even think about running towards his vehicle, and Sheila was behind him, already screaming. He turned and saw she was half-submerged in the icy water.

He couldn't let this happen.

Prunella was accelerating now, spinning the wheels of his van on the damp leaf litter. The wheels could grip again at any moment. He couldn't be responsible for another death.

He slid down the bank and gasped. The water felt even colder than last time.

Sheila was totally submerged and Prunella was still accelerating. Was she trying to kill them both – was that it? Would she go that far to protect all her dirty secrets? The bolts were all loose. He'd left them that way in case they'd jammed, but the fourth and last bolt seemed to take forever to unthread.

Sheila's eyes bulged and were locked onto him.

He could barely force his frozen hands to grip her shoulders. Then for a few precious seconds the current seemed to be working with him and Sheila was free. He forced her head up above his own. He was totally submerged while she gasped for air. A trained lifeguard would have struggled to manage what he was attempting to do, but he couldn't allow her to drown. The tenuous hold he had on her was going to have to be enough. He pushed his feet against the river bed but only found soft mud. It was taking every ounce of his energy to keep both of them near the surface. He could feel her chest heaving. She was too busy gasping and coughing to scream. He took a deep breath, kicked against the soft river bed once more, and rolled Sheila out of the water and her onto the bank.

He looked up and couldn't quite believe what he was seeing. Prunella was still sitting in his van and was still accelerating. The sluice gate and the ropes were acting together to hold his van back and prevent the cage from going any further into the water, he realised. He had misjudged the lengths by only the smallest of margins.

He grabbed at some thin, fibrous roots. The first handful broke away before he saw some stronger looking tree roots and reached out to them. He was so cold. Instinctively he pulled himself clear of the water, but then he lay still, just as he'd done the last time he'd hauled himself from this river.

His van's engine was silent. He raised his head enough to watch Prunella at the rear of his van. She was bending down and cutting the ropes from his tow-bar. For his own safety, he now needed to be much further downstream.

He slid back into the icy water and was about to push himself away from the muddy bank and swim for his life once more when he saw that the unattached ropes were allowing the cage to move downstream towards him. He kicked it away, and as it tumbled along the river bed he felt the ropes brushing against his legs. They were following the cage like two, unending, swimming snakes. Then he took an all-too familiar, instinctively deep breath as he felt them circling both of his legs. They were tugging him downstream; down into the deeper, faster-flowing water, following the tumbling cage into the centre of the river.

27

DI Lang had spent every spare moment of the past few days looking through old unsolved murder and missing persons cases, but only one that he'd studied had robbed him of any sleep.

Eight years earlier, on the outskirts of Leek, in the neighbouring county of Cheshire, the body of a young woman had been discovered in a dilapidated stone barn high up on the moors. It remained an open case, and the unidentified woman had been of Eastern European origin. The coroner had ruled that blood loss following child birth had been the cause of her death, and recorded an open verdict, but after a year of police investigations and appeals to the public, no trace of the baby had ever been found. The investigating officers had recorded their assumptions that the woman had wanted to give birth somewhere where no one would either see or hear her, and that the labour had gone badly wrong.

She'd been dead for about a month before being discovered by a hiker's dog, a Jack Russell by the name of Herman.

The door of the barn had been sufficiently ajar for a predator to gain entrance, and a small portion of the decomposed placenta was found almost a hundred metres from the barn. The assumption was that the baby had been an easy meal for a fox.

The suspected animal had been traced to its lair, but the soft cartilage which made up the skeleton of a new born baby, assuming that the fox had actually taken it to feed his family, would have been easily devoured by the predators, the detectives had learned.

A familiar name popped up on his screen. Lang's old friend DI Brixton had been involved in the case. Lang searched for contact details and found that Brixton was now a DCI, and still with the Cheshire Police force. He dialled the number on his screen.

"I remember that case all too well, and so would you if you hadn't been up to your neck in drug dealers down at the Met." DCI Brixton sounded as enthusiastic about his work as Lang remembered him to be. "There were bite marks on the young woman's legs and both her hands had been chewed off. She must have been trying to staunch the bleeding, but the autopsy showed a major rupture of a main artery so she would have very quickly lost consciousness and then continued to bleed out. The smell of blood would have drawn in the foxes. If our assumptions at the time were right, we can only hope the poor child was stillborn. A tragic case, made more distressing for those of us who worked on it because no one ever came forward to claim her remains. No one had cared that this heavily pregnant young woman was desperate enough to go out onto the moors to give birth alone."

Lang explained about Operation Lupin. "Were you convinced that your victim had died exactly where she was found, and was there really no evidence that anyone had been in the shed with her?"

"She was found lying on a blood-soaked, single duvet, which it was believed she could have easily carried up the hillside to where she was found. The wildlife had disturbed the earth floor to the extent that there were no human footprints at all, and the post mortem indicated that she had not been moved after death. We have her DNA on file along with two other unidentified samples, which I'm afraid are only partials because of their state of decomposition. But they may help identify or rule out a suspect if fresh evidence comes to light. I'll e-mail the file to you if you think it might help."

Ten minutes later, Lang was slowly pushing open the door of his superior's office, looking as though he'd rather not interrupt the thoughts of his boss. But he had news of progress on Operation Lupin and the DCI had insisted on being kept up to date. "Sir, you remember that I had the probable name of the dead female and the possible story of how she fell pregnant…"

"Get to the point Lang."

"I know that you said I should concentrate on finding the baby, but while I waited for responses from the latest television appeal I took another look at historic, unexplained deaths involving young women. And I think I've found something of interest to us. I've been in contact with a DCI Brixton from the Cheshire Constabulary. If you've got the time, sir, I'd like you to take a look at this report he's just e-mailed over."

"Donald Muir is in the cells waiting for his solicitor to return, the Oakwell females are being rounded up for voluntary DNA testing, and I haven't had any lunch." Forbes reached into his desk drawer for the family-sized, half-eaten bar of fruit and nut chocolate that he'd been saving for just such an emergency. He broke off a double row of squares, snapped the chunk into two, and pushed half of the squares across his desk. "None of us can function at our best with low blood sugar levels, and if I may say something DI Lang, you are still looking as though you could do with some building up. We haven't quite got that London pallor out of your cheeks yet. Get that down you while I have a read."

"Thank you, sir."

Forbes ran his tongue along the front surface of his teeth and swallowed before he looked up at his DI. "I agree that it's interesting, but linking these two cases, eight years apart, is a bit of a stretch, isn't it? You'll need something more in the way of evidence before I can justify spending man-hours on it."

"Sir, this might be even more of a stretch, but I was thinking there just might be a link to Oakwell. I've been reading through some of the statements we took as a result of Simon Carter's allegations. Several of the women who attended the more respectable meetings at that place mentioned regularly noticing young women who were never included in the group meetings, and occasionally hearing foreign languages being used behind closed doors. We know young homeless women were given short-term accommodation at the Grange, and I realise I'm making a bit of a leap here, but just supposing some form of modern-day slavery is being coordinated through Oakwell Grange, might that not account for the irregular spending sprees? And my victim was found only ten miles from Oakwell, so I was wondering, considering that it's only females who ever go through that place..."

"I'm ahead of you, DI Lang. The slave trade has already been mentioned in connection with this case. How many of the young females, in the slavery business, are likely to be pregnant? But even assuming that eight years ago one of them escaped somehow, Leek isn't within walking distance of Oakwell Grange for a heavily pregnant woman, is it?"

"I spoke at length on the phone to DCI Brixton. The investigating team believed the woman had been living rough for several weeks, and someone answering her description had been attending a drop-in centre less than two miles from the edge of the Leek moors, and four miles from where she was discovered. There are miles and miles of very bleak moorland to the south of Leek and if the woman had travelled across those moors on a bus, or if someone had given her a lift, then she might have considered the area as a safe place to give birth. If it hadn't been for an inquisitive dog her body could have remained there for many more months. The staff at the drop-in centre said they hadn't realised she was pregnant or they would have done more to help her, but they do remember saying at the time how nervous she was and how odd it was that she would never remove her oversized coat. She spoke very little English and refused to talk to an interpreter. They'd apparently had difficulty communicating with her on any level. They said that much of the time she appeared frightened of her own shadow."

"For your theory to hold water, DI Lang, the Oakwell Grange ladies would have had to have been involved in human trafficking for at least the last eight years. And it isn't a crime they could commit without being part of a larger organisation. If that is the case, the outlook for the baby you're searching for looks bleak."

"Not necessarily, sir. I've been checking on the internet and apparently new-born babies can fetch as much as ten thousand pounds on the open market in this country. I have a cousin who tried to adopt a young child recently, and the bureaucracy and red tape eventually proved too much for them. They ended up fostering, but it wasn't what they really wanted to do. If people are willing to pay that kind of money for a baby, you would expect it to be well cared for. With a little forward planning, desperate, childless couples can pass a baby off as their own, and documents are easily forged."

"People trafficking, baby selling and murder – three middle-aged ladies – do you realise how absurd your theory sounds, DI Lang? But it isn't beyond the realms of possibility, is it? I admire the way your mind works."

"I'd love to get my hands on the Oakwell computers. And there must be incriminating documents somewhere in that rambling old property."

"You're right that it would explain their irregular supply of cash, but unfortunately our theory isn't sufficient grounds for a search warrant. Ideally, we need a confession, or a DNA match to one of the partial samples recovered from Darya's body. Donald Muir is claiming that Prunella, Sheila, and Hannah, as well as both of his daughters, have been in and out of the front seats of his Land Rover many times during the two years it's taken him to renovate it, so getting a DNA match to the inside of that won't be worth anything in court. Getting a match, even a partial match, to material gathered from either of the dead women's remains is a different story."

*

Prunella slid most of the way down the bank, cursing her polished, court shoes. She stood over Sheila, looked through the trees for any signs of movement, and then looked downstream. Where the hell was Simon now? She fell to her knees and felt them sinking into the cold mud. How could he do this to a woman, but more importantly, what had Sheila told him?

"Try not to move while I cut the ropes." She was thankful he'd left a decent, bone-handled hunting knife on the seat of his van. When she eventually caught up with him, she would enjoy using it on him. "I'll make him pay for this. He won't get away from me again."

"He knows..." Sheila coughed and then screamed as her legs straightened. "He knows everything... you... the babies... I tried not to... he was going to kill me... I'm sorry... I'm so sorry... I'm hurt... I need a..."

"Stop babbling you stupid mare. I'm trying to think."

"My shoulder... I think it's broken... and my arm... it hurts too much. I need a doctor."

"You need to shut up. Do you think you can walk to your car if I get it a bit closer to the river? We'll find out whether you can drive. You need to get to a hospital, but you're on your own."

"What are you going to do?"

"You can't keep your mouth shut about anything. Why should I tell you? Now get to your feet." Her mind was racing. It was only a matter of time now before the police discovered the truth. Now that Jane Goodwin's mother was dead, there were only three people, including herself, who knew about the stash of bank notes in the cellars of Oakwell. If she was going to run, she was going to have to risk going back for it. Thirty thousand pounds wasn't a fortune, and the next generation of Oakwell women would be able to replace it eventually. Her own needs were the most urgent. She would have to rely on

Simon Carter not getting his story across to the police before she'd had a chance to retrieve it.

*

Adam checked his phone. He'd missed three calls, all of them from Jane. He hadn't spoken to her since fetching a jacket from her house a couple of days ago and now he was feeling guilty, because whether she realised it or not, she needed his support. And he had Ryan to consider. The boy was missing his regular sleep-overs, and he was missing Jane and Lucy. His finger was poised over the speed dial icon when he saw DCI Forbes striding down the corridor. He slipped the phone back into his jacket pocket before he made eye contact.

*

Prunella watched Sheila slowly driving away and checked her phone for about the tenth time in the past hour. She was waiting for either of the Manchester girls to return her calls or her texts. It wasn't like them to ignore her. Jasmine and Acacia were good girls who she liked to think looked on her as a mother figure. They were the future of Oakwell Grange – they were the reason for her getting up every morning. She needed to warn them about the danger they were in from Simon Carter, and she wanted to tell them to expect a call from the police. Unlike Sheila, they knew how to keep her secrets.

It was thirty minutes since she'd last seen Simon. It was time to drive away.

She had two things to do before heading up to her old associates in Northumberland, who she knew would welcome her with open arms for her particular skills and her contacts. The first was simple enough, but she was going to have to move quickly. It was getting hold of the money. The second was taking care of Simon Carter herself, as she should have done in the first place.

She pulled her car into a field entrance and pressed the speed dial icon again.

Both girls' phones went straight to voicemail.

*

Donald Muir seemed to be having difficulty sitting still on the hard chair of the interview room. And after an hour alone with his client, Donald's young solicitor was looking almost as uncomfortable. This was a task usually undertaken by less senior detectives, but Forbes wanted to conduct the interview himself. He ran through the necessary formalities and explained to Donald that he'd spoken to both of his parents. "They're in this station now, helping with our enquiries. They're being well looked after."

"They are nothing to do with any of this." Muir sounded desperate. "My parents are elderly and you've no right to go dragging them down here."

"They are nothing to do with any of what, Mr Muir?" Forbes leaned back.

The solicitor chirped up. "You should only be interviewing my client about specific matters, Inspector. He can't be expected to do your job for you."

Forbes leaned forward. "They are nothing to do with any of what, Mr Muir? You see, over the last few days, my officers have linked several serious crimes to the women of Oakwell, and therefore by association, to you, Mr Muir."

"I don't know what you're talking about."

"Well let's begin with the incident with which we already have enough evidence to charge you. On January the fifth of this year your Land Rover was involved in two incidents which resulted in the deaths of two boys and serious injuries to a third."

"You don't have any evidence that my client was driving that night. He's already told you that his garage is never locked."

"Mr Muir, your parents have told us that they saw lights in your cottage well after midnight on the night in question, and that you do sometimes take the vehicle out, illegally, onto the public road. That vehicle left your garage that night, we know that, and forensics will link it to the killings."

"Inspector, this is getting us nowhere. My client has explained that anyone could have driven the vehicle away. Have you never fallen asleep with the house lights still on?"

Forbes knew the solicitor was only trying to prove his worth. "But it was your client who drove his damaged Land Rover into one of the barns on his parents' farm the day after we'd searched them. That strikes us as suspicious. If your client wasn't driving that night, I'm sure he knows who was." He turned his attention back to Muir. "If you allowed someone to drive it, knowing that the vehicle shouldn't legally have been on the public roads that would make you a fool, Mr Muir. Is that your defence?"

"But I had no reason to hurt those boys."

"We've already established means and opportunity. I was coming to your motive next and I was hoping you would fill in a few blanks for us. Let's begin with the day before the hit-and-run incidents, and with the body of Darya Jamal, found less than ten miles from Oakwell Grange, shall we?"

Muir looked at his solicitor. He appeared surprised, but not too surprised to speak. "I had nothing to do with that."

Those few words, spoken very quietly, told him that DI Lang's instincts were spot on. The room was silent for a minute. He watched Muir's eyes close for a second and noted that the man's shoulders had dropped very slightly.

"And I now think that you know what happened to her new-born baby. I'm right aren't I?" Forbes finally said.

"I shall need to speak with my client, Inspector."

"We've wasted enough time today." Forbes spoke without looking away from Donald Muir.

"Then I shall have to advise my client to make no further comments."

His peripheral vision told him Adam was looking at him. He'd walked straight into that one; maybe his interview techniques needed some revision. He decided that while he had him in front of him, he would try to unsettle Mr Muir just a little more. "You might like to know that we are also looking into the eight-year-old case of an unexplained death in

Cheshire. You might recall the case as it attracted considerable media attention at the time."

"I don't think so."

"I'll fill you in on some of the details. A young, unidentified, Eastern European woman was found dead on the moors to the south of Leek. She'd bled to death following childbirth but the baby was never found. It was presumed that its remains had been taken by foxes."

"No comment."

"There were several partial DNA samples taken from her remains, and we thought it might be interesting to compare them to the partial samples recovered more recently from Darya."

"My client has already stated that that is nothing to do with him."

"We also intend to compare those DNA samples to those we are about to take from the women most closely associated with Oakwell Grange, and from yourself, Mr Muir. Do you think that we might find a match?"

"My client doesn't have to answer, Inspector. This is becoming repetitious."

The door of the interview room opened and DC Green poked his head through the gap. "Could I have a word, sir?"

Forbes pushed back his chair as he stood and then leaned across the table towards Donald Muir. "You can make this as difficult for yourself as you like, but I will get to the truth. We have a search warrant for the farm and for your cottage but you might be able to spare your parents some upset if you tell us what we need to know. Interview terminated at three-thirty; DCI Forbes and DS Ross leaving the interview room."

"What is it, Green?"

"Sir, we've brought Hannah Hall in for questioning, and she's given us a DNA sample, but she's claiming that Sheila has been missing since about ten o'clock this morning. She's making quite a fuss. She's claiming Sheila never arrived at

Uppertown School for her lunchtime shift but when Hannah last saw her she was almost ready to leave Oakwell. Hannah left for work first, and Sheila was expected to follow on within the next few minutes. When she hadn't arrived at the school by ten-thirty, Hannah telephoned Prunella who told her that Sheila and her car were both missing from Oakwell by the time she arrived. Prunella wasn't there when our officers called, nor was her car. We've tried both their mobiles but had no luck."

"What about the daughters of Sheila and Hannah, have you contacted them?"

"Yes sir, I just told them we needed to eliminate everyone from the Grange from our enquiries. Apparently they'd spent the weekend and most of yesterday in this area visiting family and friends, but they agreed to drive straight back down. They're providing DNA samples at the moment."

*

Jane Goodwin sat at her kitchen table with her head in her hands. It was only a few hours since Adam had told her the Oakwell finances were to be investigated, and here she was with everything the police might need to know, right in front of her now.

The files had been on the table for a couple of hours. She'd walked away from them and done a few other jobs, but she kept being drawn back. It didn't matter how long she stared at the hand-written ledgers and journals, she couldn't picture her mother pouring her heart into the task of adding up so many columns and so many pages of figures, especially since she'd never been able to recite the number of her mobile phone without first looking at a piece of paper. From the handwriting and the style of the figures, she knew she was looking at her mother's work. It was yet another part of the quiet lady's life that she knew nothing about.

She could really do with speaking to Adam, but she'd tried his phone several times already and he hadn't returned any of her calls. It seemed unlikely that the documents would prove to be evidence of a crime, but why had her mother been hiding them in her house? Could she have been involved, along with those women, in something illegal?

Phoning anyone at the station other than Adam, would make the documents a part of the official investigation, and her mother's name would be dragged into it. The people in this small community would begin gossiping about her and she didn't think she could cope with that.

The longer she sat thinking about it, the more complex her dilemma was becoming.

If she handed the documents over to the police, and if her worst fears were realised, it might reflect badly on her and affect her future career if she eventually decided to join the police force full time. And then there was Lucy – children could be so cruel. Lucy was a sensitive child who might end up being bullied because of her grandmother's actions.

If she was to put her and her daughter first, then the sensible option was to destroy all the files.

She almost wished she'd never found them.

She went to fridge, opened the wine she'd been saving for later, and poured herself a large glass.

She was being ridiculous. How likely was it that her mother would have been involved in anything illegal? Surely nothing could be gained by handing them over to the police.

Maybe she should store them in the attic and try to forget about them until the women were cleared of any involvement in any crimes, which she felt sure they would be before much longer. Or maybe she should go to Oakwell herself to enquire whether the women needed them returning for tax purposes, or whether the files were merely copies to be destroyed.

The sensible option was to go with her gut feeling and remove them from her home.

She'd decided. It would take the courage found at the bottom of another glass of wine, but she would return to Oakwell just as soon as she'd drunk it.

Returning to Oakwell Grange was her equivalent of climbing back onto a horse after being thrown to the ground.

The sooner she did it, the sooner she would recover from the fright she'd had on her last visit to the place. And she would apologise to the women for her dramatic exit the last time, and explain that she'd found the whole experience too emotional. That wouldn't be a complete lie.

28

"Sir," DC Rawlings was waiting in the corridor, "I've just been in touch with the network providers for the phones of all three women. Prunella has used her mobile to call the same two numbers several times during the last hour. None of the calls were answered. Sheila's mobile phone hasn't rung out but it received six incoming calls between eleven and one this lunchtime, all from either Hannah or Prunella, and all unanswered. The phone company's informed us that Prunella's phone is somewhere in the vicinity of Oakwell Grange at the moment. Sheila's is switched off totally."

"We need to act with caution. If Sheila has been kidnapped, then Simon Carter is the most likely perpetrator and we know that he's armed. He could also be holding Prunella. I'll alert the armed response unit. I want every available car to follow me to the area, but no one is to use a siren. DI Lang and DC Green, I want you two to go to Simon's parents' house to find out whether they've seen or heard from him since we last spoke to them. We need to gauge his state of mind. Report back to me directly, but remain with them for now in case Simon turns up there. Park out of sight, and do not, under any circumstances, take any risks. Are you comfortable with that, DI Lang?" He wanted to rebuild his DI's confidence in pressure situations. Standing behind Lang, DC

Green nodded his understanding of Forbes's concerns. They would have each other's backs, as the Americans would say.

*

From her vantage point on the darkening hillside she saw the trail of blue flashing lights snaking around the bends of the main road. Prunella wasn't surprised. Sooner or later they would be coming for her.

"The bastards must be tracking my phone." She took it from her coat pocket and threw it against the wall.

They would be at Oakwell in a matter of minutes. Her Isuzu Trooper, her trusty getaway vehicle, was still a good half a mile away, parked in a disused quarry building on the rarely used track which skirted the back of Oakwell Grange.

After taking care of Arianne, and retrieving the tin of money, she'd put on several layers of her thickest winter clothes, set light to the oil-soaked rags beside the plastic bottles of turpentine in the cellar, and then hurried back out into the cold evening air.

She felt confident she hadn't been seen. Hannah had gone to the police station to report Sheila missing, Sheila was at the hospital and most probably telling the police everything, and the next generation of Oakwell females were safely out of the way in Manchester. There was only one other person in the world who mattered to her, and he had been stuck at Leaburn police station since yesterday afternoon.

The property insurance was always kept up to date, she'd made sure of that, and Oakwell was overdue a complete makeover. The Manchester girls would enjoy doing that, and the fact that the fire had resulted in one insignificant death wouldn't upset them for too long.

She hadn't felt the usual thrill of the kill – she'd had to leave the girl merely stunned in her room. She'd hidden Arianne's key in her room and then used the spare to lock her in. They had to find smoke in her lungs if she was to be blamed for causing the fire.

It had been her intention to pause at this vantage point to watch the old place beginning to burn, but with the police already approaching, it was far too risky.

She hadn't expected Sheila to have given her away quite so quickly. She cursed her and hurried on towards her car.

*

"We can obtain a search warrant within the hour, Mr Carter." DI Lang wasn't convinced by the couple's claims that they'd had no recent contact whatsoever with Simon, but he couldn't force the information from them. "If you have any information at all, you'd be acting in your son's best interests to tell us."

"He's been the victim in all of this." Mrs Carter dabbed at her eyes again with her screwed-up handkerchief.

"We've treated your son as a victim for as long as we can, but you know as well as we do that on Monday he shot and killed a man in Bakewell."

"He was acting in self-defence... there was blood on that knife... Simon's blood... someone is still trying to kill him... we want you to find him... to keep him safe," she sobbed.

"Calm down please, Mrs Carter, we want the same thing, but we have to take any firearms incident extremely seriously. We have reason to believe that your son may have kidnapped Sheila Hall and Prunella Leath, and given that his level of violence has escalated, we could have a very serious situation developing. Could we take another look in his room?"

"Help yourselves." Mr Carter looked and sounded defeated. "He was never a violent boy, a little high-spirited sometimes, but never violent. We don't understand any of what's been happening. We feel as though no one will tell us the truth."

"His room's tidy – for a teenager," DC Green opened drawers looking for a diary, or anything else which might shed light on Simon's state of mind. He always hated going through people's personal belongings, especially when they weren't in the room with him.

"I told you – he's basically a good boy. His mother isn't handling the situation very well. He's our only child. My wife almost died giving birth to him and we decided not to risk having another. If it wasn't for her, I'd have been over to that witches coven to sort them out myself. And I'd have made every single one of them sorry for what they've put this family through."

The officers exchanged a glance but didn't respond. They could both feel empathy for the man, but both hoped he was only releasing a pressure valve in his head.

DC Green pulled a small wooden box from underneath Simon's bed and opened it. "These look like diaries." He sat down and began to read.

After a few minutes he looked up. "Mr Carter, were you aware that your son had a girlfriend?"

"No, but he's at that age when he wouldn't want to discuss things like that with his old dad. And if his mother knows, she's never said anything to me. Who is she?"

"Simon only uses the letter A. And the locations they meet in are numbered from one through to five. He's been seeing her since the early summer of last year, according to these diaries, but he's gone to great lengths to keep the relationship a secret. Are you sure you've no idea who it might be?"

"No, and he didn't start college until September, so it isn't likely to be a girl from there. It must be someone local. He never goes very far from home."

"Well whoever it is, the affair became very passionate, very quickly. Your son obviously believes that both of them are very much in love. If we don't find him tonight, may we take these diaries back to the station?"

*

Jane Goodwin parked close to the front door of Oakwell Grange. There were no other cars in the yard. She'd expected to see at least three cars, being so late on in the afternoon, but she could see light coming from somewhere on the ground floor of the building.

The heavy, cast iron doorknocker was ice-cold, and the noise it made as she released it, echoed around the inside of the old building. She wasn't sure whether she'd heard a voice, or whether it was her imagination. Gripping the equally cold, worn metal doorknob, she turned it until it clicked and immediately felt herself being pulled forward by the weight of the mammoth door.

"Hullo... is there anyone at home?"

There was a feint crackling sound. Someone was in the building, and the light was coming from the direction of the kitchen. She'd been stupid to think these women wouldn't put their cars inside one of their many sheds at night, especially during in winter. "Hullo... anybody home?" She spoke louder this time. "Hullo... it's Jane Goodwin. I only want a quick word. May I come in please?"

She pushed the door shut behind her, mainly to conserve the slight warmth. This place had to cost a fortune to heat. The light from the kitchen drew her into the bowels of the property and she felt the same intense sense of unease that she'd experienced on the other two occasions when she'd been in the dark hallway. Only on those occasions, she hadn't been alone.

The heavy atmosphere smelled similar to how she remembered it; similar but not quite the same, as though someone was burning more than just candles. Perhaps smoke was blowing back down one of the old chimneys. She'd taken a few more steps towards the light before an acrid odour caught in the back of her throat.

"Hullo, is everything all right?" Maybe someone had left a pan on the stove and forgotten about it. She tapped on the kitchen door before pushing it open. The room was unoccupied. There was no smoking pan on the black range, and the lungful of air she deliberately drew in was fresher and cleaner than the air in the hallway.

Somewhere above her, she thought she heard someone was moving about. She backtracked to the semi-darkness at foot of the stairs. "Hullo, is everything all right up there? It's Jane Goodwin. I'm coming up the stairs."

The first floor landing was long and unlit. There were no light switches that she could see, just one door after another, and every door she tried was locked. Someone was knocking, but the sounded was still coming from somewhere above her head.

Her heart thumped. She'd never suffered from claustrophobia before, but then she'd never been in a situation quite like this before. And this wasn't a good to time for it to start.

At the foot of the second flight of stairs she stood still for a few seconds and listened. Her heart thumped. The smell of smoke was becoming stronger and she considered turning back. The sounds she'd heard could simply be coming from old water pipes.

But she had to try at least once more. "Hullo, is there someone there? I think this place may be on fire. We need to leave right now."

"Help, help me, please help." A woman's voice called out from somewhere at the top of the stairs.

The glimmer of early-evening light through the cobwebbed roof window was enough to allow her to take the stairs two at a time. The voice became louder and clearer.

Breathing hard, she found the source of the voice within seconds of reaching the landing. It was coming from behind yet another locked door.

"I'm locked in. I can't find my key. Prunella has the spare one; find Prunella for me."

"There's no time. We've got to get out of here."

Instead of mindlessly charging up the second set of stairs, she should have called for help. She felt sick. She should have made the call the moment she suspected the place was on fire, but right now her phone may as well be on the moon. It was outside, in her car.

This was the one time when she could have done with the station's door opener – the yellow, weighted, battering ram that she'd only seen being used while she'd been at a safe distance from it. "Stand back. I'm going to try to kick the door down." Kick after kick, she felt adrenaline powering her muscles. The door creaked.

Her legs felt suddenly drained and she charged at the door with her shoulder, fully prepared for the pain of the impact, but not for the forward motion.

When she looked up she was staring into a young woman's blood-streaked, stunned face. "We've got to get out of here. Have you got a phone?"

"It's smashed – someone smashed it – I don't remember. Wait, please wait a moment, I have to take something with me."

*

Forbes, with Adam in the passenger seat, led the convoy of police vehicles into the driveway of Oakwell Grange. His mind took a couple of seconds to process what he was seeing. "Is that your Jane's car?"

"Yes sir, oh hell no, the bloody place is on fire. It's well ablaze. Where is she?" Adam leapt from the car.

"Adam, don't go inside." He shouted across the yard to his officers who were jumping from their vehicles. "Somebody stop him. I'm calling the fire department. Adam, no, they'll be here within minutes."

"Sir," another officer was shouting. His voice almost drowned out by the noise of a downstairs widow exploding outwards. "I see a child's car seat in the back of the car."

"Adam… is Lucy in that car? Someone get to it, now. If she's in there, for Christ's sake, get her out. Then see if you can safely push the car back from the building."

*

Jane looked in horror at the tendrils of smoke swirling and creeping their way up the stairs. Those stairs had been clear only a minute earlier. "We need to put bed sheets over our heads. We may need to breathe through them." She looked at the barred windows. "Take my hand and don't let go until we're outside." She hoped she sounded more confident than she felt. "Is there any water at all in this room?"

The young woman shook her head but the remainder of her looked frozen to the spot. She was clutching at the blanket and the plastic carrier bag she was protecting underneath it.

"Come on... we must go. My car's just outside. I've got a young daughter and I want to see her growing up." She cursed herself for parking so close to the building, but the car didn't matter, it was Lucy who was her reason for living.

It was the smoke that killed, not the actual fire, everyone knew that. Despite that, terror almost overpowered her legs when she heard a bang and felt a blast of hot air being forced through her blanket. It felt suicidal to continue downwards into the seat of the fire, but they had no other choice. The windows on the front of the house weren't barred, but her legs weren't up to kicking in another door. Who the hell locks every door in an old building like this?

"We've reached the second stairs." Her eyes stung and tears streamed down her cheeks. "When we reach the bottom, we'll crawl to the front door. There's always more air at ground level." She had to shout. There was another crash and sparks sprayed up the last few steps towards them. She desperately wanted to take in a good, deep breath – large enough to allow her to run to the door. The smoke was too thick and her lungs wouldn't allow it. She felt light headed and the woman clamped onto her right hand was crying out in some unrecognisable language.

They fell to the floor together and began to crawl.

"I can't let it end like this. I've got to get back to Lucy," she whispered.

*

"Two female bodies located on the ground floor...," a fire officer shouted across to them, "they're bringing them out now."

"Bodies...?"

Forbes watched Adam's trembling hands squeeze Lucy's rag doll against his chest."

"It's a figure of speech, Adam. If it is Jane and Lucy, it only means they've found them." A few years earlier, Forbes had felt just as powerless to help when Adam had struggled with life after witnessing the death of his first wife on the maternity hospital's delivery table. It wasn't often that he prayed, but he gave it his best shot as he waited, for the long minutes that it was taking, for the fire-fighters to emerge from the smoke.

Jane's phone was ringing in the front of her car and Forbes picked it up and answered it.

He pressed the speaker icon and held the phone out towards Adam.

"Mummy... I've had my favourite ice-cream for tea and now daddy's taking me to the bowling alley. Mum, can you hear me? Mum, what's all that noise?"

"Both breathing... both barely conscious...," the same authoritative voice shouted across the yard.

His prayers had been answered and Adam looked about to collapse. He reached out to stop him rushing towards them. The two female figures looked so small and helpless in the fire fighter's arms, both with masks clamped over their faces, both wrapped in dirty blankets, but both alive. "Let them do their jobs, Adam. She's going to be all right."

"I have to make sure it is Jane they've brought out."

He couldn't argue with that.

29

Simon's days of surveillance on Oakwell Grange were about to pay off. If he was right about Prunella he knew exactly where she would go, and this time he had the advantage of surprise.

He'd easily kicked off the wet ropes before the river and the cage combined had dragged him into deeper, more treacherous water. But after getting closer to his van, and then waiting for the bitches to leave, he'd almost suffered a second bout of hypothermia. As he waited he remembered the nurses explaining to him why he'd felt so hot that night, when he'd been on the verge of freezing to death. When the body's temperature drops below ninety-five degrees, shivering stops and disorientation kicks in. As the person loses rationality, their nerves are damaged and they feel incredibly hot. People have been known to strip off their clothes to cool themselves as they freeze to death, they told him. Thankfully he didn't reach that stage.

After he'd watched them both drive away, he'd picked up the knife that Prunella had dropped near the rear of his van, checked that his gun was still where he'd left it, and then started the engine and switched the heater onto full power. Then he changed into dry clothes, took a good mouthful of whisky, and filled his hip flask with the drop that was left.

He picked up his second phone, the one which only Arianne used, and he left a message on her voicemail. He'd never contacted her before, and he wasn't sure whether she would be able to figure out how to retrieve the message, but he had to try to warn her. Prunella was on her way back to the Grange, and she was steaming.

He was still shivering, and for once looked upon that as a good sign. His determination to resolve things in the next few hours had returned. This was the second time the bitches had left him for dead in the icy waters of his beautiful River Lathkill.

They weren't going to get a third opportunity.

The deserted quarry sheds, about three-quarters of a mile up the hillside behind Oakwell Grange, had made an ideal, if occasional base for him over the past fortnight. No one ever went there. The track leading up to them was too rough for most people to risk damaging their vehicles on, and beyond the quarry was only rough, bracken-covered land, with nothing to tempt any ramblers into exploring the area. The main attraction for Simon was that the sheds were as close to Arianne as he dared to be when he was resting.

At least, he hadn't seen anyone using the track, or the sheds, until a couple of days ago. He'd always used the smallest, least accessible building to park his van in, figuring that if anyone did come snooping around while he was there, then they would probably leave his hiding place till last, giving him sufficient time to make his escape.

Forty-eight hours earlier, on a damp Sunday afternoon, he'd been squatting in the shadows between the quarry sheds with his gun pointing into the open yard, from the moment he'd heard Prunella's Isuzu bouncing up the rugged track towards him. He'd watched her parking in the largest of the sheds, and he'd noticed that she'd shown no signs of nervousness as she'd walked out of the yard and trudged back down the lane in her wellington boots, carrying her shoes.

She'd had no idea she was being watched.

He hadn't been able to resist taking a look at her vehicle. It had been locked of course, denying him the opportunity of seeing inside any of the boxes in the rear, or underneath the blankets on the back seat. There'd been nothing particularly unusual about it, other than where it was parked.

That day he'd waited until nightfall before he'd driven back down the track, with his heater on full and his headlights off. It had been a difficult route to follow, mainly because of the thick fog which so often rolled off these moors, and which had given the illusion of following Prunella down the hillside.

He hadn't been back to those sheds since, but very soon he was intending to approach them in the same manner as he'd left, with his heater on full and his headlights off.

*

A lifetime of living outside the law had taught Prunella to always have an escape route ready. It had been a long time since she'd felt the police closing in on her, but she'd felt it for the past few days. She was very glad now that she'd hidden her Isuzu, with a full fuel tank and false number plates, within walking distance of Oakwell. And in the rear of the vehicle she'd stashed enough tinned food, toiletries, and water supplies to last her for several days. She just hadn't expected to need it quite so soon. And that was down to the loose cannon, Simon Carter.

The wind stung her cheeks. She hunched her shoulders, bowed her head, and walked as determinedly as her middle-aged legs would allow. The police would be distracted by the fire for a while. She would have plenty of time to get away.

Her legs ached. She wasn't accustomed to walking at this speed, but the sound of an approaching helicopter suddenly spurred her on. If the television reality programs were to be believed, most of them had heat seeking equipment aboard, and that was something she'd neglected to plan for. She had to keep moving.

The cold air dried her mouth and her throat, but the rest of her body tingled with sweat. She daren't even think of slowing down. Even when the thwack, thwack, thwack of the helicopter blades grew quieter, she looked up into the clear night sky without altering her pace. It was heading down the valley towards the river, but no doubt it would return. Maybe they weren't looking for her, yet. Maybe they were searching for Simon, or with any luck, Simon's body.

It disappeared from view and she could hardly hear it.

Then she smiled. One by one, the outlines of the sparse, skeletal bushes and scrubby trees along the horizon were disappearing. A curtain of dense, smothering fog was rolling down from the tops of the moors.

Her Gods were with her again. When she needed them most, they were always there for her. And she would thank them properly just as soon as she was safely away from here.

"Oh thank you, thank you, my ancient and merciful Gods." She gasped and shouted into the strengthening wind. "You really are doing everything within your power to help me tonight, aren't you? And I am so, so grateful."

They understood what was needed to keep her safe. And they were actually working with her now, fanning the all-consuming flames behind her while drawing her into their cloak of invisibility.

The breeze grew stronger. Swirling ahead of the main body of thick fog were tendrils of pale, almost transparent, shifting shapes.

They were her Gods. They had to be.

She'd never seen them in this way before, but she was in no doubt that that was what they were. She spread her arms out wide to embrace them and felt the power of their damp fingers soothing her sweat-covered brow.

She would be safe now.

*

Simon pulled clear of the trees and his headlights picked out the familiar outline of the small church at the top of the hill. There were sirens somewhere in the distance. Some poor sod was having as bad a day as he was. The sirens grew louder. Fifty metres ahead of him was the main road and on it might be the police.

They could be looking for him. He drew into the last passing place before the main road, switched off his engine, and waited. He was exhausted and in pain. He wanted his ordeal to be over, and if it was to come to an end here and now, then he'd accept it as his fate. He could tell them to look for the recording he'd thrown into the tangle of bramble bushes, and once they understood how Arianne's life was in danger, they could rescue her.

The first police car slowed as it grew nearer.

One blue car, three blue and whites, and then a police van all slowed before turning away from his junction, onto the equally narrow road almost opposite him. That was the road leading down to Oakwell Grange. His imagination leapt and twisted: Arianne had disposed of a body. Were there more bodies at Oakwell? Were there more killers at Oakwell? Sheila had driven herself to the hospital, she would be there by now, so why were there so many police for just two women, and why weren't they looking for him? He was metres away from them, waiting, watching them driving past the front of his van. They were close enough for him to see into their vehicles, so why had none of them looked his way?

He clapped his hands to the sides of his head. Nothing his scrambled brain could think of made any sense. Just when he'd finally been fired up enough to confront Prunella and Hannah, his plans had been thwarted, and by the police of all people.

He was shivering violently now. Totally out of ideas of what to do next, he restarted his engine and checked that the heater was set to full power.

He rocked steadily back and forth as the minutes ticked by.

The police vehicles had all been silent. Why hadn't he realised that straight away? He felt sick. The wailing of sirens in the distance had come from the two fire engines which were now slowing down in front of him, indicating, and obviously about to follow the police vehicles down towards Oakwell Grange.

Prunella Leath never did anything without a reason. His scrambled brain began pulling together isolated threads of the things he'd seen. Was that why she'd moved her Isuzu? He pictured Arianne trapped inside the blazing building while Prunella walked up to the abandoned quarry shed where her Isuzu truck was waiting for her.

She had intended all along to destroy Oakwell Grange if the police had ever uncovered her crimes?

Fear and helplessness together churned at his stomach as he roared his van past the entrance of Oakwell Grange. Smoke was billowing above the tops of the trees and flashing lights filtered through the branches which normally hid the property from passers-by.

He wanted to be sick. He wanted to stop, but he couldn't risk it.

They'd arrest him instead of allowing him to help. They wouldn't listen to him – not until it was too late. The fire had to have been started deliberately and there was only one person who would have done that.

He knew he was right – he just knew.

His beautiful Arianne might be beyond his help now, but if she was, he intended to do one last thing for the love of his life.

He switched off his lights and drove his van onto the dirt track.

30

"Stay with Jane as long as you need to, Adam," Forbes shouted past the backs of the paramedics. He watched the ambulance leave and then looked at his watch. Had it really only been twenty minutes since they'd arrived on the scene? That had to have been one of the longest twenty minutes of his life.

"Do we know who called in the fire?" He asked one of the uniformed officers.

"Yes sir, Miss Hannah Hall, one of the owners of the property. She left Leaburn police station with her daughter and her niece a short while ago and arrived here only minutes before us. They came straight here to find the building already ablaze. They're all sitting together in Hannah's car over there, under the trees. They're in shock."

Hannah had been interviewed briefly, and all three women had agreed to take a DNA test. With Donald Muir in custody for suspicion of murder and attempted murder, there had been no reason to detain the women.

"If we'd held them for just a few minutes longer, Jane and that other woman might not have been brought out of there alive," he said to himself as much as to the young officer at his side.

"No sir, but Hannah keeps repeating that we should be searching for Sheila and Prunella. Could they still be inside, do you think?"

"I doubt it somehow, but if they are, the fire officers will find them."

"I hope so, sir."

"Get the women back to the station and make them comfortable until we can find some accommodation for them. I want to be sure that we at least know where three of them are. I'll see you back at the station shortly. Oh, and drive carefully. This damn fog has come from nowhere, and it's getting thicker by the minute."

A third fire engine had arrived from Buxton and a minimum of six jets of water were now streaming through the broken windows. At least, that's what he hoped was happening. The smoke and steam which only minutes earlier could be seen swirling up into the early evening sky, were being held down by the thickening fog. At this rate, everyone on the site would be in need of breathing apparatus. And despite the strengthening breeze, the heat was intensifying, almost as though a blanket had been dropped over the immediate area.

Forbes was suddenly reminded of Simon Carter's hospital statement, 'some people believe the Oakwell women conjure up the Devil from the centre of a black shroud on their living room floor'. He shuddered. If he blocked out the sounds of the people around him, he could almost believe it himself.

He blinked. Fog and smoke swirled around him. It disorientated him to the point that all he could do at that moment was stand perfectly still. The smog had blocked out all but the brightest of the flashing lights when he thought he felt added warmth, and the lightest of touches around his shoulders. For a second he imagined he could detect his mother's favourite perfume overpowering the stinging smoke. "Hullo mum," he spoke softly, his lips barely moving, "I'm finding it very hard to believe that you ever came here." Another tear rolled down his cheek, but this time not from the smoke. "And I guess we'll never know for sure whether something these women gave you actually played a part in your death. It's all right mum," he smiled, "I don't think I really want to know, not after all this time. I'd just like you to know, in case you were in any doubt, that we all still love you, and we all miss you so very, very much."

The perfume – imaginary or not, vanished.

He took one backward step and tried to focus through the swirling grey mass.

He understood Jane's curiosity. Her mother had only been in her mid-sixties when she'd died suddenly – that thought had come from nowhere and he shook his head. It was a thought that he'd forever keep to himself. Voicing it would help no one, least of all Jane Goodwin.

Blurred lights flashed and shifted in front of him. His car was parked somewhere behind him, but unless the smog was less dense further away from the fire, it wasn't going to be safe to drive anywhere for a while. He'd seen no mention of thick fog on the weather report this morning, and the police helicopter, which had been scrambled and asked to search the River Lathkill and the Oakwell Grange area for three missing people, had taken off in reasonably clear conditions. It had been forced to return to base until conditions improved, but with daylight just about gone, realistically that meant tomorrow.

Wind coiled the fog around him and he began to see snapshots of the smouldering building and people trying to prevent the flames from springing to life again. From what he'd read and been told about the history of the building, it had been built with the best of intentions, but had since witnessed varying degrees of abuse.

Perhaps the place ought to be allowed to burn to the ground.

Fog or no fog, there were still three people unaccounted for, and the fire officers hadn't located any other bodies in the building.

"Has anyone checked the sheds?" he shouted to his officers as he walked towards them.

"Not yet, sir, we thought it best to wait until the fire service had things a bit more under control."

"We'll check them now." He beckoned to four of his men to follow him.

The sliding doors of the largest garage rattled on their overhead metal runners, and dismissing fears of a desperate teenager with a loaded gun, Forbes stepped inside. Prunella's empty, blue Ford Mondeo faced him. He placed his open hand onto its bonnet. It was slightly warm, but whoever had driven it and then parked it there was long gone.

Simon parked his van behind a hedge, about four hundred metres ahead of the old quarry, to continue his journey on foot. He pictured himself as a young Rambo as he pulled on his thick coat and a black woollen hat, and then patted the fabric on each side of his body where his weapons were hidden. He was tempted to shout 'yo', but he didn't.

He had to move cautiously. He walked on the grass verge, alongside the hedge, to reduce the chance of being seen.

He'd parked up not a moment too soon. Thick fog was rolling down the hillside towards him, and right on the leading edge of it was a solitary figure. Only a couple of hundred metres ahead of him, someone else was walking up to the sheds. The figure disappeared into the fog, but he could hear a familiar voice. He walked faster. It was Prunella all right. The bitch was singing – no, she was chanting something.

She was predictable, and she was no match for him. He climbed over the next field gate and followed the line of the hawthorn hedge which took the shorter route to the rear of the quarry sheds.

He heard her puffing and grunting before he heard the slap, slap, slap of her wellington boots on the concrete yard.

The stupid bitch had even left her car unlocked for him this time. He opened the door and with only seconds to spare he managed to scramble half-way underneath the pile of blankets on the back seat.

He knew how her mind worked. She believed she was going to be the one who got away with murder – well not if he had anything to do with it, she wasn't – especially not if she'd harmed his Arianne.

The shed doors rattled open and a wave of rage surged through him. It was a physical, intense, almost painful emotion. His heart pounded and his fingernails dug into the palms of his hands. Arianne could be lying dead, or disfigured, and with the blood of John and Philip already on her hands, Prunella was going to pay for her sins tonight.

He forced himself to lie still and quiet. He bit into his bottom lip until he tasted blood, and he listened. The driver's door opened and he heard something being placed on the passenger seat, followed by the sound of wellington boots being thrown into the foot well. The car rocked slightly and he felt the seat being pushed back against him when she took her place in the driving seat, with the door slightly ajar and the interior light still on.

He knew now that he was capable of killing her, because despite being the most unlikely killer imaginable, that was what she had turned him into. But first he wanted her to experience real terror.

His fingers squeezed the bone handle of his grandfather's knife; the same knife that Prunella had conveniently dropped on the ground earlier today, and the rage he'd felt only minutes earlier was replaced by an urge to feel the blade moving through the air towards her throat.

It was time.

She gasped, but she didn't move.

"A wise decision, Prunella," he spoke slowly, savouring the moment. "You imagined you'd conveniently disposed of me today, didn't you?"

"You can't hurt me," she seemed to be sneering.

He looked into the rear view mirror and saw her face reflected back at him. She was smiling at him – she was actually, genuinely smiling.

"No, really, you can't hurt me," she added. "You see, I'm being protected by forces too powerful for you to even contemplate. You and your girlfriend really should have realised that by now. I didn't set out to hurt you today. If you had died, it would only have been as a result of your own stupidity."

He leaned towards her until his mouth was an inch away from the back of her neck. He wanted her to feel his breath on her skin. "Where is Arianne? Tell me."

"That shouldn't matter to you now. She'll never be yours."

"I'm the one holding the knife here. Are you so bloody arrogant that you think you can defy me?"

"To the death, Simon Carter – to the death, but it will be your death, not mine – you'll see."

"You don't scare me. I'll ask you once more. Where is Arianne?" He pressed the knife harder into the soft flesh of her throat but she didn't flinch.

"In the name of all of the ancient Gods of this mother earth, I forbid you to injure me. I promise you, I will live to witness that knife being turned from me and plunged into that firm young flesh of yours. And I will enjoy hearing your screams, yeah; I will revel in the sound of your agony."

"You crazy bitch," he drew the sharpened edge of the blade across her skin as he spoke and felt her pulling away from it. "Stay perfectly still." He gripped the opposite side of her neck with his free hand.

"Do you really think it's an accident, Simon, that your life has involved so much chaos? Do you believe you and your dead friends have simply been dogged by bad luck for so many years? If you do, then you are sadly deluded. It was I who asked the Gods to disrupt your miserable lives, and with their help, it was I who killed your friends, and I who will destroy you."

"No, not this time Prunella. This time you are going to pay for what you've done. There are no Gods here helping you, ancient or otherwise. It's just you and I."

"You're wrong. You may believe you're in control of this situation, but really, you're nothing of the sort. The Gods, my Gods, are all around us. You survived your first ordeal by water for a reason. I used to wonder what that reason might be, but now I know. The Gods wanted us to come face to face for one final challenge. You see, occasionally they like to have some fun, they like to play with us mortals – their servants, and they obviously wanted at least one of your group to witness their powers before they destroyed you."

He felt a rush of cold air on his face. It came from the partly open door, but it was unexpected enough to make him want to look beyond the confines of the car. Not that there was anything to see beyond the light cast by the vehicle's feeble interior light. He shivered, but this time as much through fear as through cold.

"Close your door and start the engine. I want you to drive to where you almost killed me today."

The car edged out into the darkness and a few remaining wisps of fog swirled around the sheds.

"Switch on your headlights."

"Are you afraid of the dark, Simon Carter? You know, you really ought to be."

He couldn't believe she was laughing as she changed into second gear. The woman was more unstable than he'd realised. He squeezed her neck with his left hand, just to remind her who was the one in control.

How do you terrorise someone with such obvious mental problems, he suddenly thought, much less kill them in cold blood? "Tell me where Arianne is right now, and I'll consider letting you go free."

"Burned beyond all recognition, as far as I know, in what remains now of Oakwell Grange. You surely didn't think she would be allowed to live, did you? The ancient Gods never leave any alien witnesses to their work. You'll realise that soon enough. Are you having fun now, Simon? You should be – I am."

He opened his mouth but no words seemed adequate.

They travelled the rest of the short journey in silence, seeing only one police car on the main road as they turned down towards the river.

He was thankful he'd left the gateway wide open.

"Well, here we are again," Prunella said, almost triumphantly.

"Switch off the engine. I'm going to give you exactly ten minutes to explain to me why you wanted the three of us dead." He looked at his watch but it had stopped working. "Take a look at the clock on the dashboard. You can watch your life ticking away if you don't tell me what I need to know."

He wanted to know how much of Sheila's story had been true, but also now, he was struggling with the prospect of killing a deranged woman in cold blood. His almost uncontrollable rage had deserted him and he wished it would resurface. "If I think your answers are reasonable enough, I might spare your life. Start talking, bitch."

"You were fools, all three of you. When you have dangerous knowledge about someone, you shouldn't write to them to tell them. What did you expect me to do? I was protecting my family. Any self-respecting woman would do the same."

"You have nine and a half minutes left. And the Oakwell females aren't your family."

"That's where you're wrong."

"What do you mean?"

"I am one of the only two direct descendants of the man who built that fine property, over two hundred years ago. He was a respected peer of the realm, a powerful freemason, and I'm proud to have his blood in my veins. Because of some wrongdoings, his stupid daughter-in-law gave Oakwell Grange away for absolutely nothing, when it ought to have remained in the family – in my family. That place is my birth right."

"You've just set fire to it."

"It's insured. The stonework will stand up to the fire and the next generation will rebuild it."

"None of that means that the property should belong to you."

"You haven't heard my complete story."

"I'm listening, aren't I?"

"My father was killed in a hit and run incident when I was a teenager. He was the one who'd researched our ancestry, and because of what he found, had been offering to invest in Oakwell Grange in exchange for having our family name put back on the deeds, and for a small share in the property. At that time, four elderly ladies had been running the place into the ground and they hadn't been able to agree with one another about accepting my father's generous offer. His killer was never found, but I always knew it had to be one of those four women. That's when I made it my mission in life to get my family's blood back where it rightly belongs – in Oakwell Grange."

"You've less than eight minutes now – go on."

"I earned good money when I was in my twenties, but property prices rose far faster than I was able to save. I knew I'd never have enough to be able to offer anything like the market value, so I came up with another plan." She paused. "This is difficult for me."

"Seven minutes remaining."

"Different people know different parts of my story. No one has the whole picture. I'm only telling you everything because I know you won't be permitted to live long enough to repeat any of it."

"Bullshit... only six and a half minutes remains."

"As you like, but remember, you've been warned not to underestimate my powers. Shortly after my father was killed, I was sent to live with relatives in Manchester. I have a brother, Donald, who's two years younger than me. He was allowed to stay with our mother, who then married a farmer called Jacob Muir. Donald was adopted by Jacob and took the surname of Muir, but Jacob hadn't wanted a girl cluttering up his farm and so I was left to rot in Manchester. Only three people know that Donald and I are brother and sister. I haven't spoken to my mother for thirty years, though I take a walk around their farmland occasionally, but I've always kept in touch with Donald. It was amusing for a while to let people think we were an item. His new father had expected to gain a cheap farmhand, but Donald was never interested in farming, so I guess the old bastard got what he deserved."

"Five minutes left, and I'm losing the will to live. What has this got to do with anything?"

"I needed to ensure that Oakwell went to the next generation with our blood in their veins, so I befriended the two young sisters and the old witch who ran Oakwell. It was easy to persuade Sheila into a relationship with Donald. They were married when she was two months into her pregnancy, and to celebrate we had... well let's just call it an old-fashioned orgy, with myself, Sheila, and Hannah, but with only one male in attendance. Ironically, it wasn't Hannah who fell pregnant that night, but me. I found myself carrying my brother's child." She smiled as she spoke.

"That's sick."

"Not really. It kept the bloodline even more pure. That's how the old aristocracy used to do it, and some of the old ways are the best – I've realised that many times over the years. And don't forget, the sisters didn't know, and still don't know, that Donald and I are brother and sister. I never was the maternal type, so I persuaded Hannah to pretend that the baby was hers. She shoved cushions under her clothes and I attended a hospital in Manchester, where no one knew Hannah, and used her name. Everyone could see Donald was the father, but no one realised that Hannah wasn't the natural mother of the girl."

"You're down to your last three minutes, and now I know that your niece and your daughter will inherit the Grange. But even if John and Philip found that out, which I don't believe they did or they would have told me, that doesn't justify killing them in cold blood."

She continued as though he hadn't spoken. "I groomed those two girls. People remarked on how I treated them as though they were my own." She laughed. "When the old lady wouldn't let me move into Oakwell I even married that surly old gamekeeper so that I could live nearby. And I ensured that the girls grew up understanding the history of the property, and the responsibilities that came along with owning such a place – a place sacred to women and with special, magical powers."

"Cut the crap... you're time has just about run out."

"I don't expect a runt like you to understand, but I was a respected figure in the underworld of Manchester for many, many years. My name was spoken in hushed tones and was feared. As the two girls grew, they both lived up to my expectations. I wanted to turn around the fortunes of Oakwell Grange for them. People trafficking had become the newest and most lucrative source of income for some of the people I'd once worked for, and when I saw a gap in the market, I offered to fill it. Years later, Donald and I set the girls up in a health food shop in the city so they would be in the best possible place to make contacts of their own."

"You groomed them to become criminals?"

"I saw it more as them as offering a service, just as I had done when I was their age."

"Doing what?"

"Many of the illegal female workers fall pregnant each year, often through no fault of their own, and a few of those die in childbirth, often in dreadful conditions. The live babies are euthanized and the women put back to work straight away. Even you must see that that isn't right. At Oakwell, we took in some of those women, delivered their babies in a safe and clean environment, and then nursed them back to full health before we sent them back. Only one girl ever escaped from us and she gave birth alone on the moors, miles from here. The Gods ensured that her and her baby perished. But that happened years ago."

So Sheila had been telling the truth. "And Arianne...?"

"She came to us heavily pregnant, as they all do, but after a long and difficult labour, she lost her baby. Did she tell you that?"

"What happens to the babies you deliver?"

"We take good care of them and sell them to the highest bidder. People will pay good money for new-borns."

"Sheila talked about a letter. It was written and posted by John and Philip, but I never saw it. It was meant as a joke and I really don't believe they knew anything damaging about you or they would have told me."

"It may well have been a joke to them, but it had a ring of truth to it. I couldn't take the risk of ignoring it, could I? I was forced into taking action."

"Everyone knew that you took in and cared for homeless and sometimes pregnant girls."

"Yes, but only a handful of people knew what happened to a few of them after the births. If that had got out, Oakwell would have been finished. You do see that, don't you? I had to protect the rightful inheritance of my girls – my bloodline."

"But why did you have to kill Arianne?"

"She disposed of a body. She knew too much. That was Hannah's fault."

"A body...?" He'd prayed that Sheila's account had been a lie.

"The body in the ditch – the one that they've just identified, was placed there by your precious Arianne. That woman's death was sort-of accidental. She tried to take back her baby, and in the struggle she fell down the stairs. I wasn't at Oakwell that day or I would have disposed of the body myself, not given the job to that useless girl that you're so besotted with. When that letter arrived I assumed Arianne had told you everything. I had to act quickly. I knew I could control her until I'd taken care of you three boys. Then I would have disposed of her and no one beyond my family would have missed her. She will be dead by now anyway, and that only leaves you, Simon Carter."

She was watching him through her rear view mirror.

"You're an evil bitch." The rage was finally returning.

*

Forbes shivered as he entered the incident room. The fog had cleared enough for him to drive away from Oakwell, but the damp air had seeped into his clothes and taken the stench of the burning building in with it. He wanted to speak with his officers before he went home to shower, change, and refuel his body, knowing that when he did return to his office in an hour or two, most of his team would be at home with their families and preparing to retire to their beds.

"Is there any news on Jane?" DC Green asked.

"I've heard nothing yet, but Adam's with her. He'll let us know as soon as he's able. Now, while we're waiting for a report from the chief fire officer, I think we should assume that today's fire was started deliberately." Heads were nodding all around the room.

"Simon Carter…?" DC Robert Bell asked what the others were obviously thinking. Heads were nodding again.

"He could be the arsonist, but until we find him we can't be sure. Prunella and Sheila are also still missing, remember. We may still have a hostage situation, or, as DI Lang has suggested, if the women realised we were looking into their affairs more closely, and Darya Jamal was killed at Oakwell, it's possible one or both of them were aiming to destroy any evidence, and have disappeared of their own volition. Until we find them, we won't know. Have all the nearest hospitals been checked for any of the three missing people?"

"Yes sir," DC Emily Jackson answered, "about an hour ago."

"Then check again, now."

"As I understand it, all three women lived for that place," Emily continued, "and from what I've learned about Prunella, I think she's far too devious and intelligent to have been taken by Simon Carter. If the three of them are together, as Hannah is suggesting, then I'd say that it could be Simon's life which was in serious danger, and not the women's."

31

"Shut the fuck up, Prunella."

"What's your next move going to be, Simon Carter? Do you really think you have the bottle to slit my throat with that rusty knife, because if you do, I promise you, you'll live to regret it? The ancient Gods..."

"I said, shut the fuck up. I've heard enough of your rubbish. It doesn't scare me. Now give me the goddamn keys."

She moved barely an inch before the keys flew past his left shoulder and landed beside him on the rear seat. He reached for them.

A flash of light, an explosion of noise, and then an excruciating pain in his left shoulder all happened before he could close his fingers around the keys. Another noise followed. It was the sound of his knife falling onto the metal doorstep of the car.

His breath came in short, fast spasms. He couldn't speak. The initial sharp pain began to feel more like a vice being tightened around his shoulder and he turned to face Prunella.

Blood was trickling down her neck onto the collar of her coat, but she seemed oblivious to it. She was smiling again, but this time she was pointing a tiny, silver pistol directly at his face.

The rage boiled up inside him again until he could no longer contain it. He spoke through gritted teeth. "If I'm to die here, then I'm taking you to hell with me."

His breathing slowed. She was just staring at him. He heard the click of the trigger, but this time there was no explosion. Before she could try again, his right arm was locked around her throat. He squeezed her neck until his own body was running short of oxygen.

When he released his grip, Prunella's torso slumped sideways onto the passenger seat and her head collided with the door. He slumped back and stared at the blood soaking into his own clothes from his shoulder. The effort it had taken to defeat her had drained his energy, along with his blood. Then he remembered her pistol and leaned towards the front of the car. He had to find it. She was still breathing, and the stupid little pistol that she'd managed to conceal from him had misfired once. He might not be as lucky a second time.

He groped around on the floor until he found it. There was no wonder she'd been able to keep it hidden; it was the smallest gun he'd ever seen. His face was close to hers. "Now whose side are your Gods on?" he growled into her ear, but she didn't respond. What if she had more hidden weapons? It hurt like hell, but he held his left hand across her throat while used his right to search her clothing. She had no more weapons.

He flopped back into the rear seat and listened to her rasping breaths. A rat in a sewer would make less noise. He reached into his inside pocket. There was nothing to be gained by trying to bring her round yet, and a long swig of whisky from his hip flask might help with his pain while he cleared his thoughts.

With her gun and her keys safely in his coat pocket, and his knife in the least painful of his hands, he slowly clambered out and walked to the rear of the Isuzu. One of those boxes must contain something he could use. He'd no idea what he might need next, but while Prunella was unconscious it wouldn't hurt to take a look.

The rear interior light came on as he swung the back door open.

The first two boxes contained only tinned food and bottled water. "So you really were planning your escape, you devious bitch." The third held a small disposable barbeque and a plastic bag containing matches. The forth box was different.

A smile, the first he'd managed since waving to the night watchman the night before, spread across his face. "Perfect, bloody perfect, an eye for an eye. Arianne, this will be sweet justice or you. She's going to regret destroying you. Tonight, I'll make certain of that." Tears rolled down his cheeks and he brushed them away with his blood-stained hand. He was going to have to improvise with a few things, but he had everything here that he needed.

He slammed the back door of the Isuzu shut and listened.

Apart from the occasional eerie screeches and hoots from a pair of communicating tawny owls somewhere fairly close by, and the disgusting, snorting noises coming from Prunella, he could only hear the reassuring roar of the river. If people were searching for them, they were searching in the wrong places.

His left side felt warm and his sweat shirt was sticking to his skin. He had to pull Prunella out of her vehicle while he still had the strength.

She was easier to move than he'd expected. She gasped as her back, followed by her head, hit the soft, wet ground beside the track. Her eyes remained shut.

He leaned against the vehicle for a few minutes; the effort of getting her onto the ground had exhausted him and left him feeling light-headed. He closed his eyes and pictured Arianne.

Thoughts of her charred body were more than he could stand. He bent down, grasped Prunella's ankles, dragged her to the front of her Isuzu, and then positioned her very carefully. After tying her up with what he'd found beside her boxes of supplies, he very reluctantly poured a small amount of his whisky into her open mouth.

"Wake up, bitch, this is show time."

She spluttered and coughed.

"Wake up; I don't intend to waste any more of my alcohol on you."

He watched as she blinked at the headlights shining onto her, and as she realised her hands were tied with her own rope and her feet were bound together with plastic, supermarket carrier bags. Slowly he lifted one of the cans of petrol that he'd taken from the forth box until it was over her stomach. For the first time since he'd taken her hostage, he saw genuine fear in her eyes.

"This is for Arianne." The fumes stung his eyes as he poured a straight line of the liquid across her middle. He blinked, but didn't close his eyes for long enough to stop them from watering. He wanted to watch her fear developing into terror.

"You will regret this, Simon Carter," she yelled upwards into the tree branches. "By the laws of the Gods and the Goddesses of this mother earth, you will pay dearly for this day."

She actually looked pathetic, squirming and flopping from side to side on the ground like a dying fish, yet still attempting to intimidate him. He took two small steps back, struck three matches together, and tossed them towards her.

Ignoring her screams, he walked to her car, took out one of the duvets, and sauntered back to her.

"Here," he placed the folded duvet over the last of the flames. "It's more than you deserve, but the burns are payment for only one person – they are for my Arianne."

Her eyes rolled back until he could no longer see any colour other than white, and she whimpered.

"Don't lose consciousness yet. I haven't finished. Now you're going to pay for what you did to John and Philip. Don't move."

He checked her position on the ground, returned to her vehicle, and slowly eased his injured body into the driving seat. He hadn't had enough energy left to place her where he could see her face at the precise moment the engine roared into life.

He selected the reverse gear and seconds later she was staring up at him.

Her mouth opened and closed, but no intelligible words were coming from it. He selected first gear and accelerated. Bump, bump, the sound was just as the old guy from the Legion in Ashtown had described it on the night that John and Philip had died. He selected reverse gear and accelerated again. And again he heard the same bump, bump.

All that he lacked were the screams.

He felt slightly cheated as he switched off the engine.

If she was still conscious, she had to be in tremendous pain. That thought made his own pain more bearable as he staggered from the seat and leaned against the front wing of the car to take a closer look at her.

She saw him and whimpered. Her head rolled from side to side, but because of where he'd positioned her, just as he'd intended, only her legs had been crushed. There was no blood, only wet tyre marks across her thighs.

"Please..." she croaked. "Enough... sorry... hospital..."

"Not a chance. It will never be enough for what you've done. But I do have an idea."

"I... help... please."

"Maybe, if you have a pen and some paper in your vehicle, we can come to a deal."

"Front..." she arched her back and stifled a scream.

He turned his back on her. She wasn't going anywhere.

He pulled a red notebook and two pens from the glove box and then leaned back into the seat to catch his breath. He looked at the box on the floor beside the passenger seat. When he'd pulled her out, he hadn't noticed it. He remembered hearing her placing it onto the seat before she'd got into the car, but it must have been caught on her coat and dragged off by her body. Apart from her boots, that box seemed to have been the only item she'd brought with her from Oakwell. He'd take a look at it when he'd finished with her.

"If I untie your hands," he said as he walked back to her, "and if you agree to write and sign a full confession to the murders we both know you've committed, I'll consider taking us both to the nearest hospital. Do we have a deal?"

"How can I trust you...? I'm in so much pain... You might kill me anyway." She spoke through clenched teeth and her breathing was becoming more rapid.

"And I might drop dead while you're writing it. It's a risk we'll both have to take, isn't it? But if you refuse, then you'll be forcing me to take justice into my own hands, and my need for revenge for Arianne will mean an agonising death for you."

With his knee against her back, he supported her so that she could write. He watched each word being written and then ordered her to sign it.

"There are store cards in my bag...you can check my signature...I've written the truth... now please... I'm in agony... I need a hospital before I pass out."

He smiled, leaned forward to take the confession, and then quickly withdrew his knee.

She fell back, groaning, "Please... please... you promised... I've done what you asked."

"You don't seem to realise, Prunella, that you turned me into a killer that morning in Bakewell when you sent a hit man after me. And you of all people should know you can never trust a killer." He opened his jacket to put the confession safely away on the side which wasn't drenched with blood.

She was alternately sobbing and moaning and the noise was beginning to irritate him. But that was good. It was another reason to shut her up for good.

He had a decision to make. He could either leave her here to slowly die, but she might be found, or he could use one of his three remaining bullets to put an end to her. Or he could simply roll her into the water and let the River Lathkill deal with her.

But why contaminate such beautiful, clear water? That river had saved his life today when it had pulled him clear of the knife-wielding Prunella. And besides, he'd loved this river and this valley from the very first day his parents had moved here.

Over the years he'd found many secret, quiet places along the valley sides – places where the tourists never ventured, and he liked to think of those areas as his own. Now that John and Philip were gone it was his own serene valley.

How could he contaminate something so beautiful with such evil?

He'd lost a lot of blood; he knew he wasn't thinking clearly.

He staggered back to Prunella's Isuzu to sit down and rest while he weighed up the two remaining options.

32

Forbes had managed a couple of hours of solid sleep on the small sofa in his office when his phone rang. It was Adam calling from outside Calow hospital.

"Sorry it's so early, sir, but I knew you'd be in your office. I grabbed an hour of sleep in my car. Have you been home at all?"

"Never mind about me, how's Jane doing?"

"She's going to be kept in for a few days. The other girl has a minor head injury and both are suffering from smoke inhalation, but both are out of danger. If we hadn't arrived on the scene when we did, it would have been a different story. And, sir, I have news."

Adam sounded cheerful so he played along. "Don't tell me you've proposed to Jane, not when she's in that state?"

"Sir... what...? No, I had a call from DI Lang late last night, enquiring after Jane, and he told me he'd taken possession of Simon Carter's diaries. Have you seen Lang this morning?"

"I'm not expecting him in for a couple of hours yet. What have you learned?"

"Simon has had a girlfriend since early last summer. He's been very secretive about it – his parents knew nothing, and he only referred to her in his diaries with the letter A. And guess what, the foreign girl pulled out of Oakwell with Jane yesterday is called Arianne. She's in the next bed to Jane so I've been talking with her."

"And is she the girlfriend?"

"She certainly is. She's a bit strange. She's got a thick, plastic carrier bag with her which she won't let go of. When she slept she had it tucked down in her bed between her thighs. She won't say what it contains."

"It could contain evidence to a murder."

"I tried that one on her. She says not, and short of arresting her, I can't force her to give it up. But listen to this – I only found out a few minutes ago that Sheila Hall is in the next ward. She was operated on last night for a dislocated shoulder after driving herself to the hospital yesterday afternoon. Her medical records have her named as Sheila Muir, that was her married name, and that must be why we couldn't find her last night when we were calling round the hospitals. That just leaves Simon and Prunella missing."

"Good work, Adam." He didn't want to share the news with Adam that Simon and Prunella had been found – not for a few hours – not while Adam was still in shock from thinking that he'd lost another partner.

*

Brian Leath was sitting in the interview room, looking flushed. Presumably he was also still in shock. "I got a phone call from a good friend and neighbour of mine, late last night," he told Forbes. "His property overlooks the River Lathkill, and he has views right down the valley, and he'd been taking his dog out for its last walk of the day when he noticed stationary lights down by the river, well away from the road. He thought nothing of it at first, but then when he had to get up to the bathroom at about midnight, he looked through his bedroom window and saw that the lights were still there. He knows I normally watch the sports channels till gone midnight, and that being the gamekeeper for the estate, I'm always alert for poachers, or gangs of druggies, so he telephoned me."

"Do you get many poachers in that area, at this time of the year?"

"Aye, you'd be surprised, and idiots on drugs don't seem to feel the cold as much as we do. Anyway, I did what I always do. I loaded two shotguns, put all three dogs into the Land Rover, and headed off to where the lights were supposed to be. You could have knocked me down with a feather when I saw it was my Prunella's old Isuzu sitting there."

"You knew we were looking for her."

"Aye, but when I saw it I couldn't work out what it might be doing down by the river. I found Simon first. I've known Simon and his father for years, and he's a good lad. I drove back up to the top of the hill to get a signal to phone for help, and it wasn't till I got back down that I saw my Pru on the ground in front of her truck. I really thought she was dead. As the lad was just conscious, I returned to him and did what the emergency services had told me to do. I tried to keep him still and warm. I should have phoned his parents while I had a signal, but I didn't think."

"It's all right, they're with him now. He's lost a lot of blood, but thanks to you he's in good hands. Are you sure you don't want to go to the hospital, Mr Leath? I understand your wife's in a critical condition."

"Quite sure, thank you."

"Then please, carry on."

"Well the lad just kept on repeating that he'd tried to phone for help but couldn't get a signal. After a while he began mumbling about a confession and a notebook. He made me take this notebook out of his pocket to give to you. He was so cold and soaked in so much blood that I was starting to think he wouldn't last until the paramedics arrived."

Forbes read the first page, conscious of the man watching for a change in his expression. "Is this your wife's handwriting, Mr Leath?"

"Aye, it's a bit shaky, like, but it's hers all right. And the signature's right. While we waited for the ambulance Simon insisted that I read it. He trusted me, you see. I know some people are against him, but after reading that I think he was a brave lad to tackle my Prunella the way he did. And I hope he isn't punished too severely for it."

His phone rang. It was Adam again from the hospital. This time he sounded tired. "Sir, I've just been informed about Prunella. I thought you'd like to know that they're taking her down to the operating theatre in the next few minutes. I believe it could still go either way."

He pressed the speaker icon and placed his phone in the centre of the table. "Adam, I've got Mr Leath with me. Is Mrs Leath conscious? Has she said anything?"

"No to both questions, sir, but at least she isn't in any pain. Her injuries sound particularly nasty."

"Hmm, pity about the pain bit," the gamekeeper muttered, "I wouldn't have minded inflicting some of that on her myself. I've told the doctors I want nothing more to do with her."

"Thank you, Adam. Keep me informed."

"Just one more thing, sir, Arianne has gone missing. She left the ward before breakfast, over an hour ago, with the plastic bag she's been so fiercely protecting, and no one knows where she is. She told Jane she'd be returning in a few hours."

"Then I'm sure she will, but thank you for telling me." He put his phone down.

"How is Simon, mentally I mean?" Brian Leath asked. "He seemed in a bit of a state before the ambulance arrived, but that could be down to his injuries, couldn't it?"

"I'm told he's relieved his ordeal is over, and when he learned that Arianne was alive, in the same hospital, and out of danger, it was all the nurses could do to prevent him from going to find her."

"I'm glad about that. The lad deserves some luck. But he kept that girlfriend of his quiet for a reason, didn't he? Will she be in trouble for moving that poor woman's body?"

"We'll need to question her before we decide how best to proceed, Mr Leath."

"Will it be all right if I get off home now? I could do with some sleep."

"Yes, but we'll need a full statement from you later today, or tomorrow."

"No problem, it's not as if I'll be making any hospital visits."

Forbes took another brief phone call from the hospital before he walked into the incident room. Only Adam was missing from his team.

"Morning, sir," DC Robert Bell greeted him. "Donald Muir has been informed of Prunella's critical condition, and that we now know she is his sister. He says he's ready to co-operate. How is Jane doing?"

"She'll be in hospital for a few days, but she's going to be fine. Adam's blaming himself for not keeping her fully in the picture and warning her how dangerous we were beginning to think those women had become. She shouldn't have gone there alone, but none of us could have predicted that fire.

Unfortunately, Prunella Leath passed away just a few minutes ago. On the strength of her written confession, which I trust you've all read by now, we can at least begin to unravel some of what's been going on at Oakwell Grange. DC Bell, will you make it clear to the lab that we need the results of the women's DNA samples as soon as possible? It will be interesting to see if they confirm Prunella's account of the group's relationships."

"Yes sir."

"Simon Carter is responding well to treatment and is due to have a bullet removed from his shoulder this morning. I think he's been through enough so we'll delay trying to take a statement from him until tomorrow. We already know most of what happened, partly thanks to the video on the phone we retrieved from the bramble bushes."

"What will happen to Oakwell Grange now, sir?" DC Jackson asked.

"That will be up to the courts to decide. DI Lang, it appears you were right – we now believe Darya Jamal did die at Oakwell, and her baby was sold on. The women had been in the business of selling new-born babies for at least the past ten years. Do we know if there's any way of tracing where any of the infants might be now?"

"I didn't go home last night either, sir. Before studying Simon's diaries I had lengthy conversations with Hannah and the two young women. They all claimed that only Prunella knew the final destinations of the babies and they also said there should have been a large sum of money in a tin, down in their basement where the fire was started. It was money from the sales of the infants, and they believed there should have been at least thirty thousand pounds hidden away down there. This morning I spoke to the chief fire officer but he knew nothing about any tins, other than those which had contained paint. We've searched the internet history of all five women, but found nothing of any use. If there was any documented evidence it was most likely destroyed in the fire. If you want my opinion, sir, considering how long ago these children were taken, and assuming they went into loving homes, it might be cruel to remove them just because they weren't legally adopted."

"You may well be right DI Lang, but that shouldn't prevent us from trying."

"Sir," DC Green said, "I attended last night's crime scene by the river. I checked the inside of the vehicle before securing it for scenes of crimes officers this morning and there was a locked tin on the passenger seat and a key inside a wellington boot. Inside the box were just folded newspapers. I left it there of course, but I thought it worth mentioning. Prunella had enough provisions and clothing to last for several days, but no cash. Could one of them have been trying to cheat the others out of the money and swopped the cash for paper?"

Jane Goodwin adjusted the clip on her nostrils. She longed to lie down flat but she'd already been told off once by the nurses for trying. It was like trying to sleep with the window open while sitting in a slowly moving car. She heard Adam's voice, and then two nurses wishing him good luck.

She opened her eyes but couldn't see him. Instead, the largest bouquet of pink, red, and white roses she'd ever seen, was slowly heading towards her bed. "Adam, you fool, what are you doing? The hospital no longer allows fresh flowers on the wards."

"I've been granted a special concession to bring them in, but I've got to take them away with me when I leave." His voice came from behind the bouquet. "I'll put them in water for you at home. They'll be waiting for you. Now I want you to close your eyes, smell their perfume, and imagine the sun warming your back as you lean over to smell them in your own garden, with me and Ryan and Lucy by your side."

She closed her eyes, aware of everyone in the ward watching. "My mother loved her roses, and so do I."

"Are you there yet, can you feel the heat and hear the bees?"

She giggled, self-consciously. "Yes I can."

"Now open your eyes."

The flowers were only a foot away from her face. She glanced at them and then looked up at Adam's flushed face and sparkling eyes. He winked at her and then looked down at the flowers, so she lowered her gaze. The tightest and darkest rosebud had been positioned perfectly in the centre of the bouquet. On it, a shining gold band contrasted perfectly with the velvety, blood-red petals, and a single stone sparkled from the glare of the overhead lights.

"Jane Goodwin, you know how much I love you. I've told you often enough, and I promise I'll never stop reminding you of that fact. Yesterday, when I thought I might have lost you, I literally couldn't breathe. You are my life. You, Lucy, and Ryan are all I live for and I want you in my life very minute of every day."

He rested the bouquet on her bed and dropped to his knees. "Jane Goodwin, would you do me the great honour of marrying me?"

She hadn't expected that. Suddenly she needed the toilet, but now wasn't the time to ring the bell for a nurse. Besides, the ward seemed to have miraculously filled up with nurses and patients from other wards. And everyone was watching, waiting for her answer. She needed a moment to think.

"I don't expect an answer straight away – not until you're feeling better." His smile had slipped slightly and his cheeks had gone an even darker shade of pink.

"I... I need a minute."

Despite his words, he had obviously been expecting her to say yes instantly. And she wanted to, she really did. There was just one problem. From the very beginning of their relationship they had promised to always share their problems, never have secrets, and always talk openly to each other. Her mother's secret life and the contents of her mother's bedroom had tested her ability this week to be able to do that.

Before she could give him an answer, she had to decide.

In her mother's handwriting were possibly the answers to some important questions in a major police investigation. Adam was a respected detective and she liked to think that she was a capable special constable. How could she even consider not handing the files over? That was easy. It was because if her mother had been involved in anything criminal, her name would be dragged through the courts, the press could potentially damage both Adam's career and her own, and her daughter would almost certainly be taunted and bullied at school.

She was going to burn them at the first opportunity.

Decision made, she gently removed the ring from the rose bud, handed it to Adam, and held out her left hand.

"Yes Adam, I would dearly love to marry you."

33

"Adam, good of you to join us," Forbes said sarcastically, but with a supressed smile, "and there are still three hours of the working day remaining."

"I've been talking with Sheila and Arianne. The girl reappeared after about an hour and a half and climbed back into her bed as though nothing had happened, but without her package."

"That isn't all you've been doing today though, is it? I hear congratulations are in order."

"How did you know?"

"I've lived in this town for most of my life. I have a lot of friends and some of them just happen to be nurses. They couldn't wait to phone and tell me all about your proposal. I expect to be on your guest list."

"We haven't got that far yet, sir, but I'm sure you will be."

"Where did Arianne disappear to, did you find out?"

"She went to see Simon in the recovery room. His parents were with him and they met her for the first time. I'm told it was a very emotional meeting and they took to her straight away. When she's discharged from the hospital she's going to move into their home, and as soon as Simon is well enough the couple intend to marry. She won't then be deported."

"Technically, she's a witness and an accessory to a crime. She was aware of the selling of babies and she moved a woman's body. We'll need to formally interview her as soon as possible."

"She understands that. The nurses told me that she handed the package she's been clinging onto to Simon's parents for safe-keeping. And she's still insisting that it's her own property."

"How large was the package, did you get a good look at it?" Forbes clicked on his computer and brought up the photograph of the tin box on the passenger seat of Prunella's Isuzu. "Would it have fitted inside this box?"

"Yes sir, I'd say it would have been a perfect fit for that."

"We may never know where all, or indeed any, of the babies sold from Oakwell have disappeared to, but I think we know where some of the proceeds of those sales are right now." He explained to Adam about the missing thirty thousand pounds.

"What about Donald Muir," Adam asked. "Has he admitted to playing a part in the deaths of John Lewis and Philip Booth, and the attempted murder of Simon Carter?"

"He's admitted to knowing that his Land Rover was taken by Prunella, but still insisting he knew nothing of why she'd needed it that night or he would never have allowed her to use it. And he admits to covering for her when he realised what she'd done. He's confirmed they're brother and sister and that he fathered a child with her which was then passed off as Hannah's, as well as having a child with Sheila. He was drawn into Prunella's schemes without realising what her long term plans were."

"They're all as sick as each other."

"He says his mother couldn't cope with Prunella when she was a child, and that that was why she was packed off to relatives in Manchester. After her father was killed she became even more unmanageable, fixating on the property he'd been trying to invest in and delving into her family history. She'd always been an extremely difficult child who'd obsessed about things."

"She may have had some sort of obsessive compulsive disorder," Adam said. "Conditions like that weren't recognised thirty or forty years ago."

"Possibly, also she'd convinced herself that she and Donald were the only legitimate descendants of the original owner of Oakwell Grange, a Lord Reynolds, and that she should somehow have been a baroness. Donald says he'd tried to persuade her that she was mistaken, but that she was a difficult woman to deal with once she'd made up her mind about something. All her years of scheming had been designed to get her bloodline back into the Grange."

"Was she ever really a contract killer for the mobs in Manchester?"

"I've passed her information on to the department dealing with cold cases in the Manchester area. We'll have to wait for news on that, but the pistol she used on Simon had originally been registered and owned by the wife of an American mobster who was stabbed to death while visiting England, almost thirty years ago. So maybe she will turn out to be everything she claimed to be in her written confession. It will be interesting to find out."

"Sheila and Hannah both played a part in the selling of new born babies, even though Prunella set everything up and dealt with the human traffickers. Do you think their daughters would have continued the trade when they took over?"

"It's not something you can extricate yourself from, being involved with organised crime, is it? They might not have been given the choice. They claim not to know about the baby trafficking, and they don't seem to want anything more to do with Oakwell Grange now. Their paternal grandmother, Mrs Muir, is saying that they will now inherit the farm, so they won't struggle financially."

"Let me get this straight, sir. Two weeks and two days ago, we thought we were beginning the year badly with a mini-crime wave. Since then we've solved the case of the woman in the ditch, and also the eight-year-old case of the woman on Leek moors which was a cold case on the books of the Cheshire Constabulary. We've solved the hit-and-run murders and the attempted murder of three teenage boys, and we've smashed a baby selling organisation. On top of that we've provided the name of someone responsible for possibly dozens of contract killings going back over thirty years. And we're still in January."

"I think that's a fair summary, Adam."

"The only thing we haven't been able to do is find the missing baby. Let's hope it's being well cared for and loved, wherever it is."

"I'll second that, although with the publicity this case is bound to create, we may yet find it."

"I was thinking on the way over here, sir."

"Well that's good to hear," Forbes joked. "I've always liked to encourage that in my team. Go on..."

"Are you familiar with the butterfly effect?"

"I've heard of it. It's something to do with the chaos theory, isn't it, whereby something small or insignificant can have far reaching effects?"

"That's right sir, it's the idea that a tornado could be caused by the flapping of a butterfly's wings, weeks earlier, in another part of the world."

"What are you getting at?"

"That letter we've heard about but never seen represents the butterfly's wings, sir. Before Christmas, just for a laugh, two teenage boys sent a hoax letter to a woman that they didn't like. Everything I've just mentioned has happened as a result of that letter. How could anyone possibly have imagined the effect that that letter was going to have?"

"That's a profound thought."

"Thank you sir, but there's just one other thing."

"And that is...?"

"What are we going to do about the thirty thousand pounds that we believe Arianne gave to Simon's parents today?"

"Don't you think that young couple deserve some compensation for everything they've suffered at the hands of the Oakwell women?"

"Maybe they do."

"Arianne did say it was her personal property in that package, didn't she? Only you and I know that it looked a perfect fit for the box in Prunella's car. And neither Sheila nor Hannah can prove that the money was in that cellar, let alone that it was stolen, or even that it existed, come to that. That's the drawback to having illegally gained money."

"So we ignore it?"

"For all we know, if the money did exist, it was destroyed in the fire."

"I'll go along with that, sir."

"I thought you would."

ENDS

64697453R00151

Made in the USA
Middletown, DE
19 February 2018